Totally Bound Publishing books by K.E. Turner

The Wolves of Langeais
Wolf's Keep
Wolf's Prize

The Wolves of Langeais

WOLF'S PRIZE

K.E. TURNER

Wolf's Prize
ISBN # 978-1-80250-775-1
©Copyright K.E. Turner 2024
Cover Art by Erin Dameron-Hill ©Copyright May 2024
Interior text design by Claire Siemaszkiewicz
Totally Bound Publishing

Published in 2024 by Totally Bound Publishing, United Kingdom.

Totally Bound Publishing is an imprint of Totally Entwined Group Limited.

WOLF'S PRIZE

Dedication

To my dad: My biggest and most devoted fan. You showed me what a real partnership should look like between a husband and his wife. You and Mum — 60+ years of marriage and still going strong.

Acknowledgements

Once again, thank you to the wonderful team at Totally Bound Publishing who've helped me bring Aimon and Kathryn's story out into the world. To my editor, Nicki Richards, who helps me get my head around where the commas are really supposed to go, and who makes sure I don't embarrass myself by catching any grammar or plot errors. This book wouldn't be the same without her input. To my cover designer, Erin Dameron-Hill for bringing to life my character and the lengths she had to go to making sure the armor fit the century I write about. As someone who has no clue how to make a decent cover, I am in awe of your ability. To my beta readers and fellow authors — Dani Mclean, D.D. Line and Victoria Brown, for your time, your advice, your ongoing support and your 'tough love.' I firmly believe my books are better for it. To my family for your ongoing and unflagging support. And to my hubby, Mark, who answers all my questions about men, even though sometimes he finds them a little embarrassing.

Author's Note

Dear Reader,

When I encounter foreign words I do not know the meaning of in a book, it causes me to pause each time I see them in the text, taking me out of the story. Here is a brief list of foreign words and meanings I have used in this book.

Bretaigne: Britannia/Brittany/Britain
Archeveque: Archbishop
Amonier: Chaplain
Chevalier: Knight
Comte: Count
Comtesse: Countess
Demesne: Land attached to a manor
Eveque: Bishop
Franceis: Old French
L'enfer: hell
Ma belle renarde: My beautiful vixen
Ma dame: My lady
Mademoiselle: Miss
Merde: Shit/fuck
Mon Dieu: My God
Monsieur: Sir
Mon Seigneur: My Lord
Mon Seigneur Comte: My Lord Count
Sacre bleu: Damn it!

As Old French is, well, an old language, there are many variations. I've chosen the terms I think best apply. In some instances, when I've not been able to confirm a word or phrase in Old French, I have taken the liberty of using modern French.

Langeais Keep and Langeais are real places. However, they have been used in a fictitious manner. There isn't, and has never thought to have been, an underground cell in the ruins of Langeais Keep. *Oubliettes* are now believed to have been used for storage, not prisoners, but the latter makes for a far more interesting story.

There were many comtes de Anjou over the centuries (none named Lothair that I am aware of, although Lothair was a popular name at the time). One of them, Comte Foulques de Noir, built Langeais Keep to guard the crossing point of the Loire River.

Comte Foulques de Noir, The Black Falcon, was notorious for his wars with other comtes — as were many comtes of that era. His power base was in Tours, and Langeais Keep, one of the first stone keeps built, was just one stronghold for him. An important one.

He did, however, dress his wife up in her wedding gown and burn her at the stake. She was also his cousin. They did things a little differently back then. Burning people at the stake was a popular way of ridding yourself of your enemies while making a statement to the masses at the same time. He wasn't the only one to use such methods.

My Comte Lothair is a fictitious Comte de Anjou created from a compilation of many comtes of that era.

And, as much as there were myths and legends of the *loup garou* (werewolf) in medieval France, there are no documented instances of werewolves in 10th-century Langeais. In case you were wondering.

For a dreamer is one who can only find his way by moonlight,
and his punishment is that he sees the dawn before the rest of the world.
~ Oscar Wilde

Prologue

Langeais, Frankia (France)
Year 988

Twelve-year-old Kathryn Beauchene, red hair loose and in disarray, poked her freckled face out of the window to keep track of the woman in the green dress crossing the street.

Where is Aunt Elise going? To the stables? To the pond?

Kathryn would love to go to the pond. The sun shone, not a single cloud dotted the sky and warm air shimmered across the thatched roofs of the village. A swim would be just the thing.

Her aunt paused, casting a furtive glance up and down the lane, then darted past the stables. Kathryn's eyes narrowed. *How intriguing.* She gripped the window ledge with impatient fingers, her body thrumming. If something exciting, some adventure were to happen, Kathryn *would* be part of it. But she could not be too hasty, for it would not do to get caught. She could do without another scolding. Her father had already given her two lectures since this morning, and she wrinkled her nose at the prospect of a third.

As she jiggled about, eager to be on the move, her keen gaze followed her aunt as she slipped down the lane beside the Cadieux's residence, heading for the west gate.

Yes. She is going to the pond.

Kathryn abandoned the window, flung open her chamber door and raced down the corridor.

"Watch where you are going, child," scolded a maid as Kathryn flew past her. "And where are your shoes? And your head-veil? It is unseemly for a young lady to be gallivanting about so."

Kathryn laughed, taking the stairs two at a time.

"Oooh, child. Your father needs to take a firm hand to you. You have become wild. People will talk."

Kathryn snorted. She pushed into the street, her bare feet dirty and a fresh rip in her dress from scaling a fence this morning. What other people thought of her was the last thing on Kathryn's mind. She skipped past the Cadieux's home, careful not to attract the attention of their beastly son, Jean-Luc, and exited the west gate, taking the path into the forest.

The breeze carried the scent of blossoming spring wildflowers and rustled the leaves in the trees as she picked her way along the grassy trail. Why would she want to stay inside all day learning how to embroider violets and roses? She would rather be out here, enjoying the sun and the fresh air.

Her bare feet made no sound on the damp, leafy undergrowth as she ducked off the path and into the trees. She knew of a perfect vantage point overlooking the pond, ideal for this situation—a large flat rock shrouded in sapling trees. Last summer, some of the older village boys had come down to the water to swim.

Pressed flat against its rough surface, remaining unseen, she had spied on them as they had stripped off their clothes and frolicked in the cool water. She had never seen a boy naked before. The sight had thrilled her no end. They had not suspected a thing. Not once.

Careful not to make a sound, she slipped through the trees and clambered up the large, sloped rock above the pond. Her dress snagged, and she tugged at it, the material tearing.

Oh dear.

If only she had brothers. A pair of men's breeches would be just the thing. She grimaced at her damaged dress. Brothers or no, she would never wear anything but a dress. Her father might view her dirty feet, her unkempt hair and a few tears in her skirts with amused forbearance, but for certain he would forbid her from wearing boys' clothes.

She plastered herself against the rock and crawled to the edge.

"What are you doing here?"

Kathryn froze. The breeze ruffled her hair, and she cursed its bright color. It always caught her out.

"Why did you not come and visit upon me at my brother's? Why all this secrecy?"

Kathryn expelled a silent sigh, slumping against the rock. Her aunt did not address her, rather someone else. She risked a peek over the rock's lip and spied her aunt frowning at a man. A chevalier with armor like her father's. Tall, in a dark fur-lined surcoat, the chevalier stood with his back to Kathryn and his sword belted to his waist, the large yellow-brown stone decorating its pommel bright in the sun. *A nobleman.*

She wriggled a little farther up the rock, trying to get a better view, and to see the face of the man below. A leafy branch obscured her vision, but she dared not move it, lest her aunt see or hear her.

"I needed to see you, Elise," said the man. "Is that too much to ask? We were always so close, inseparable. Now I never have a moment alone with you. I have missed you. Missed us."

His voice was tender, like that of a lover, or so Kathryn imagined. Who was this man? Was he handsome? Was it her aunt's husband, Uncle Jacques? Kathryn could not picture Uncle Jacques speaking to anyone like that, not even his wife. He always seemed so stern and forbidding. Dark and brooding, her father called him, and she had to agree.

"I thought the message was from Jacques," said her aunt. "That is why I came."

Not Uncle Jacques? Then who? And why would her Uncle Jacques not simply come to the house if he wanted to see his wife?

Kathryn grinned. *This is the best spot for spying.*

The man growled. *Growled.* Like a real, live animal. Kathryn's eyes widened.

Her aunt's expression grew stern. "I should not be here with you alone. Jacques will find out, and he will be furious."

Oh my, yes.

Even Kathryn knew how wrong it was for her aunt to be here, meeting a man in secret. A man other than her husband. The man stepped forward, raising his hand to touch her aunt's face. Long, brown hair hid his features.

Kathryn clenched her fists. *L'enfer! Who is this man?*

Good thing her father, or the maids, could not censor her thoughts. They would scold her for cursing, for certain.

He brushed his hand against her aunt's cheek. "Jacques need never know."

Her aunt slapped the chevalier's hand away and stepped back from him. "He *would* know, and you are making a presumption I want to be here. Alone. With you."

The chevalier huffed. "Come now, Elise. You knew I sent the message. That is why you came. Why you snuck out of the house without your brother knowing. Do you not miss the time we had together? Before Jacques took you away from me? We grew up together, spent all our time together. We had a connection, you and I."

With one large step toward her aunt, he swallowed the distance between them.

Kathryn's hands clenched tighter.

Her aunt snorted. "We were children and we played in the meadow. All of us. Not only you and I. And we had fun, but I am a married woman now with two grown boys. Men."

"All the more reason for it to be our time. You have done your duty. Provided Jacques with male heirs, and I have built up my fortune. It may not rival Jacques', but you would want for naught, Elise. Now I can give you all you crave."

From the shock on her aunt's face, the man had misjudged the situation. And her aunt. He leaned closer, perhaps to kiss her, and her aunt's expression darkened. Kathryn had seen that look on her aunt's face before. The man was in imminent danger of getting a tongue lashing.

And I will witness it firsthand. How exciting!

Aunt Elise, with her red hair and fiery temper, brought an energy with her every time she visited, but this was a whole new level of interesting.

"I have caught the heated looks you send my way when you think Jacques cannot see," said the chevalier.

"You cannot possibly deny this heat between us. You have hungered for this, for us, as much as I have."

Oh boy. Here it comes. Kathryn could not look away.

But Aunt Elise did something Kathryn did not expect. She laughed.

The man growled again.

A shiver ran up Kathryn's spine. How *did* he make that noise with his throat? *Could I learn how to do that?* She could come back to this very spot, when the village boys were here again, and scare them silly with it. Let them think a wild animal lurked close by in the forest. She smothered a giggle, clamping her hand over her mouth just in time.

Unperturbed, Aunt Elise stood her ground. Respect for her aunt's courage swelled in Kathryn's chest. She would be terrified in her aunt's place.

"I really do not know what I have done to give you the impression there is something between us. Yes, I care for you. You are one of my closest friends, but it is Jacques who I love, and Jacques I mated." Her aunt reached out, rubbing the man's arm in a comforting gesture. "One day you will find your mate and you will see what we share is naught more than a friendship." She turned to leave.

With a snarl, the chevalier grabbed her shoulders, wrenching her aunt around to face him. "Do not turn your back on me. He may be a d'Louncrais, but Jacques does not get to have everything."

"Let. Me. Go. If Jacques hears of this, he will punish you no matter how much your friendship means to him. Think about what you are risking."

"I have. And I will not be denied what is mine any longer."

He pulled her against him. Her aunt struggled, and his hand gripped her throat.

Kathryn's lungs seized and panic fluttered in her chest.

Aunt Elise's cheeks flushed. "I am not yours. I never was and I never will be."

The man growled again, deeper, angrier. "You will not fight me forever."

Kathryn had to do something. But what? Her father would know what to do. He would put a stop to this. Scrambling down the rock, no longer concerned about keeping quiet or being caught, she raced for the trail.

At her aunt's scream, she skidded to a halt, her heart thudding in her chest. What should she do? Run to her father as fast as she could, or race to the pond to help her aunt?

A vicious snarl from the man, and another scream from her aunt, turned Kathryn toward the clearing. She flew down the trail toward them. Fear for her aunt overriding her instinct to flee, she launched herself at the unknown man, her fists flying as she threatened him with the wrath of her father, her uncle, le Comte de Anjou and anyone else she could think of.

Startled, the man shoved her aunt to the ground and turned on her. Kathryn's breath whooshed from her lungs.

His head! Mon Dieu! His head!

Large, furry, with an elongated snout and lethal canines, it bore down on her. She raised her arm to fend off the slavering jaw and sharp teeth. It latched on to her arm. Pain flared. Kathryn screamed.

Her aunt launched herself at the beast, and it let go.

"Run, Kathryn. Run!"

Kathryn fled, bleeding, pain burning along her arm, not knowing it would be the last time she would see her aunt alive.

Chapter One

Eleven years later…

If the scuff of her boots on the road matched the pace of her thundering heart, Kathryn would complete the short walk to Langeais Keep in record time. Instead, she dragged her feet, her father beside her, his arm slipped through hers. Summoned by the Comte de Anjou! Nothing good could come of that.

"Are you tired, Kathryn? Did you not sleep well?" Her father's concerned gaze focused on her.

She smiled, patting him on the arm. "Just the usual nightmare, Father."

"Again? They seem to be increasing. You have not had so many in a row for several years now. Not since…" His jaw clenched. "Was it the same one?"

Kathryn avoided her father's eyes. "Always."

The scar on her arm burned, and she resisted the urge to rub it. It remained a constant reminder of the attack, of the darkness that now resided within her, finding release only in her sleep. For eleven years, the same nightmare had plagued her — a clearing, a pond, a woman with red hair and a man, but not a man. A man with no face, who morphed into a terrifying combination of man and wolf, fangs and fur. Snarling, snapping, it came for her, again and again and, without fail, her body would refuse to move.

Eleven years and it had never deviated. Not once. Until last night. With eyes the color of blue flame, chevalier Aimon Proulx, looking like one of God's warrior angels, had invaded her nightmare. Long, white-blond hair loose about his shoulders, his blue surcoat with its white dove insignia rustling in the breeze and his hand on the pommel of his sword — he'd drawn her to him, made her heart race and her body quiver.

She had awoken this morning feverish, with a desperate longing for Aimon Proulx. Her body thrummed with remembered heat. She blew out a breath. Aimon had occupied her waking thoughts a lot of late. She could only presume that to be the reason for his presence in her nightmare, but it unnerved her all the same. Most likely, she was one of many young women who dreamed of Aimon Proulx, but only *her* dreams contained monsters.

"Do you know why Comte Lothair has summoned us, Father?"

Farren Beauchene shrugged his shoulders. "I do not. They gave me no indication as to the nature of the comte's request. It is most likely a minor matter." His frown betrayed his true thoughts. Her father was worried.

"Perhaps it has something to do with Mademoiselle Erin Richardson."

They passed through the gate into the outer bailey, dodging a chevalier on horseback as they joined the crowd of people making their way to the keep hall. The comte would hear all public matters today, and the outer bailey had begun to fill with people — peasants, merchants, farmers, chevaliers and noblemen. Most would wait in line to petition the comte. Some, like Kathryn and her father, were responding to his summons. She spied Manette Chapet with her two friends, Odila and Lisette. She scowled. They had come for the spectacle, the chance to gossip and the opportunity to forge connections above their current station.

"Mademoiselle who?" Her father guided her around a group of farmers who had paused to discuss the likelihood of rain.

"Oh, Father, you must stay abreast of things. Mademoiselle Erin Richardson is all the talk in the keep."

He grunted. "I do not hold much for gossip. Too much trouble can come of it."

"I agree. You are lucky you do not have to endure hours of it like I must, but Erin Richardson is not gossip, Father. She is Gaharet d'Louncrais' newly betrothed."

"What? You say Gaharet d'Louncrais is taking a wife?"

They stepped aside for a Baron and his wife to pass.

"Yes, and a woman no one has ever heard of. Rumor has it, and it is purely rumor," she said, as they trudged up the hill toward the keep, "Comte Lothair is unimpressed. Gaharet did not consult him when choosing his bride to be."

Her father grunted again. "Gaharet is only *the* most powerful chevalier in this county. Lothair would want to be secure in Gaharet's allegiance. A bride not chosen by him, or at the very least vetted by him, would not have pleased the comte at all." He narrowed his eyes.

"His father did much the same when he wed your aunt, marrying a woman far beneath his station."

"He married her for love?"

Her father's gaze drifted away from her and over the people moving through the gate into the inner bailey. When he finally answered, his voice was soft and his eyes distant, caught up in his memories.

"Yes," he said. "I believe Jacques did marry Elise for love, God rest their souls. Much as I did with your mother. I guess some of us are born with that inclination."

Kathryn gave him a sad smile. Her father's stories, his memories, were the only things she had of her mother, and he infused his words with the depth of his love for his wife. He still missed her, even after all these years. Would that she could find a match such as her father, such as her aunt.

Her mind turned again to Aimon Proulx. She quashed the childish notion. She might fancy Aimon, but with a plethora of appealing options to choose from, would he even consider her? She had never fit society's expectations of a demure, proper lady. Less so since her attack. No self-respecting man would find those attributes appealing.

Still, Kathryn clung to her father's promise she could choose the man she wed. If she could not have love, then at the very least she would marry a man she did not despise. One she hoped would accept some of her wayward behavior.

"What would Gaharet's betrothed have to do with us?" her father asked, guiding her around a group of nervous young men waiting to be considered for training to become the comte's newest chevaliers.

"I met her in the keep this week past. She certainly brightened up the monotony of embroidering flowers and talking of the latest young man to pledge investiture." Kathryn rolled her eyes. She loathed those days. When she must behave as any well-bred daughter of a chevalier should. "I like her and I mentioned I would be very appreciative if she could put in a good word for me with Gaharet."

Her father jerked to a halt, pulling her out of the flow of people entering the keep. His brow furrowed as he rounded on her. "Why would you wish to do that?"

Kathryn raised her eyebrows at the gruffness in his voice. "Father, you may not have noticed, but I am not a little girl anymore. In a few months I will be a score and three years. I need to find a suitable match. People are beginning to talk."

"Yes, yes, I understand that. But how is it Gaharet can help with that? *Why* would you want Gaharet to help with that?"

"Apart from him being my cousin, and the most influential person in the county after the comte?"

Her father shook his head. "It is not wise to court attention from the d'Louncrais."

"Why ever not? Half the people in the court are vying for his attention. Why not us?" Her father would not meet her eyes. "Father, all Gaharet's men are unwed, and any of them would be a much better prospect than those who have indicated their interest in me. So far, most of my suitors are twice my age, fat, balding, mean, illiterate, unwashed or a combination of all the things I find abhorrent. Through Erin, I may have a chance to once again move in the same company as Gaharet and his vassals, perhaps secure the attention of one of them."

All Gaharet's vassals were a power unto themselves. No one questioned them or defied them. Would a wife of such a man be allowed certain liberties?

Her father's brow furrowed further. "It appears you have given this some thought, Kathryn. Have you set your sights on a particular vassal?"

Kathryn's cheeks heated. She had given the matter much consideration. Gaharet had six vassals—Lance, Ulrik, Godfrey, twins Aubert and Edmond, and Aimon Proulx. Lance was older than her father, despite looking no more than two score years, and he had a reputation for being stern and hard. He would want to discipline her and bring her under his rule. Definitely not an option.

Aubert and Edmond were huge with forbidding countenances. Not once had she witnessed a smile grace either of their faces, and they nary said a word that was not accompanied by a scowl. Kathryn found them rather intimidating. Ulrik had a reputation with the ladies, so Kathryn would steer clear of him, and Godfrey was a quiet, reserved, scholarly man. People often described her as willful and untamed. Not a good match. That left Aimon Proulx.

Like all Gaharet's men, he was as impressive physically as he was in his position in society. The second son of a baron from an old, noble family, his reputation, unlike Ulrik's, was above reproach. Neither studious like Godfrey, stern like Lance, nor as unapproachable as the twins, he had an aversion to political intrigue and showed a fervent loyalty to Gaharet. If gossip were to be believed, Gaharet had saved his life.

Barely a few years older than her with bright blue eyes and a clean-shaven face, he set the hearts of many a young woman aflutter, including Kathryn's. That his presence made her thoughts jumble, and her body tingle only added to his attraction. Whether his lack of a beard would signify better personal hygiene, Kathryn could not be certain, but it did appeal to her. Many of her would-be suitors had little familiarity with bathing. Sitting in the same room with them had been repugnant. Agreeing to wed them was out of the question. She could never marry a man she did not respect, and she could never respect a man whose stench made her stomach churn.

"I have to marry somebody, Father, despite my..." Kathryn cast her gaze around "...problem."

Problem? More a curse. The darkness within shifted, as if merely thinking of it roused it from its slumber. She forced it down.

Her father offered her a weak smile. "I know, but—"

"You wish to see me marry someone for love, like you and Mother." She gave him a wan smile. "Believe me, Father, I would like nothing more than to have what you and Mother had, but I must be realistic. The chances of that happening are not good. I must choose soon or risk the comte's attention." Her chest tightened. "Could this be why he has summoned us?"

Her father considered it. "It is possible, but unlikely. If, as you say, Gaharet has announced his betrothal to a woman the comte does not approve of, I think we would garner little attention by comparison."

"I hope you are right." Comte Lothair would not take her feelings into consideration when deciding who she should wed. Indeed, he would not care what she needed or wanted in a husband, nor would her father have any influence. "Marrying someone of Comte Lothair's choosing could prove disastrous."

Her father nodded, leading her into the hall. "Do not fear, Kathryn. We will find you a man you can trust and, with any luck, one you like."

A nervous flutter stirred in her stomach. She must marry, she had no other option, but she must also be careful. For should anyone find out her secret, should the church or the comte become aware of the beast she hid inside her, it would cost Kathryn her life.

Chapter Two

Unease clawed at Aimon Proulx as he rode his warhorse toward the gate of Langeais Keep. Fisted in his hand was a directive to present himself to Lothair, Comte de Anjou. After all that had occurred that cursed night Gaharet had fled with his betrothed, being summoned by Lothair did not bode well. Treachery surrounded them, tied his stomach in knots and left him bewildered and unsure of whom to trust.

He had not wished to leave his self-appointed position guarding Gaharet and Erin, but Gaharet had ordered him to return home, to pretend he knew little of what had happened. Hidden away in the forest, Gaharet was blind to what transpired with his men, the unpredictable Comte Lothair, or the scheming Archeveque Renaud. Gaharet needed him to be his eyes and ears. A task he felt wholly unsuited for.

At the gate ahead of him, he spotted Lance dismounting from his horse. Had Lothair commanded his presence, too? Had they all received a similar summons? Lance passed his horse's reins to a waiting stable hand and unbuckled his sword, handing it to the gate guard. A moment later, he retrieved a dagger from his boot and another from beneath his surcoat. Lothair would want to be certain they were not armed, at least not with human weapons.

Aimon reined his horse in and dismounted beside Lance, eyeing his fellow chevalier, his pack member. Could Lance be the one who had betrayed them, selling their secrets to Archeveque Renaud? Who, in turn, had exposed them to Comte Lothair? Lance, who had stood by Gaharet, advised him and supported his ascension to pack alpha? Was he the one who had faked grief at the murder of their kind — men, women and children, even his own family?

Lance shifted and turned to face Aimon, placing his back to the wall. Lance, it seemed, held his own concerns.

"Any word of the others?" His face grim and a haunted look in his gray eyes, Lance appeared tired and worn, as though their situation had aged him more than time ever had.

Aimon shook his head. "You are the first I have seen in days." Aimon hesitated, his hand on the buckle of his sword.

Lance held up his empty hands. "Troubled times. It is hard to know who is friend and who is foe."

"Agreed." Aimon unbuckled his sword, his gaze never leaving Lance. He handed his weapon to the gate guard.

The guard raised an eyebrow. "Any other blades?"

Aimon removed two daggers concealed on his body. He had other weapons at his disposal, but none he could reveal in such a public place.

Lance frowned. "We cannot let them turn us against each other. If they succeed in that, then they have already won."

Aimon caught a scent in the air and turned. Two large men rode toward them. Aubert and Edmond. All their kind were larger, more muscular than most, but Edmond and Aubert were truly daunting in their sheer height and breadth. Rarely seen apart, the twins made a fearsome pair. Could they have turned on the pack? Gruff in manner and brutal in battle, Aimon had always thought them steadfast and loyal.

They reined in beside him, dismounting and handing their weaponry to the gate guard. Edmond forced a tight smile. Aubert glowered. The four of them moved within the walls, away from listening ears.

Godfrey entered the bailey and joined them, his movements cautious, his expression wary. Always careful with his words, considered in his approach, could his quiet, thoughtful ways hide a deceiver?

An awkward silence hung between them, each man looking to the others, suspicion darkening their faces. One of these men had betrayed them all. He must discover who. The weight of Gaharet's expectations fell heavily on Aimon.

"It appears we have all received a summons. Has anyone seen or heard from Gaharet? Ulrik?" asked Lance.

A shake of heads. Aimon kept still. He could not afford to be caught in a lie.

"Perhaps they are already here." Edmond's words lacked conviction.

Lance turned his head to the breeze and his nostrils flared. Aimon did not deter him, though Lance would not catch their scent. Neither Ulrik nor Gaharet would appear, no matter how long they waited.

"We cannot linger. If we keep Lothair waiting, it will only add to his displeasure."

Aubert huffed. "We can well do without that."

They made their way to the keep. Whispers circulated as they entered the crowded hall, and Aimon noted the preponderance of keep guard in the room. Men moved out of their way, gazes dropping to the floor as they deferred to their authority, their power. Women smiled and batted their eyelids. One reached out and touched his mailed arm. Aimon did not even glance in her direction, brushing past her, all his focus on the man seated at the end of the hall surrounded by guards. Comte Lothair.

They halted, five abreast. Movement to the right of Lothair snagged Aimon's attention. A black-robed priest, his pectoral cross dangling about his neck, moved to stand beside Comte Lothair. Archeveque Renaud. Cold, hard eyes stared out of his lined and cadaverous face, a malevolent grin twisting on his thin, bloodless lips. Aimon swallowed his disgust. He had never encountered a man of the cloth as devious and manipulative as Renaud. The man was a disgrace to his profession.

An expectant silence settled over the hall. The crowd waited, almost salivating.

Lothair motioned to his guard. "Clear the hall. I want everyone out."

An undertone of disappointment rumbled through the crowd, and a prickle of unease flickered along Aimon's spine. Whatever Lothair had in store for them was not for public dissemination, and yet Lothair had ordered them to appear here, in the hall, rather than in his private chambers. His message was clear. You are mine to command, and I wish all to know it.

The guards stepped forward, ushering people out, the hum of conversation, the curious whispers fading to a murmur, the hall emptying with reluctant shuffles and curious backward glances.

"You too, Renaud."

"Mon Seigneur?"

Lothair's lips thinned. "I said out!"

Edmond gave a low chuckle, and Aimon dared to smirk in Renaud's direction. The archeveque scowled and opened his mouth, perhaps to argue his dismissal. Lothair glared, and Renaud's mouth snapped shut. With an angry swish of his robes, he stalked from the room, the thud of the large doors closing behind him echoing through the now empty hall. The alliance between the comte and the archeveque was more precarious than they had thought.

Aimon shifted his attention back to Lothair. The comte sat in his chair, his body draped in mail, his sword buckled about his waist and his keen gaze settling for a moment on each one of them. He had come to this meeting fully armed. Archeveque Renaud posed a significant threat, but their more deadly opponent sat before them.

Tension radiated from the men to Aimon's left, the stench of it coating his nostrils, but they made not a sound, standing firm. Aimon's heart swelled. That he was one of them, despite so few of them left, filled him with pride.

Lothair reached beneath his mail and retrieved a small gold disc on a chain. He held it out for them to see. A howling wolf's head on one side, a blood-red jewel glinting in the firelight, on the other. The throb of his pack members' emotions reached him—anger, disbelief, shock. Despite knowing Lothair had the binding amulet, having witnessed Lothair take it, seeing it in his hand unnerved him, too. He did not doubt the others would scent his unease.

"Interesting little thing, this," said Lothair, swinging the amulet on its chain. The alpha's amulet. "What it represents. What it does. I believe you all have one, though not quite like this."

A muscle ticked in Aimon's jaw. Did Lothair know the significance of the bloodstone set in its center?

"Renaud tells me your amulets have an inscription. That you can recite it and" — he snapped his fingers — "disappear."

The air crackled, like the moment before lightning struck, but no one said a word.

"But this one... This one is special. This stone" — he grasped the amulet, staring at the bloodstone — "denotes the alpha of your little...pack."

Aimon exhaled long and slow. Lothair had yet to discover the true purpose of the bloodstone, that it bound all other amulets to it. When they activated their amulets with blood and the words of the inscription, the bloodstone acted as a beacon, drawing them in. A safeguard for when they were at their most vulnerable. They may appear to disappear, but in reality, the bloodstone brought them home to the safety of their alpha, the strongest of them all.

Some of the tension eased from the men beside him, but they must wonder how Lothair came to possess the binding amulet.

"This one," continued Lothair, "belonged to Gaharet." He clasped the amulet in his hand and ran his fingers over it, examining it. His gaze flicked back to them. "Gaharet's dead."

A throaty rumble, a gasp, a ripple of anger from the men beside him. Aimon tried to tease out the different emotions from them, searching for one of triumph, a hint of satisfaction, but he sensed nothing untoward. He gritted his teeth. The traitor was adept at concealing his emotions from humans *and* their kind.

"It might surprise you to know," said Lothair, "he did not die by my hand, or at my orders. I took this…" he said, tossing the amulet in the air, catching it in his palm, once, twice, three times, "…off Ulrik."

The pulse of anger turned to fury and a low inhuman growl rumbled deep in the throat of one of them. Aubert? They had swallowed Ulrik's deception. In that godforsaken clearing, Gaharet and Ulrik had conceived a plan to fool everyone into thinking Gaharet was dead. Ulrik and Gaharet's past altercation making it easy for them to believe. Aimon smothered his relief, masking it, he hoped, with his fear for Ulrik. His skill at deception was somewhat lacking.

And what was Lothair's game? He knew Gaharet lived. Had seen him with his own eyes in the clearing. Aimon's brow furrowed. He caught Lothair's gaze, and a slight widening of the comte's eyes, before his attention flicked back to the other men.

L'enfer. Have I given myself away? Did Lothair now suspect he, too, knew Gaharet lived? That he had witnessed the exchange in the clearing. Observed Lothair and Gaharet come to an agreement?

Again, Lothair's gaze settled on him, and Aimon kept his face blank, opening his senses, reaching out to the comte.

Merde.

He dropped his gaze. Lothair reeked of curiosity. Because of him? Aimon could not tell.

"If my understanding of how this works is correct, then Ulrik is now your alpha," said Lothair. "But I am afraid you will not have the opportunity to congratulate him on his new position. He is resting. In a cell beneath this keep. Bound in silver."

The others shifted uneasily beside him.

"And what is it you want from us?" asked Edmond.

Lothair snarled. "Mon Seigneur."

"What?"

"What is it you want from us, *Mon Seigneur*?" Lothair leaned forward in his chair, his voice rising. "I am your comte, and I *will* have your allegiance *and* your obedience. You will yield to *me* and no other. When the next lot of squires comes before me to swear their investiture, you will kneel beside them. I will have it known no matter how powerful a chevalier becomes, he is *mine* to command. I will not tolerate any less than your full submission to my will, and *my* will alone."

The echoes of his voice bounced off the walls of the hall, fading to an eerie quiet. They were to be made a spectacle of. The indignity of it rankled, but Aimon would bend the knee for Lothair if he must.

Lance stepped forward and broke the unsettled silence. "Mon Seigneur Comte, I speak for all of us. We are loyal to you, as we have always been. If you wish us to re-pledge our allegiance to you, we will."

Lothair settled himself back into his chair. "Very well. You will continue to serve me in whatever capacity I deem fit. Any misguided attempt to rescue your new alpha will fail. I know how to control your kind. I know how to neutralize your…werewolf side. Renaud has told me all about your weakness to wolfsbane and silver."

He stared them down. Aimon had to give Lothair his due. Brave or crazy, few would have the courage to confront five of their kind at once. If but one of them made a move toward Lothair, it would not end well for the comte. As tempting as that was, they would not leave this hall alive if they did. Too many of the keep guard awaited them beyond the doors. Lothair was many things. Stupid was not one of them.

"I have what I want chained beneath my keep," said Lothair. "Ulrik will give me all I need. He will have little choice. He will bite someone, or he will die. I *will* have my werewolf army."

Aimon swallowed hard, the enormity of Ulrik's sacrifice now clear to him.

"And Archeveque Renaud will cease his attempts to kill us, as he has killed our brothers and our kin?" asked Lance.

Lothair glowered. "Leave the archeveque to me. Dismissed."

They turned to leave, all but Lance. Aimon paused.

"Mon Seigneur, what of Mademoiselle Erin? Gaharet's betrothed?"

Aimon tensed. What did Lance want with Erin?

Lothair's eyes narrowed. "What of her?"

"Gaharet would have wanted us to see to her wellbeing."

Aimon relaxed. Lance could not know Erin rested safely in Gaharet's care, hidden away in the forest. He was right to be concerned about her. His experience and steady guidance would serve them well in the coming days.

Lothair grunted. "Very well. You may do so."

"Thank you, Mon Seigneur Comte."

Dismissed, they retreated. Aimon exited the heavy doors, following along behind the others, his head down and lost in thought, he weaved his way through the throng of people pushing to return to the hall. He brushed against a woman and an unexpected scent invaded his nostrils. Aimon's head jerked up. He turned and took her in with all his enhanced senses. Small, feminine, with a dusting of freckles across her nose, she stared up at him. Dark shapes flitted within the depths of her hazel eyes. Bold eyes. Unashamed, they held his stare and his wolf stirred, rising to the surface. Aimon frowned. *Who is she?*

He tried to place her, unable and unwilling to look away. Kathryn, Gaharet's cousin. Kathryn Beauchene. Was it possible? Could they have overlooked her? Surely Gaharet would have been aware? If his nose did not lead him astray, then she was precious. Something they had feared lost.

He tried breathing in her scent again, but she turned away from him, and he lost any trace of her in the miasma of rank smells from the keep—of unwashed bodies, soiled meadowsweet rushes on the floor and smoke from the oil lamps. He looked toward Lance and the others. Had they caught her scent? No. Their faces grim and their focus elsewhere, they had moved too far away.

Aimon turned back to the woman in time to see her disappear through the doors into the hall. She glanced up at him and offered him a tentative smile. He smiled back, pondering this new possibility. For the scent he had caught, so briefly he could almost think he imagined it, was that of a female werewolf.

Chapter Three

Kathryn slipped into the hall, her cheeks burning. Aimon Proulx had smiled at her. For a moment their gazes had locked, and she had stared into the bluest eyes she had ever seen—intense, bright and looking straight at her. As she walked away, she had dared a backward glance and a coy smile. When he had smiled back, her heart had faltered. She caught Manette's scowl as the woman leaned in to whisper to Odila. Kathryn smirked. Out of all the women whose gazes followed Aimon's every move, hoping he would glance in their direction, *she* had been the focus of those piercing, blue eyes. Not Manette, or Odila, or even Lisette, who had yet to secure a husband. But her. Kathryn Beauchene. Perhaps she did have a chance of garnering his attention.

Her unease returned, their reason for being here tempering her triumph as she found a place in the crowd beside her father. Smells from the keep, from the people that crowded around her, jostled her—the stench of their emotions, their unwashed bodies overwhelmed her senses. The beast within stirred, and it pushed perilously close to the surface. What if word had reached the comte of all the suitors she had spurned? She clasped her hands together so tight her nails bit into the flesh of her palms.

"All will be well, Kathryn. It is certain to be a minor matter," said her father, patting her on the arm.

She gave him a wan smile, forcing the inner presence down and locking it away tight.

The doors closed, and quiet descended on the hall. The keep guard called up five young men, and Kathryn narrowed her concentration on them—on the stiffness of their shoulders and the sour taint of their nervousness. They stood before the comte, hoping to be found worthy of being a squire to a chevalier. No doubt wanting to be a chevalier themselves one day. Fearing the comte would reject them. The comte stepped forward, running his gaze over each of the young men, sizing them up, their jubilation and pride ringing loud in Kathryn's mind when Comte Lothair accepted them. She applauded absently along with the crowd.

A cloth merchant came next, dragged forward by the keep guard. Accused of cheating his clients, his fear and guilt clogged her nostrils. He received seven days in the stocks. The comte was no more deceived by his vehement protestations of innocence than she was. Next, Baron and Baronne Cousineau were called on. For services rendered, the comte announced their daughter's betrothal to his second cousin, elevating the family's status. From the gleam in the baron's eyes and the haughty tilt of his wife's chin, they were most satisfied. From her unshed tears and the sting of sorrow only Kathryn could taste, their daughter was not.

Bile rose in the back of Kathryn's throat, the clamor of the crowd's whispered gossip receding in the fog descending over her. Was this to be her fate, too? A husband chosen by the comte? Any one of the many men whose proposals she had rejected could have petitioned Comte Lothair.

"Farren and Kathryn Beauchene." The keep guard's voice rang loud across the packed hall.

Kathryn snapped to attention, her nerves fluttering in her stomach, as she stepped forward with her father. Manette's open curiosity did little to quell the dread hounding her every step.

"Mon Seigneur Comte." Kathryn bowed her head and curtseyed to the man sitting at the apex of the hall surrounded by his guards. Scores of eyes watched them, the weight of their stares bearing down on her, eager to see if the comte rewarded or punished them. Or, as with the Cousineau's daughter, would the reward be its own punishment?

Comte Lothair's gaze assessed her, running up and down her body before settling on her face. Kathryn straightened her shoulders a little and lifted her chin. Amusement flickered in the comte's eyes, his fingers thrumming against the arm of his chair. Kathryn gritted her teeth and kept a tight leash on her temper.

His fingers stilled, and the comte's attention switched to her father.

"Farren Beauchene, I am granting you the lands and monies once held by your nephew, Gaharet d'Louncrais."

Startled gasps and a low muttering skittered about the hall. Kathryn, wide-eyed, turned to her father. His stunned expression matched her own incredulity.

"But...Mon Seigneur Comte... What of Seigneur Gaharet?" asked her father.

Comte Lothair waved a dismissive hand. "Gaharet is not your concern."

Gathering himself, her father bowed his head. "As you will, Mon Seigneur Comte."

"I have organized men from my guard to escort you to the d'Louncrais demesne," said Comte Lothair. "I expect you to take up residence there today."

Kathryn fidgeted beside her father, the envious and calculating stares from the throng of courtiers and chevaliers disconcerting. In her wildest dreams, she could not have foreseen this. Her marriage prospects had certainly improved. But at the expense of her cousin? Why? She opened her mouth, but her father's warning glance had her clamping it shut.

Comte Lothair rose and stepped away from the dais, coming to stand before her. Taking her chin in his hand, he tilted her head from side to side. Kathryn's body trembled with the effort to not snatch her face away. Her father's hand settled on her arm, cautioning her against any rash action.

"I expect you will see many a man eager to take advantage of your change in fortune, looking to secure your daughter's hand in marriage." His voice barely above a whisper, the comte addressed her father, not her. "You will turn them all away."

Heat burned Kathryn's cheeks, and her nostrils flared.

Her father nodded. "As you wish, Mon Seigneur."

No! Why? What does the comte want from us? From me?

"With the exception of Gaharet's vassals. Should any of them call upon you, and I suspect they will, I will know of it immediately. You may allow them to court her, but you will make no agreements without my consent."

Kathryn wrenched her face from his grip and glared at the comte. How dare he take her choice away? One she clung to with every breath in her body.

"Kathryn." Her father's tone brooked no disagreement. "Come. We have a household of belongings to prepare. By your leave, Mon Seigneur."

Comte Lothair nodded, a sharp intelligence glittering in his eyes. She would have considered him handsome if not for his mocking smile. Kathryn gave a perfunctory curtsey before turning on her heel to follow her father from the hall. Shoulders tense, she strode past Manette, too incensed to gloat over the woman's chagrin.

Pushing through the doors and out into the bailey, she halted and took a deep breath to reassert calm. Her father took her elbow and led her from the keep grounds toward the home they were to vacate. She suspected he wanted a bit more privacy before she vented her feelings.

"This is not what I would have wanted for you, Kathryn, but you yourself had set your sights on one of Gaharet's men. You should be happy with our change of circumstances."

"Happy?" Kathryn glared at her father, her nostrils flaring. "Yes, I want access to Gaharet's circle, to his vassals, but I also want the right to choose. Now the comte has taken that away."

"Keep your voice down, Kathryn."

She pursed her lips but acknowledged his caution with a stiff nod. "Why has he done this, Father? Why has he given us Gaharet's estate? And what has happened to Gaharet?" She blew out an unladylike sigh. "Clearly, Comte Lothair has some plan that involves his vassals. Did you see them leaving as we arrived?"

"I did. Did you also notice Ulrik's absence?"

She shook her head. Heat burned her cheeks. No, she had not. She had been too busy focusing on one vassal in particular.

"Something is most definitely afoot. Granting us Gaharet's demesne was done with a very specific purpose in mind. Lothair could have bequeathed it on any of one of Gaharet's vassals had he chosen to, yet he did not. My guess is he wishes to see which one of Gaharet's vassals is ambitious enough to take the bait."

"And I am the bait?"

"In part, yes."

Kathryn's shoulders slumped. Her father halted and took hold of her hands.

"Though I would never have chosen one of Gaharet's vassals for you, all is not lost, Kathryn. You wanted their attention. Now you have it. The comte may wish to be informed if any of them come calling, but we have some control over who we allow to spend time with you."

"But Comte Lothair said to make no agreements without his consent."

"So, we ensure only one vassal has access to you."

Kathryn stared at her father. *He would defy the comte? Circumvent his command in order to affect the outcome?* Her father had never been one to challenge authority. He smiled at her and brushed his hand across her cheek.

"Now, come, child. Tell me which of Gaharet's vassals has caught your fancy."

* * * *

The business of running his county concluded and the hall now empty, Lothair sat, chin resting in his hand, ruminating on his decision regarding the

Beauchenes. Regret twinged in his gut at giving away all the d'Louncrais' had amassed. Especially knowing his vassal still lived. But he saw no other way. Gaharet's wealth was reason enough for any of his vassals to betray him, but would making it readily available to them reveal Renaud's informant?

One thing he knew for certain—it was not Aimon. Young and unpracticed in court politics, his unguarded expression had given him away. Aimon knew Gaharet lived, and yet he had not informed his fellow werewolves. *Interesting.* How he would use this information Lothair did not yet know but use it he would if it served his purpose.

And what of Gaharet's betrothed? Gaharet had eschewed any manner of eligible matches in favor of a woman with no background at all. Who was she that Lance now sought to find her? And that girl of Farren's... Feisty, and pretty, too. Marrying her to gain the d'Louncrais wealth would be no hardship for any man. He stood and adjusted his sword. He had set things in motion. Now all he need do was wait. Which of Gaharet's vassals would try to claim the prize?

Chapter Four

"We will have a month at most, no more," said Lance, as the five of them sat astride their horses at the crossroads beyond Langeais village. Horses trained to take their kind. "Lothair will want us re-pledging our allegiance as soon as he can. He will usher in fresh, unprepared squires if need be. It will be nice and public to remind us of our place."

Edmond's low rumble penetrated Aimon's thoughts, and he looked up at the disgruntled faces of his pack.

"I do not like it any more than any of you do, but we will do it. We will kneel before him like green young men, humble in his presence, if that is what it takes to appease him," said Lance.

With their mood tense, and anger a living presence amongst them, they had positioned themselves close enough to hear each other talk, yet a distance existed between them not present before. The bond he had once thought unbreakable, of shared knowledge and understanding, had fractured.

Aimon's attention drifted from the grumbles of complaint back to Kathryn Beauchene, and the moment she had brushed past him. He could not *stop* thinking about it, about her — her freckled nose, her pretty hazel eyes, her smile, her musky werewolf scent that teased his nostrils. How had her presence gone undetected by werewolves more experienced than he? Werewolves born, not made. Was he wrong? Could the wolfsbane still be affecting his nose?

He knew of Kathryn. His mother had once considered her a suitable match for him a few years back. Before he had become a werewolf. Before he had sworn allegiance to Gaharet. When his mother had sought advancement for the family through his marriage. Kathryn had caught his mother's eye not because of any wealth, titles or standing of the Beauchenes'. Her suitability stemmed from her connection to the d'Louncrais. Save for that, his mother disapproved of Kathryn, thought her outspoken and a little wild. A woman with no talent for the approved activities for ladies of her station.

Gossip did not speak kindly of Kathryn, and his mother reveled in gossip, breathed it in like oxygen and dispensed it with equal veracity. He had defended Kathryn and chided his mother on believing rumors most likely unfounded. It had only encouraged a lengthy lecture on how, should he secure Kathryn's hand in marriage, he would need to bring a firm hand to the girl and make her conform. No more unchaperoned forays into the forest, or swimming in the mill pond in her chemise. If not for his mother's distaste, he may not have remembered Kathryn at all.

"It is possible Lothair will drag Ulrik out in chains and parade him around," said Edmond. "Force him to kneel beside us. This statement of his is not only for our benefit."

The mention of Ulrik snapped Aimon's focus back to the conversation. He would be of no use to Gaharet if he did not pay attention.

"If he is still alive," muttered Aubert, shaking his head.

"Better he dies than give Lothair what he wants," said Godfrey.

"Better he dies, anyway. He betrayed us. He must have told Renaud of our weakness to wolfsbane. It is a fair bet he also told him about our amulets." Edmond's voice was little more than a growl. "And he killed Gaharet."

Edmond's horse pranced, reacting to the tension and anger resonating from its rider. The other horses stirred. Aimon held his reins firm and edged his own horse a foot or two further away. Emotions, sharp-edged, simmered in the air.

"We are all angry about what has taken place, but it is better we free him from Lothair's keep. We are too few." Lance's serious gray eyes took them in. "We need every single one of us if we are going to survive."

Edmond shook his head. "He betrayed us. We do not need him and I, for one, do not want him with us."

"I do not like it either, but he is still our alpha." Lance's jaw set firm and his eyes dared them to disagree. "No matter our feelings, he has won that right. Unless one of you wishes to visit Ulrik's cell and challenge him, he will remain so. It is our way, as it has been for centuries. It is not for us to question. Agreed?"

Aimon conceded with a brief nod. Lance's seniority in the pack was not something easily ignored. Godfrey also nodded.

"Agreed?" Lance fixed his stare on the twins, their resentment clear on their faces. After a pause fraught with tension, they, too, nodded in assent.

"You can challenge him once we have him out of Lothair's clutches, but for now he is our alpha." Lance paused, taking in a deep breath. "We also must stop Lothair's plan for an enhanced army. I do not believe any of us want to see an army of our kind under Lothair's command."

No, we do not.

"So, we rescue Ulrik," said Aimon. "It would be a blow to Lothair's plan if Ulrik were to escape. I imagine Renaud would not be too happy either."

Godfrey gave a shrug of his shoulders. "I have no objection to foiling Lothair's plan. If we can go one step further and lay the blame for his escape on Renaud, it would be to our advantage. That Lothair excluded Renaud from our meeting suggests the alliance between them is already crumbling. Perhaps we can sever it completely."

"Then once Ulrik is free, we kill him ourselves," growled Edmond. "Our way."

Aubert nodded. "He betrayed us. He deserves nothing less."

Aimon gritted his teeth but kept his silence.

"We have to free him first," said Godfrey. "With silver, and possibly wolfsbane to contend with, that is no easy feat." Godfrey rubbed his chin, frowning. "There is something I do not understand. Something bothers me about all this."

Lance cocked his eyebrows. "Such as?"

Godfrey rubbed at the back of his neck. "Did any of you witness what took place in the rendezvous clearing? I saw two score of mounted men heading for it, so did not dare venture there."

"They saturated our clearing in wolfsbane. I could barely make out who had been there. It completely addled my senses," offered Edmond. "The closer I got, the more dulled my senses became, and I struggled to control my form. My body wanted to shift without me willing it."

"Same for me," said Aubert.

Lance nodded. "Archeveque Renaud and Comte Lothair were there for certain, but I could discern little else."

"There were mercenaries. Hired by Renaud? They were all dead when I arrived." Aimon chose his words with care, heedful not to tell a lie.

"What are you thinking, Godfrey?" asked Lance.

"Each of us saw something or caught the scent of wolfsbane and managed to avoid the trap. Yet, Ulrik did not. Ulrik is hot-headed and impulsive, but he is far from being a fool. If he told Renaud about wolfsbane, why would he have been careless enough to get caught by it?"

Lance leaned forward in his saddle. "What are you suggesting?"

Godfrey shook his head. "I am not sure. I cannot envision Ulrik allying with Lothair. Not after what happened to his family. Or with Renaud. Ulrik has his faults, but I would sooner believe Lothair gentle and kind than Ulrik would aid them."

"Would you doubt, too, he killed Gaharet?" demanded Edmond.

Godfrey pursed his lips, and Aimon waited, tense. Ulrik and Gaharet's deception could be for naught if Godfrey questioned it.

"No," he said, after a long silence. "That I can believe. He challenged Gaharet for the pack once before and lost. Perhaps he saw an opportunity and took advantage of the situation, of Gaharet's vulnerability with the woman."

"And then got caught in Renaud's trap?" Lance inclined his head. "It is a possibility?"

"Then who betrayed our weaknesses? How does Lothair know about the amulets?" asked Edmond.

Aimon studied the mounted men, his friends, his pack mates. Who could he trust, and who lied with every word that came from their traitorous mouth? The twins, Aubert and Edmond, were livid, their anger visible in every movement they made and every word they spoke, their sense of betrayal very real. Godfrey's quiet, thoughtful words were not out of character and about Lance hung an air of defeat, as though news of Gaharet's death had extinguished the fight in him.

None of them gave him cause to doubt their loyalty. And yet one of them was lying and telling them all what they expected to hear. How could he uncover the traitor when Gaharet, who had known these men all his life, could not?

"Are we certain Gaharet's dead?" asked Godfrey.

Lance's shoulders slumped. "Lothair has the binding amulet with the bloodstone. Gaharet would never relinquish it to Ulrik, not willingly. But you are right, Godfrey. We cannot presume Ulrik is responsible for everything. It is another reason we must free him. We need answers. And there is also the matter of Gaharet's betrothed. We must ensure her safety. Gaharet would want that of us."

Edmond tugged at his beard. "Gaharet would have kept her close. Perhaps Ulrik has taken her somewhere."

"All the more reason to find her," said Lance.

"Now Gaharet is gone, one of us should have her at least," muttered Godfrey.

Lance's eyebrows shot up. "You surprise me, Godfrey. I would not have expected such sentiments from you."

Aimon glared at him, uncomfortable with where Godfrey's thoughts had gone. "You are no better than Ulrik."

"For all his faults, Ulrik was right. We are not in a position to be choosy. If she was willing to mate with Gaharet, she should be willing to mate with any of us." Godfrey stared at Aimon. "How many women have you found who would accept what we are, what they would have to become?"

Aimon remained silent.

"None. Like the rest of us. They are few and are hard to find. Unlike you, we have waited years, some of us decades, to find a mate. Gaharet is dead, and if she is not with Ulrik... Why waste a resource?"

Aimon looked away. Ever the reminder of his origins—turned, not born.

"Whatever the situation," said Lance, giving both Aimon and Godfrey a warning glance, "we need to find her. Either Gaharet, or Ulrik, may have begun the turning. She needs our help."

"I crossed paths with Gaharet and Erin early on that night," Aimon spoke up. "I can return there and try to track where they went. Erin may recognize me."

Lance nodded. "If her turning has begun, you are also the best to understand her suffering."

A cart trundled into view and all of them tensed, hands hovering near the hilts of their swords. The conversation turned to innocuous talk of training horses and commissioning of equipment until the wagon had passed beyond their sight. They breathed a collective sigh and relaxed back into their saddles. Aimon's lips curled. They were worried about a farmer and his wagon, while a traitor lurked in their midst.

"When we pledge allegiance to Lothair," continued Lance, picking up their conversation, "I plan to petition him for Gaharet's demesne."

Aimon struggled to keep his expression neutral. Could it be that simple? Had one of them schemed, all along, to gain what Gaharet had had — leadership of the pack, power, immense wealth and now a mate?

"We cannot leave it open for anyone to take. It should remain within the pack," said Lance.

Edmond snorted. "You may want to rethink that idea." He leaned back into his saddle and crossed his arms across his broad chest.

"Oh?"

"Have you not heard? Lothair has already redistributed it."

"What? So soon? To whom?"

"It is the talk of Langeais. Lothair has made no secret of it. He has handed the entire estate to Farren Beauchene. Did you not see the keep guard in the village loading up wagons?"

"Gaharet's uncle?" Aimon's mind flitted back to a freckled nose and a bold stare.

Well, that makes things more complicated.

"Yes. I talked to the guard. Lothair insisted they occupy Gaharet's keep from today."

"They?" asked Lance.

"He has a daughter, Kathryn, of marriageable age." Edmond cast them all a knowing smile.

Aimon's wolf shifted within, a restless energy beneath the surface. He frowned. Did his wolf know something, sense something, he did not? An image of Kathryn's smile hovered in his mind, and his darker half pushed to the surface with more force. He willed it away. Now was not the time.

"What game is Lothair playing at? He has to know every eligible man will petition for her hand," said Godfrey.

"Including us," rumbled Aubert.

"I would imagine that is the point. Perhaps there is some truth to your theory, Godfrey. That the blame for all our circumstances does not rest entirely with Ulrik." Lance's eyes grew troubled. "If you are right, then this may be a ploy to draw out Renaud's informant."

Aimon's blood froze. Clever, but damned inconvenient. If his suspicions about Kathryn's true nature had foundation, Lothair's gambit put her in danger from the very person who had brought about the loss of all the pack's females.

Edmond shrugged. "A clever trap, but easily avoided."

"Not if we want to keep the d'Louncrais wealth in the pack," muttered Godfrey.

"Spread the word the Beauchenes are to be left alone, that they are under our protection for now," commanded Lance. "Make it clear any who seek them out will face our wrath. Few would dare challenge us, and the ones who do we can deal with. If need be, we can consider one of us taking Kathryn as a wife in time, but for now, we will all keep our distance. I will speak to Lothair and see what can be done. If nothing else, we must ingratiate ourselves back into his favor."

Aubert huffed. "I do not like your chances. He turned on Gaharet, the closest person he had to a friend."

Edmond snorted. "Lothair has friends? This is the first I am hearing of it."

"That may be so, but I must try. Aimon, you will track Gaharet and Erin's last movements. Aubert and Edmond, you look into Renaud. Find out anything you can on him. Let him see you doing it. Let him know we have him in our sights." Lance turned to Godfrey. "Godfrey, we cannot get access to the d'Louncrais library, but your father kept an extensive collection of scrolls and tomes. See if you can find anything on circumventing wolfsbane and silver. We need to free Ulrik from Langeais Keep."

"One of us should talk to the witch in the forest," suggested Edmond.

Lance frowned. "The witch in the forest?"

"She has herbs that could help with a turning. We mentioned her to Gaharet. Ulrik was there. Aimon, too. Perhaps Gaharet sought her out that night."

"I will visit her," offered Aimon. Gaharet and Erin were still there. He could not risk another of the pack sniffing around. "Perhaps Gaharet's trail will lead me to the witch, and, with any luck, Erin as well."

"Very well. Ask the witch about wolfsbane, too. We will meet again in fourteen days hence. Unless any of us finds something important, it is best we all lie low." Lance gathered his horse's reins as another wagon loaded down with hay trundled into view. "Stay safe. We cannot afford to lose any more of our kind."

Taking up their reins, they separated and cantered off to their respective tasks. As soon as he was out of sight, Aimon changed direction and headed for Gaharet's keep. To see Kathryn. He had to know for sure. He wished he could tell the others of his suspicions. It pained him more than anything that he could not trust them. But if Kathryn were a werewolf, keeping her secret was the only way to keep her alive.

Chapter Five

Dusk eased across the sky as the three wagons carrying all their possessions wound their way toward the d'Louncrais keep. The clop of the horses' hooves slowed, and the idle chatter of the keep guard escorting them petered out. The walls of Kathryn's new home loomed before her, a formidable barrier to protect the inhabitants. A barrier to confine her to her new circumstances. Her throat tightened.

The unfairness of it rankled. Her choice of the man who would be her husband now taken away from her. Despite her father reassuring her they had some sway, that they could manipulate Gaharet's vassals into an outcome of her choosing, Kathryn was far from convinced. Would Lance Vautour defer to the much younger Aimon if she expressed a preference for him? Everything she knew about Lance told her no. Would they fight over her? Or would they simply decide amongst themselves who would claim the prize of the d'Louncrais estate, and her along with it?

Her darker half roiled inside her, feeding on her emotions — a persistent force determined to break free. When her emotions ran high, the surging call of the curse was stronger — a rush of heat through her body, an aching in her bones and an overwhelming compulsion to change. Right now, with the beast closest to the surface since her turning, it would only take a moment of inattention for it to gain the upper hand. If she could not regain some measure of equilibrium, she might lose control. She could never allow that to happen.

She eyed the expanse of forest stretching beyond the walls. Its shadows beckoned her, offering sanctuary and a temporary relief. The forest soothed the beast and helped give her the strength to resist it.

"Father?"

He smiled at her. "Go on, then."

Her father understood her, understood her need. She stepped from the slow-moving wagon, ignoring the startled looks from Lothair's guard, and darted toward the trees. A muttered oath from a guard, and hoof beats followed her.

"Let her go," her father called out. "She wishes to explore a little. She knows not to be too long."

"Willful girl," muttered the guard, but the hoofbeats retreated.

Leaving the wagons behind, Kathryn slipped past the tree line, pressing into the forest and out of sight. Breathing in the pine and earthy scent, feeling the cool darkness of the woods on her flushed skin, the beast ceased its restless pacing. Kathryn removed her head-veil and unpinned her hair, letting it cascade over her shoulders. She unlaced her boots and discarded them, reveling in the earth beneath her bare feet. She closed her eyes, and a smile tugged at the corner of her lips. Relief.

A bird screeched, and Kathryn's sensitive hearing caught the subtle brush of wings in flight. A rodent, a dormouse by its scent, scurried nearby in search of food. The creak of limbs and the rustle of leaves in the breeze whispered their soothing song in her ears. Kathryn had long grown accustomed to the enhanced senses her curse afforded her. She resisted using them, terrified calling on them too often would allow the beast a foothold on her consciousness, one it could use to consume her. But being here in the forest, the one thing that never failed to placate it, she relaxed. Opening herself to them, she let the sounds and smells of the forest wash over her, a balm to her agitated mind.

She tilted her head back, pointed her face to the leafy canopy above, stretched her arms out wide and turned in slow circles. A laugh bubbled up inside her. Mayhap her father was right. Perhaps they could turn Comte Lothair's bequest to their favor, and determine the man she would marry. And with the forest this close, she may even find contentment.

The breeze shifted, bringing with it a strange yet tantalizing scent. She halted her spinning and turned her head toward it, breathing in deep through her nostrils. The scent grew stronger, filling her lungs, its tendrils curling through her body starting an unexpected tingling between her thighs. Strong, musky and animal, but with a hint of...human? Her nipples tightened, and the beast writhed, pushing forward.

She gasped and her eyes popped open. *What is it?* She had calmed the beast and yet it stirred again. What was this...this intoxicating aroma? Her eyes darted about, searching the shadows for its source. Her gaze locked on a figure shrouded in shadows.

Aimon Proulx.

Standing in the gloom of the trees, he watched her. Silent. His long white-blond hair fell about his shoulders, his blue surcoat rustled in the breeze and his hand rested on the pommel of the sword belted to his waist. There he was, the chevalier from her dream, looking every bit the angelic warrior she had imagined him to be.

Her pulse raced and her thighs clenched. The beast hammered at her consciousness. A bone in her hand cracked and claws extended from two fingers. She hid them behind her skirts.

No. Please, no.

Aimon stepped closer, his musky scent intensifying, and his gaze fixed on her with a fervor that stirred feelings in her no man had ever elicited before.

The beast thrashed within. Another bone popped in her finger. Kathryn held her breath. If she looked, she would see coarse red hair sprouting across the back of her hand. She fought the change, and it halted, but it did not regress. Aimon could not be here with her. Not now. Not with the beast so close to breaking free. She must make him leave before she lost all authority over the darkness within. Before she lost the battle and shifted into a slavering monster. Before she attacked him.

"I suspected my change in circumstances would attract men to our door," she said, attempting to keep any hint of her panic from entering her voice. "I did not imagine it would begin so soon."

He stepped closer, his gaze never leaving her face as though mesmerized. Never had she been the focus of such scrutiny. It unnerved her and scratched at the frayed edges of her control. The sharp point of a canine scraped against the inside of her mouth. She willed it to recede, testing it with her tongue to ensure it had.

"Perhaps you would do me the kindness of visiting the keep, Monsieur Aimon." She pointed in its direction. "My father and I would be happy to receive you."

The breeze floated his scent to her, and her nostrils quivered. His scent. Like the siren song of mermaids, it called to her monster, luring it from the depths of her mind. Oh, why did he not smell like other chevaliers? Of horsehair, stale sweat, blood and steel? She wished he did, rejoiced he did not.

Why is this happening? Now? He came. The one vassal out of all of them she had hoped to attract. She wanted to smile at him, converse with him, but for his own safety, he must leave.

"Have you gone mute, Monsieur Aimon, or do you often skulk in the forest, catching unsuspecting women off guard?" She cringed at her harsh words, but he had left her little choice.

He tilted his head to the side and raised an eyebrow at her. "Do you often wander the forest unaccompanied and barefoot?" he countered.

She flushed and snatched up her boots and veil from where she had discarded them. If he would not leave, then she must. "Good evening, Monsieur Aimon. I suggest you call on us in the morning."

She spun on a barefooted heel and headed toward the keep. Of course he had noticed her state of undress. How long had he stood there watching? Had he seen her alight from the wagon? Spied on her as she had spun around, barefoot and her hair loose, reveling in her freedom? Kathryn's heart ached. In all likelihood, after witnessing such wanton behavior, after the way she had spoken to him so rudely, he would decide against presenting himself to the keep, and she would never see him again. She had ruined everything.

A rush of air whooshed past her, and suddenly Aimon stood in front of her, cutting off her retreat. Her momentum propelled her into his chest.

"Oh!" She stumbled away from him.

He reached out and grasped her arm, steadying her.

"How did you...?" She looked back over her shoulder to where he had been, then back at him, clutching her boots and veil to her chest. "You moved so fast, I..." Intent on fleeing, had she not noticed his pursuit of her? She raised her eyes to meet his, much closer now. Too close. A shiver raced up her spine and a soft growl rumbled in her chest. She sucked in a panicked breath. If he heard it, he gave no hint.

He reached out and touched her hair with a gentleness that was almost reverent. "You have the most glorious hair." He let the strands slide through his fingers. "The color is like nothing I have ever seen on a woman before. Like the leaves of the maple tree in the autumn."

Her knees wobbled. *He likes my hair.*

His fingers delved into her hair again, brushing against her neck, and his gaze dipped to her mouth. Her tongue flicked out to lick her lips, suddenly gone dry, and his blue eyes flared with heat. Her breath came in shallow pants, and she leaned closer. Would he kiss her?

His hand slipped from her hair, down to cradle her neck, and he drew her closer. Another bone in her hand cracked, but she could not make herself move. She swallowed hard. He stilled, his mouth hovering a mere breath away from hers, her lips tingling in anticipation.

This may well be the only chance she got.

Kathryn bridged the gap between them, and he pressed his mouth to hers. She gasped, her lips softening, and her eyes fluttered closed.

L'enfer.

Her heart's pounding beat echoed in her ears. She leaned into him without thought or conscious effort, her hand reaching up of its own volition, and she placed her palm on his chest. This one kiss, this light touching of lips, stoked a fire within her she had not dreamed could exist.

The change roared up, powerful, insistent and threatening to strip away the last shred of her humanity. She wrenched herself from his grasp. Hiding her shifting hand beneath her veil, she pushed past him and slipped beyond his grasp so he could not stop her.

Hand over her mouth, her lips still warm from his kiss, she sobbed as she raced from the forest. She had to get away from him before she let the beast loose. He would not like her hair then. Not when she had the power to hurt him, to physically tear him to pieces.

The color draining from her face, and the fear in her eyes, had Aimon letting Kathryn go. His breathing labored, he clenched his fists to his sides to stop himself from reaching for her.

"Please do not run," he whispered after her, not certain he could hold himself in check.

As soon as Kathryn cleared the tree line, she broke into a run. Aimon gritted his teeth and sunk his claws into a nearby tree trunk, resisting the primal urge to chase after her, bring her down beneath him, and seduce her until she cried out his name in the throes of passion.

Merde. What am I thinking? Have I lost my mind?

Panting, reinstating the control Gaharet had taught him how to master, he steadied himself—his human brain, and his conscience, reasserting themselves.

Only three years a wolf, he did not yet suffer the growing desperation of the others who longed for their mate. Their desire to find the one they would cherish for life a consuming force, only stronger now their pack teetered on the verge of extinction. Gaharet assured him, in time, it would engulf him, too. But, catching Kathryn's werewolf scent, seeing her fiery auburn hair tumble about her shoulders—a beacon of flame in this cool forest of greens and browns—hunger had stormed through him stronger than he had ever experienced before. It made his heart pound and his cock as hard as stone.

She was beautiful, from the smattering of freckles across her nose down to her tiny bare toes. Her musky werewolf scent mingling with the tantalizing notes of her innocence had called to him, to his baser half. The change had roared up on him fast, catching him by surprise, and he had struggled to keep it in check. Aimon could only surmise the combination of her innocence, her werewolf scent, and a spirit with a vibrancy to match her hair, were the reason for his powerful response. And she was, most assuredly, a werewolf. He could not mistake it, not here in the clean air beneath the trees.

He straightened himself, retracted his claws and pushed his wolf into the deep, dark recesses of his mind. Kathryn, innocent Kathryn, deserved more than a single moment of pleasure. His way forward was clear. An untouched, previously unknown female werewolf, Kathryn needed safeguarding. From Lothair, Renaud, from his pack mates, perhaps even from him. Gaharet would expect nothing less. He would not let his urges jeopardize her wellbeing. Whatever the cost to himself, Aimon must protect her. Keep her safe. Keep her alive.

Chapter Six

Aimon entered the keep walls as the guards were unloading the last of the Beauchenes' possessions from the wagons. Stable boys unhitched horses and servants hustled the Beauchenes' belongings up the hill to the keep. They scarce glanced at him, but the gazes of Lothair's keep guard followed him as he rode up the hill. By the morrow, when the guard returned to Langeais, Lothair would know of his attendance here.

He ignored them, making his way past the stables and the smithy to the large entrance doors of the tower. He could do little about their presence. Delaying until they were gone would have been the wiser course of action, but Aimon feared he did not have time to wait. Kathryn would not fail to inform her father of their encounter in the forest. What would she have told him? Would Farren be angry to know Aimon had kissed his daughter? He had every right to be. Delaying the inevitable confrontation would not make any easier the conversation he must have with Farren. And there was no telling if another of the pack would come calling on Kathryn.

He dismounted, and a stable boy came running to take his horse as the head servant, Gascon, stepped from the entryway to greet him.

"Good to see you again, Monsieur Aimon," said Gascon, ushering him inside.

"I am glad to see you here, Gascon. It is a relief to see a familiar face." Aimon looked around. "Is it still the same servants here, or have the Beauchenes brought some of their own people?"

"It is still all my family, Monsieur Aimon," Gascon assured him. "I believe the gifting of the demesne includes us all. Whether the Beauchenes plan on keeping any of us on, we will know in time."

"Good. I may have need of your help before the night is through."

Gascon motioned for Aimon to follow him, and led him to the vacant hall, the central fire pit lit and the large, oak table empty. The last time Aimon had been here, all seven of them, including Gaharet, had sat at this table. They had shared a meal, discussed their concerns about Archeveque Renaud and experienced hope upon Erin's arrival. It seemed like a lifetime ago. *How strange to be in this room now without Gaharet's anchoring presence.*

"You mean with the girl, Mademoiselle Kathryn?" asked Gascon.

Aimon started. "What do you know of Mademoiselle Kathryn? Has Gaharet mentioned her?"

"I am afraid I know very little. But she entered the keep in a state of distress and, while she hid it well from most, I caught glimpses of her hands transitioning back and forth between one form and the other."

His presence had affected her as much as hers had affected him.

"We have seen neither her, nor her father, since the death of Dame d'Louncrais, Monsieur Gaharet's mother. But prior, when she visited with her father, there was never any suggestion she was one of your kind."

Then Kathryn was not born but bitten. When? And by whom? Aimon was not certain which he found more disturbing—that it had happened at all, or that the pack had no knowledge of it. "Do you know why the Beauchenes stopped visiting?"

Gascon shook his head. "No, Monsieur Aimon. The death of Dame Elise devastated the d'Louncrais. Seigneur Jacques grieved to the exclusion of all else, and Seigneur Gaharet absorbed himself in the running of the estate and the pack. I suspect, over time, without the presence of Dame Elise, the connection with the Beauchenes simply lapsed."

"Mmm. Where is Kathryn now?"

"In her chamber. I have sent Anne to make some of her calming brew and to minister to her. She seems the most suitable for the task."

Aimon smiled. He had come under Anne's care when Gaharet had sheltered him during his own turning, and the subsequent months after. A good choice, motherly and caring, but she would take no nonsense from recalcitrant werewolves. Of that, Aimon had personal experience.

"Anne is just the person to care for Kathryn. I must talk to Farren first, but this may prove a difficult night for his daughter. Kathryn is in grave danger. Can I count on you? And Anne?"

"Of course, Monsieur Aimon. Without question. May I know the nature of this danger?"

Aimon thought for a moment. "She is not safe, not even from us. Especially not from us. One of our own has betrayed the pack. We have a traitor in our midst."

Gascon's face paled and he slumped onto a seat. "Oh, my."

"That is not all. Comte Lothair and Archeveque Renaud are now aware of our existence. There are schemes afoot, and I fear Kathryn has unwittingly become a part of it all."

"Do they know she is—?"

Aimon shook his head. "I do not believe so. And I am certain I am the only one of our kind who knows, too. We must keep it so. We cannot risk her being discovered. Not until we find and deal with the traitor."

"Of course, Monsieur Aimon. You have my word."

"Can you keep me informed if any of the others should try to see Kathryn? You cannot refuse them entry. Even I could not stop them. It is unfortunate, for as soon as they enter these walls, they will sense her, but we must do all we can. Ensuring her safety is our priority."

"Leave it to me. I will organize our people. And I will inform Anne of the situation. Perhaps she knows of some strong-smelling herbs that may help disguise her scent."

"Thank you, Gascon." Aimon moved toward the door.

"Monsieur Aimon, if I may ask? What has happened to Seigneur Gaharet and Mademoiselle Erin?"

Aimon turned to Gascon, perhaps the most loyal servant in the whole county. His extended family had served the d'Louncrais for generations. "Hiding," he said. "The others believe he is dead, and his mate missing. It is the only thing keeping them safe."

"Thank you, Monsieur Aimon. They will not hear it from me. I will not tell a soul. Not even Anne. Come, I will show you to the library. I should warn you, Seigneur Farren encountered the distraught Mademoiselle Kathryn when she burst into the keep. He is expecting you."

* * * *

Aimon found Farren Beauchene seated beside the brazier, a goblet of wine in hand, his expression dark and his brow furrowed. The d'Louncrais' vaunted collection of tomes, books and scrolls filled chests lining the walls, but Farren showed no interest in them. His dark hair, graying at the temples, gave no hint of where Kathryn's vibrant, copper locks had come from, but Aimon saw her in the hazel eyes that bored into him as he entered the room.

Farren did not offer him either a chair or a drink, eyeing him up and down. Aimon stood his ground. Old enough to be Aimon's father — quite an accomplishment under Lothair's rule — Farren deserved respect for that alone. And he was Kathryn's father. Aimon would need his help with keeping Kathryn safe. He would take whatever tongue lashing Farren gave him. And apologize for his behavior.

He sampled the air, catching Farren's scent. Human. Whatever had occurred had happened to Kathryn alone.

"I understand us being here in Gaharet's home must be difficult for you." Farren took a long sip from his cup. "It is difficult for us, too."

Aimon held his silence.

"We did not ask for this. We are here only because Comte Lothair has ordered it so." His face flushed, and his fist thumped down on the arm of his chair. "There was no need to upset my daughter."

"You have my apologies, Farren. Upsetting your daughter was not my intention. But I did come to see her."

Farren nodded. "Comte Lothair suggested some of Gaharet's vassals might." He waved Aimon to a seat.

Aimon hesitated, puzzled by Farren's easy acquiescence. Had Kathryn not detailed their interaction in the forest? Mentioned their kiss? He pulled up a chair, adjusting his sword aside, and sat opposite Farren.

"You have come for Kathryn, and the d'Louncrais estate?"

Aimon gave a slow shake of his head. "No. We know Lothair is using you as some form of trap for us."

"Then why are you here?"

Does Farren know what his daughter is? As sheltered as he had kept her, how could he not? Aimon leaned forward and clasped his hands in front of him. "Farren, I...I came here to confirm something I suspected. Something about Kathryn." He paused, unsure how to broach the truth. "I believe...I believe she is different. Not entirely...human."

Farren choked on his wine. "You know?"

Relief washed over him. He did not have to tell a father his daughter was a werewolf.

Farren's shoulders slumped, and he put his head in his hand. "I thought we had hidden it well. That no one knew, that—" He groaned. "I should have anticipated a vassal of Gaharet's would recognize the signs."

Aimon gaped at Farren. "What did you say?"

Farren shrugged. "You would know. Of course you would know. You are one of *them*."

Aimon's head jerked back, and his muscles tensed.

"It surprises you I know?"

A wariness crept over Aimon. It *had* caught him by surprise. Was the knowledge of their existence more commonplace than they had thought? "How?"

"Gaharet's father, Jacques, married my sister Elise." He waved a dismissive hand at Aimon when he frowned. "She tried to hide it from me, but I could tell she had changed. Then one day I saw her. Quite a shock, as you can imagine. But she was my sister, and I loved her. I swore I would keep her secret. I did and I still do." Farren locked eyes with him. "You will keep Kathryn's secret? Protect her from Lothair?"

Aimon dropped his gaze to his hands. "I am sorry, Farren. It is too late for that. Lothair is aware of our existence. As is Archeveque Renaud."

Farren's face paled. "Mon Dieu." He crossed to a small table and refilled his goblet. With a glance over his shoulder, he poured a second one and handed it to Aimon.

"I am sorry, Farren, I need to ask. How did Kathryn become one of us? What befell her?"

Farren grimaced. "It happened many years ago," he said, resuming his seat. "She liked to run in the forest and swim in the pond. After losing my wife, I confess I indulged her and gave her freedoms perhaps I should not have." His hands fiddled with the stem of his goblet. "One day she returned from the forest, bleeding from a deep wound in her arm—an animal bite. She was hysterical, not making much sense, telling me a wolf-man had attacked her. She was always an imaginative child, prone to flights of fancy. I thought a wolf had attacked her. A real wolf. Elise had promised me your kind were of no danger to Kathryn. That she was safe with them, with the d'Louncrais. That they would never hurt a child."

Farren dropped his gaze to stare at his wine. "But then she took ill — her body burning hot, then freezing cold, convulsions, extreme pain. At first, I thought the wound had turned bad, but her body began to change into..." He drank deeply from his goblet. He sighed. "It was then I knew. I knew what she had seen, what had attacked her and what she was becoming."

Aimon shook his head. "I...I do not understand. You knew what Elise was. Why did you not seek help from the d'Louncrais? They could have helped you, helped her. Why did you not tell your sister?"

"Elise died in the attack! Who was I supposed to trust? I lost my sister to one of your kind. I was not about to lose my daughter." Farren stood, turned his back to him. "Perhaps I could have trusted Jacques, but he was in mourning, and my daughter was distraught. She believed herself to be a monster. She does still and I...I cannot say I blame her."

"One of our own attacked Kathryn *and* Elise?" Aimon slumped in his seat, the enormity of Farren's words sinking in.

Farren spun around. "You did not know?"

Aimon shook his head, the implications of Farren's words rendering him speechless.

"I thought the d'Louncrais invented the story about bandits to hide the truth."

Gaharet must know of this. Aimon would see he knew the truth about his mother's death, but he did not relish being the bearer of such news. Aimon raked his hands through his hair. It would have consequences far beyond Gaharet's pain, but that would be for Gaharet to determine.

"I am glad you told me this, Farren. And I will take this to the pack, but right now it is important I know all about Kathryn. How is she coping? How did you train her? Without the help of the d'Louncrais? She clearly has the ability to hide her true nature. Did your sister explain it to you?"

"Train her?" Farren looked puzzled as he resumed his seat. "What do you mean?"

"Like Kathryn and Elise, I was not born a wolf, but turned."

Farren's eyes widened and understanding flashed across his face. "The Battle of Montsoreau?"

Aimon nodded. "Yes. I would have died if not for Gaharet. The first few months after my turning I spent here, with Gaharet, learning to call on my wolf, and to banish it at will. Gaharet insisted I master it before he would allow me to leave this keep. It is not something that comes naturally to those of us who are turned."

Farren shrugged his shoulders. "Kathryn never calls on it. She has suppressed it."

Aimon sucked in a breath. "Farren, no, that is not possible."

"I beg your pardon, Aimon, but it is, and she has."

Aimon shook his head. "No, it is not. Her wolf is irrevocably entwined with her psyche. One body, one identity, two forms." He counted off on his fingers as he spoke. "It cannot be subdued, not entirely. She should not even try."

Aimon remembered too well his own turning. The agony, the fear, the night terrors, and, once complete, the lack of control he had over his ability to change.

Every time he experienced any strong emotion, the urge to shift would consume him. It had taken him months to manage some form of mastery over it.

"You are wrong, Aimon. It *is* possible. Kathryn has managed well so far. She needs no training. She is content."

Aimon gaped at him. Kathryn's appearance in the forest—stripping off her head-veil and shoes, the fear in her eyes when she pulled away from him—told Aimon Kathryn was *not* content. She had not found peace with her wolf. Instead, she feared it. Farren himself said she believed herself to be a monster. With the Beauchenes' new circumstances, her problems with her wolf would only increase. Aimon tilted his head back and stared at the ceiling. How could he make Farren understand?

He leaned forward, his elbows on his knees. "What did you plan to do when she wed?"

"We had hoped to find someone we could trust to keep her secret, someone of Kathryn's choosing, but..." Farren sighed. "Lothair's decision to grant us this estate will force us to act sooner than we had hoped."

Aimon reared back. For all his love for his daughter, Farren had no inkling of the turmoil in Kathryn's mind, no concept of the internal struggle she must face daily. For her to have lasted this long, to retain her sanity while repressing what her body and mind longed for with every fiber of her being, astounded him. Her strength of mind must be phenomenal. Could it be the reason she had survived the turning at such a young age?

It might also explain the rumors regarding her behavior. Her wolf would always push for release, and Kathryn would need to appease it in any way she could. Aimon had no desire to repress that side of himself, but if he did, he would surely fail. That Kathryn had not, with no training at all, was staggering. *What a remarkable woman.* And given her expression as she raced away from him, a frightened one. One in desperate need of help.

"She may manage her wolf now, within the safe company of those who love her, but she will struggle if those circumstances change. Your move here could affect her. Emotions, strong emotions, can trigger it. Because she has repressed it, I suspect she will find it more difficult to cope than if she had not. Emotions such as stress, anger, excitement, fear...desire. Especially desire. Those urges are *much* stronger in our kind for both male *and* female."

And do I not know that now.

Being made aware Kathryn had no control or understanding of her wolf, Aimon's shame at his behavior burned within him, leaving a sour taste in his mouth. He should have controlled himself, leashed his wolf the moment he scented Kathryn's innocence. In future, he would take more care.

He forced himself to relax. Kathryn needed his help, but he needed her father in agreement. "Her secret is safe with me, but she needs training."

"No." Farren gave an abrupt shake of his head, his lips pursed.

"Farren, her life is in danger. She must have command over her wolf. I came here because I scented her at Langeais Keep. But that does not mean the others will not come. Perhaps the one who attacked her will be one of them. He will only need to set foot in this keep and he will know what she is. I knew for certain when I encountered her in the forest."

Farren inhaled a sharp breath. "That is what upset her, is it not? You told her what you are."

"What? No." Aimon stared at Farren. "Wait. Are you telling me she does not know about us? Does not even know her aunt was one of us? That she thinks she is the only one, save for her attacker?"

"Of course I did not tell her. We do not need the d'Louncrais, or any of your kind. She is my daughter. She belongs with me. *I* can take care of her."

"*Mon Dieu.*" Aimon jumped to his feet and strode to the door, flung it open and beckoned over Gascon, who stood waiting in the corridor. "Please fetch Mademoiselle Kathryn. It is important I speak with her. And Gascon, do not take no for an answer."

"Of course, Monsieur Aimon." Gascon disappeared down the corridor.

"What are you going to do?" demanded Farren.

"I need to show her what I am. It is time she learned she is not alone. For her to know this is not a curse." He regarded Farren's alarmed expression. "I do not regret what I have become, and neither should she. She must stop repressing her wolf and embrace it. Your daughter will not find peace until she does. Believe me, I know."

Chapter Seven

Kathryn stared at the wall, counting the stones from the top down, then the bottom up. And again. She gave a little hiccup and a sniffle and brushed away her tears, her hands still shifting back and forth.

"Sixty-seven, sixty-eight, sixty-nine."

Aimon's blue eyes flashed into her mind. Brilliant blue, with dark indigo shadows flitting in their depths. She could lose herself in those eyes.

Coarse hair spread past her wrist. She uttered a sob.

"Seventy, seventy-one, seventy-two, seventy-three."

The feel of Aimon's soft lips against hers. The gentle, but firm pressure of his hand on her neck.

L'enfer.

Three fingernails became claws. She trembled, another sob wrenched from her throat, and she inhaled a shaky breath. She could do this, had done so many times before.

"Seventy-four, seventy-five."

This bedchamber was far larger than her previous one, so it took her longer to count all the stones. She all but ignored the opulent furnishings, the clean smell of fresh, untainted meadowsweet rushes, and the plush blankets on the enormous bed. It stood to reason the d'Louncrais would have better, larger, more luxurious rooms than the Beauchenes could ever have afforded.

Kathryn kept counting. She would stand here all night if she had to. After her reaction in the forest, that was a distinct possibility. Was it the stress of the day, Comte Lothair's announcement and the move to a new home with new servants that made it so difficult to control her curse? Or her encounter with Aimon?

"Seventy-six, seventy-seven, seventy-eight, seventy-nine."

The coarse, red hair slowly receded, and fingernails replaced claws. His scent—she had never smelled anything so... Heat pulsed through her body, and her hands tingled with the beginnings of a shift to paws once more. She gritted her teeth.

"Eighty, eighty-one, eighty-two."

She stared at her hands and waited. They remained human, with fingernails and skin. Human hands. Her shoulders sagged, and she flung herself on the bed and stared at the ceiling.

What should she do now? She had placed all her hopes and dreams on Aimon Proulx, and one whiff of his clean, musky scent, one gentle kiss, had swept all her control away. If she could not keep the beast at bay in his presence, she could not marry him.

But if not him, then who would I choose?

Startled, she sat up as the door swung open and the largest woman Kathryn had ever seen bustled in carrying a platter of food and drink. Prodigiously round, with the most enormous bosom and gray hair pinned back in a neat bun, her friendly smile lit up her lined face.

"Come, child, this will warm your blood and fill your stomach." The woman set the platter down on the table and wiped her hands on her food splattered apron. She brought a mug to Kathryn and urged her to take it. "The name is Anne, dear. I am the cook. And you must be Kathryn."

Kathryn took the cup foisted on her. She sniffed. A faint, sweet, herbal smell filled her nose. "What is it?"

"Chamomile brew laced with honey. Good for calming the nerves. The d'Louncrais put great stock in it. I make sure there are always chamomile flowers growing in the garden. Come now, drink up."

Too drained to offer any resistance, Kathryn complied.

"Tsk, tsk, tsk. Look at that pretty face of yours. All red from crying. We cannot have that."

Kathryn glanced over her cup at Anne. The woman was bold for a cook.

"There is naught to be bothering yourself about here, Kathryn. It is a new home, I know, but we will take good care of you."

Kathryn forced a smile. "Thank you, Anne."

"Now, I have organized for a nice big barrel to be brought in from one of the other chambers. I will have it filled with hot water so you can bathe, relax and wash away the weariness of your journey here. Nothing like a good soak to ease the old bones, I always say." She chuckled, and busied herself around the room, straightening the covers on the bed, stoking the coals in the brazier and lighting the candle. "The boys from the yard will bring up your belongings soon so you can get settled and make yourself right at home."

Kathryn's gaze followed the rotund woman's ministrations to her chamber. Would she not leave? She was the cook. Did she not belong in the kitchen? She was behaving as if she were Kathryn's personal maid. Kathryn wanted to be alone. Needed to be alone.

A sharp rap, and her attention snapped to the open doorway. Another servant entered — tall and slender, with graying hair at the temples. The same man who had shown her to this chamber.

"Mademoiselle Kathryn." He gave her a slight bow. "I am Gascon, head servant of the keep. Monsieur Aimon Proulx wishes to speak with you in the library. May I escort you there?"

Kathryn gripped the mug. She could not face Aimon, not yet. Perhaps never. She had barely settled the beast. She remained resolutely in place, sipping her drink.

"Oh, here it is," said Anne, beckoning in yet another servant.

Kathryn's eyes bulged. Her room was becoming a veritable thoroughfare of unfamiliar faces. This would not do.

Gascon stepped aside as the servant rolled an enormous barrel into the room and placed it by the brazier at Anne's direction. This must be what she would bathe in. Despite herself, Kathryn smiled. It did look appealing. She had never had the luxury of an actual bath before.

"Shall I escort you to the library now, Mademoiselle Kathryn?"

Kathryn's shoulders sagged. "I...I cannot..."

Anne held up her hand. "One moment, Gascon." She poured water into the washbasin, dipped a linen in and began fussing over Kathryn's tear-stained face.

Startled, Kathryn moved to pull away.

"Keep still, child." Anne grasped her chin, not unkindly. "It will take but a moment. You want to look your best. He is a handsome one, is Aimon Proulx."

Kathryn blushed.

"You noticed that, too, did you?" Anne smiled, dabbing the cool wet cloth around her reddened eyes. "He is a good man."

"You know Monsieur Aimon?" asked Kathryn, looking up into Anne's face, her motherly attentions not entirely unpleasant.

"I have known him for a few years now. When Gaharet brought him here, wounded from battle, I cared for him. He nearly died. Would have been a damn shame if he had. He has a good heart, has Aimon Proulx. You would not find one more loyal than he. You could trust that young boy with your life."

Kathryn considered Anne's words. Could she trust Aimon with her secret? She stared down at her mug. Maybe, but what use would it be if his very scent triggered her curse? The mere thought of being in the same room with him, or kissing him again, heated her face and her body. It stirred a hope for a marriage based on more than security, wealth or titles.

But if she could not control the beast in his presence, it could never be. Tears threatened to form again. If, as Anne professed, he was a good man, would he be an honorable man and accept her rejection? Her father would think she had gone mad.

"There, much better. Now you go talk to that handsome young man, and I will bring you some more chamomile and honey brew." She shuffled toward the door, turning back to look at Kathryn. "And if Aimon upsets you, you tell me. Old Anne will take him to task for certain," she said, before disappearing down the corridor.

Kathryn finished the brew and set the mug on the table, aware of Gascon's presence behind her. Staring at her hands, she brought to mind an image of Aimon. No changes, no shifting bones or fur sprouting from her knuckles. Her hands remained human. She inhaled a tremulous breath. Best to finish this now. After what had happened in the forest, Aimon would be certain of a welcome reception. Who knew what her father had already promised him, believing he helped her cause by encouraging Aimon's favor. She would need to put a stop to that before things were beyond retrieval. She squared her shoulders and turned to Gascon.

"Please show me to the library, Gascon."

"Of course, Mademoiselle Kathryn."

Gascon led her from the room and down the stairs to the library. Pausing at the doorway, he turned to her.

"No harm will come to you here, Mademoiselle Kathryn." His voice was kind and his expression sincere. "We will look after you and your father, as my family has done for the d'Louncrais for centuries."

"Thank you, Gascon."

Lifting her chin, Kathryn entered the room.

A small, cozy space with chests stacked full of books and scrolls, the library seemed to shrink further when her gaze fell on Aimon Proulx. He sat in a chair near her father, regarding her. She struggled to prize her gaze from him, from his broad shoulders and his white-blond hair. A powerful physical presence, he dominated the room. But it was his eyes that captivated her. Piercing and direct, they stared into her soul as though laying her every secret bare.

He had removed his mail and sword and looked relaxed in a black tunic and breeches. Seeing him without his armor softened him, made him appear less intimidating.

"Father, Monsieur Aimon."

"Please come and sit down, Kathryn," said Aimon, rising to place a chair next to her father.

Avoiding his gaze, she sat, the weight of his regard burning into her. Kathryn fought the urge to place her arms across her chest. She summoned her courage and lifted her gaze, meeting his. Her heart stuttered, and her wolf surged to the surface. She clutched her fingers tight in the folds of her dress.

"We need to talk. There is much to discuss."

He leaned toward her. Kathryn pressed herself hard against the back of the chair and forced a polite smile to her face. Inside, she wanted to burst into tears.

"To the contrary, Monsieur Aimon, there is very little that needs to be said. I believe we met earlier under false pretenses. It has been a long and arduous day, and I am fatigued. I have, perhaps, given you false hope."

She kept her true feelings buried deep, something she had become skilled at over the years. She could not falter. For Aimon's sake. In the periphery of her vision, she caught her father's confused expression, but she continued on. "I understand the recent change in our circumstances presents an opportunity for you to obtain the d'Louncrais estate."

If only I...

Kathryn brushed the thought aside lest it weaken her resolve. "I appreciate it is likely you have come here with that very purpose in mind. Perhaps you have already discussed the possibility of a marriage with my father. I am sorry to say you have wasted a journey."

Aimon's eyebrows rose, and a suggestion of a smile curled at the corner of his mouth. Her smile faltered. Would he be so uncouth as to not accept her rejection? Did he think to circumvent her wishes by securing an agreement with her father? Kathryn gritted her teeth. The man tested her, surely?

"I have no desire to wed you, Monsieur." She gathered her skirts and stood. "I am not for sale."

"Kathryn!" Her father glanced between her and Aimon. "Sit down."

"Father, I will not—"

"Sit. Down."

Kathryn slunk back into the chair and glared at her father. He had promised her she could choose. Yes, if circumstances were different, her elation at Aimon Proulx wanting to marry her would know no bounds, but she could not change her reality, no matter how much she wished it.

"Kathryn," said Aimon. "I need to show you something." He glanced at her father. "Something you should have been aware of a long time ago."

"Father?" Her father dropped his head and stared at his hands.

"I want you to know," Aimon continued, "I will not hurt you. I promise."

No, but I may hurt you. Please, Aimon, accept my rejection.

"Focus on my hands, Kathryn."

Aimon held them out toward her, palm down, his gaze fixed on her face. The man was too damn handsome. Even his hands were enticing. Long slender fingers, clean nai—

Oh, dear God!

They were changing, slowly at first, then faster. Bones cracking and popping, white fur sprouting from knuckles that receded and nails turning to claws. She shrank back from him, her throat constricting and her heart pounding out a ferocious rhythm. Her gaze flicked up to meet his steady, blue one, but only for a moment, before being drawn back to the horror of his transforming hands.

He is as cursed as I am!

Her hands flew to her mouth, and she stumbled to her feet, knocking over her chair. A whimper escaped her. Her fear, a living entity, overwhelmed her. Her beast roared to life, and she did not have the fortitude to stop it. Her body contorted and began to change. Through a roaring of blood and heat, she spied Aimon moving toward her. She put her arms out to fend him off.

Her hands shifted into paws. "No!"

"It is all right, Kathryn. Let go. Let it happen." Strong arms surrounded her, drawing her to him. "I am here. I will keep you safe," he whispered, holding her firm.

She struggled against him, his musky scent filling her nose, irresistible to the monster inside of her. It accelerated her transformation, the timbre of his voice sending shivers down her spine. She shook her head and tried to protest, but she could no longer speak. Her vocal cords were changing. Her face elongated and became a snout. She slunk to the floor, and Aimon came with her, her clothes ripping and tearing as her body continued to reshape.

"You will not hurt me, Kathryn." Aimon's warm breath ruffled the fur of her face, his voice calm and sure, and she focused in on it. "You are not a monster. *We* are not monsters. Relax and let it be."

Against the warmth of his body, his gentle voice soothed, and Kathryn's terror melted away. She stopped fighting him, leaned into his comforting presence, and did what her body had longed to do for years. With a soft sigh, she completed her transformation. She lay cradled in Aimon Proulx's arms, a very large, auburn-furred wolf.

"Everything will be well, Kathryn," he murmured, stroking the fur on her neck. "I am here now. I will look after you and keep you safe. You have no need to fear."

She placed her big, furry head against his chest, his heartbeat steady and strong against her ear, and she found comfort in it. An unfamiliar quiet descended. The two warring factions that had fought for supremacy in her mind, for once were silent. Free of the restrictions she had placed on herself, she relaxed.

The sense of peace did not last long.

It started as a whisper and built to a roar in her ears, a heat in her blood and an undeniable longing she could neither contain nor ignore — an insistent urge to be in her beloved forest, running through the trees.

Struggling to free herself from Aimon's grasp, she growled deep in her throat, resenting that which only moments ago had comforted her. Now it kept her from what she craved. She snapped at him. Her large canine teeth barely missed his face, her only thought to escape, to run. He tightened his grip and whispered words she struggled to comprehend. Desperate to heed the call of the forest, her claws raked his chest and her teeth snapped at whatever she could.

"Kathryn. Listen to me. Listen to my voice."

Kathryn. She recognized the word. He said it again and its meaning swirled close. *Kathryn. She* was Kathryn. She stopped snapping at him. Her lips peeled back in a snarl, but she listened. A part of her recognized he spoke to *her*, was trying to reach *her*.

"I know you want to run, to feel the earth beneath your paws and the wind in your fur. I *know* the forest calls to you. It calls to me, too, Kathryn, but you must be patient. Now is not the time to run."

Run. Yes, I want to run.

"Kathryn, focus on my voice. You need to return to human form. Now."

No. I do not want to.

She growled and bared her teeth at him, but he kept repeating the command over and over. For it was a command, not a request.

"Find the place inside your mind where your wolf cannot reach, the space where only you can go." As he spoke, he stroked her fur. "You can do this, Kathryn. Find your center and will your wolf away."

She stopped fighting him, and the quiet place in her mind, the dark space where Kathryn lurked, heeded his words and clawed back control. As her wolf retreated, awareness of the intimate way he held her against his broad chest, cradled between his muscular thighs, seeped in. She *wanted* to be human again.

Her snout shortened, her claws and canines retracted, her spine and hips transformed and her wolf slowly receded. Her dress torn and her shoulders bare, she clung to Aimon.

"That is it, Kathryn." He smoothed her hair off her face. "You are doing well. You are almost there."

She did not look at him, could not face all that had transpired. She snuggled closer, hiding her now human face in his tunic, her secret as exposed as her shoulders.

Aimon held Kathryn close as her body continued its shift from wolf to human, letting her press her face into his tunic. He had expected her transformation, had been ready for it when it had happened. His own reaction he had not. If he had thought her captivating as a woman, as a wolf, she took his breath away. Never had he seen one of his kind with such beautiful fur. His own wolf had stirred, pushing for its release, and it had taken all his concentration to focus on aiding Kathryn.

A strangled groan had him glancing up at Farren's horrified face. Aimon cut him a glare, and Farren turned away.

"Gascon," Aimon called out.

Farren gaped. "No!"

Gascon entered the library, his gaze falling on Kathryn, her clothing torn from her transition and her fur slowly receding. He disappeared back out the door.

"Look what you have done." Farren clasped his head in his hands. "Now everyone will know. They will hunt her down." He covered his face with his hands as Gascon returned with a blanket. "I should never have let you do this, Aimon. My daughter is ruined."

"Please calm yourself, Seigneur Farren." Gascon handed the blanket to Aimon. "My family has served the d'Louncrais for centuries. Believe me, Seigneur, we have witnessed far stranger things than this over the years. We helped care for your sister during her turning. Monsieur Aimon, too. And we will care for your daughter now."

Aimon wrapped the blanket around Kathryn's shoulders and pulled her close, rocking her gently. He ignored Farren's agitated pacing.

"You have done well, Kathryn. You made it through a change and back again. I am proud of you."

And he was. The last decade would have been pure hell for her, resisting the call of her wolf, hiding her true nature and believing herself all alone with this terrible secret. Aimon marveled at the woman in his arms. The force of her will was astonishing. It took mere moments for her to find her way back. It had taken him much longer when he had first transformed, to listen to Gaharet's voice and to fight the overwhelming call of the wolf threatening to consume him. For all her strength of mind and self-control, right now Kathryn clung to him, seeking comfort. And he gave her what she needed.

Anne shuffled in with steaming mugs of chamomile and honey. She offered a cup to Farren.

"Go on, drink. It will do your nerves good. Here, Kathryn," she said, wrapping Kathryn's hands around a mug. "There, there, child. It is all done now. Drink this. It will help calm you. One for you too, Aimon?"

He smiled but shook his head. "No, thank you. I have drunk more than enough of your chamomile and honey in the past."

"Very well. Now come, Kathryn. You must be exhausted. You have had quite an emotional day. Drink some more of my brew, and you will sleep like a babe tonight with not a care in the world." She reached for Kathryn.

A fierce urge to protect washed over Aimon and his arms tightened around Kathryn, pulling her closer. His jaw shifted—the slide of his canines sharp against his lips. He growled at Anne. *He* would comfort her, protect her. Only *he* could do so, like no one else.

"Do not go all wolf on *me*, Aimon Proulx. I will rap you over the knuckles if you do. You know I will." The old cook stood over him with her hands on her ample hips. "I will take good care of her. She needs time to collect herself, time to sleep. You can prowl outside her chamber door all night if you wish, but I am taking her with me now."

Aimon contemplated resisting, but one look at Anne's determined face and he repressed his wolf's need to protect. He retracted his canines and released Kathryn into Anne's care. The moment she left his embrace, he itched to gather her back into his arms. But Anne was right. Kathryn needed rest, and Anne would make good on her threat. It would need a braver man than him to take on Anne, so he let her take the now fully human Kathryn from his arms and lead her from the room.

Chapter Eight

Clutching the blanket around her shoulders, Kathryn trailed along behind Anne. A heavy numbness settled upon her, and exhaustion tugged at her mind, yet the burden she had carried since the day of her attack was gone. She no longer had to hide who, or what, she was. Not from everyone. Not from Anne, Gascon or Aimon Proulx. In her heart, something new had taken root. Hope. If Aimon could tame the beast within, control when, where and how much of his body he could shift, maybe she could learn to do it, too. And perhaps being a…werewolf…did not mean being a monster.

Werewolf. A word Kathryn loathed to even think of in the dark recesses of her mind. A word she dared not utter aloud. It screamed of feral beasts, base thoughts dominated by bloodlust and a killing rage, uncontrollable and savage. Aimon had shown no hint of those things, epitomizing the refinement of his noble birth.

When his hands had shifted, his composure had remained the same. Neither had her uncontrolled shift wrought a change in his calm demeanor. His words had soothed, and his gentle touch reassured. She raised her fingers to her lips, their kiss in the forest lingering in her mind. If only she had not rejected him, not behaved in a manner more befitting the village shrew.

Anne pried the blanket from her fingers, slipped it off her shoulders, and helped her shed the torn dress. As promised, they'd filled the bathing barrel with heated water, and Kathryn stepped into it, slinking down into its scented warmth. The water soothed her aching body, and she closed her eyes. She had not completed a full transformation since the months following her attack. She had forgotten how it made her bones ache and muscles throb.

"Relax now, child. The worst of it is over. The first few times are the hardest and the most frightening. You are safe here to be who you truly are."

Kathryn screwed up her face and pulled her scattered thoughts together. *Who I truly am? Who is that?* Kathryn did not know anymore. She hugged her knees to her chest and sifted through everything that had happened in the library. She had so many questions. Kathryn opened her eyes and turned her attention to the old cook.

"Did you...? Did I hear correctly? Did you really threaten to rap Monsieur Aimon over the knuckles?"

Neither Anne nor Gascon had balked at the scene she had created in the library. No fear, no horrified screams, as though a person turning into a wolf was an everyday occurrence in the d'Louncrais keep.

"Of course, dear. I told you I would have words to say if he did not behave himself."

"But… Were you not afraid he would attack you?"

She ran her fingers over the scars on her forearm, following the gnarled skin. She shuddered and dropped her arm beneath the water.

"Oh, good Lord, no. He is a good boy, is Aimon Proulx. They all are. None of them would attack a woman. It is not in their nature. And if they did… Oh my… There would be hell to pay with the rest of the pack. And most certainly with their alpha."

"But…" *There are more like me? A whole pack? An alpha? Is that their leader?*

She slumped further into the water until only her head remained above its surface and watched Anne busy herself sorting through her clothes in the trunks now lining the wall.

"One of them attacked me," she said, leaning her head against the edge of the tub, her hair cascading over the rim. "That is how I became…you know…what I am. How my aunt died."

Anne spun around. "What did you say?" Eyes blinking rapidly, she cast aside the blue dress she held in her hands and stared at Kathryn. "Are you saying one of her own kind killed Elise d'Louncrais?" Her hands flew to her face. "Oh, my. Something needs to be done about that."

Kathryn started upright, her sudden movement slopping water out of the giant tub onto the floor. "My aunt was like me?"

Anne patted Kathryn's arm absently, turning away. "Of course, dear. She *was* married to the alpha, Jacques d'Louncrais, Gaharet's father. She was not born that way. Jacques turned Elise. Like Gaharet turned Aimon. That is a whole different thing from being attacked." She met Kathryn's gaze, her expression serious. "These wolves do not attack women or children. They protect them. Cherish them. Especially ones of their own kind. Especially family."

Kathryn gaped at Anne.

Anne sighed. "Seems to me," said Anne, eyeing her with a shrewdness Kathryn found disconcerting, "you have a lot to learn about your own kind."

Anne picked up the discarded blue dress, clutching it to her chest, a visible tightness about her lips and a frown marring her brow. Kathryn swore she could see tears misting in her eyes. The old cook blinked, straightened herself and went back to sorting clothes. Perhaps she should not have mentioned her aunt.

"Kathryn, I assure you, Aimon only growled at me because he was protecting you. He, of all people, would understand exactly what you are going through. He wanted to keep you safe. From yourself if need be. He may have had a go at me once or twice, when he was turning, but he could not help that. He had yet to learn to master his own wolf. Gaharet spent a lot of time teaching him that."

Kathryn rested her arms on top of the barrel and her chin on her arms and stared at Anne. Her aunt had been a werewolf. *And* her Uncle Jacques. And Gaharet, too. She would never have guessed. Although... Memories of her Uncle Jacques, dark, brooding and a little frightening, made a lot more sense now.

Kathryn rubbed her forehead. It was a lot to take in. Only this morning, she had believed herself alone with her curse. Now, everything she knew, and all she understood about herself, had lost its certainty. There were others out there, an entire pack of them. With an alpha. How many of them were there?

K.E. Turner

"You said Gaharet turned Aimon. Why?" Aimon would not have wanted to be a werewolf, surely? And how did that differ from being attacked?

"Gaharet found Aimon on the battleground, grievously wounded and dying. The only way to save him was for Gaharet to turn him into one of his own kind — a werewolf. Werewolves are stronger, they live longer lives and they can heal from injuries a human could not possibly survive." Anne held up a deep green gown of Kathryn's. "This is a lovely dress," she said, with forced gaiety. "It suits your coloring perfectly."

"So, are some...born this way?" Did that mean any children she had would be like her? Kathryn grimaced at the idea of it. How could she inflict this on her children?

"Most are," said Anne. "Your aunt and Aimon are two I know of who were not born but turned."

"And me," said Kathryn.

"No." Anne pointed a stern finger at her. "You were not turned."

"But..."

"You were attacked." Anne's firm tone and the pinch of her lips brooked no disagreement. "Gaharet did not make the decision to turn Aimon lightly. The turning process, as I am sure you would remember, can be quite horrific. There are tales of those who went mad because of it and had to be confined. Of others who died, not strong enough to withstand the turning. Never seen it myself. I only heard the warnings passed down through the centuries. Turning someone is not something these wolves do on a whim. Only when taking a mate outside of the pack or, in Aimon's case, because he would have died had they not done so.

Aimon's turning was as difficult for Gaharet watching on, as for Aimon going through it."

Anne held out a linen for Kathryn to dry herself on. Kathryn stepped out of the tub and stood in front of the brazier, toweling down her body. She could languish in the scented bath water all night, but she was too tired, too spent, to argue with Anne. If Anne was brave enough to take on a seasoned werewolf like Aimon, threaten to rap him over the knuckles, then Kathryn was no match for her.

"What happened to you, and your aunt, was wrong. Very wrong," said Anne. "If the pack had known, they would have taken steps. They would have helped you through the process and tracked your attacker down. They would have dealt with him most severely. Killing one of their own, attacking a human and leaving that person to suffer through a turning on their own... It would horrify Gaharet if he knew. He would not stand for such behavior. Nor would have Jacques."

With the cloth wrapped around her, she sat by the brazier, her hands twisting together in her lap as Anne's deft hands combed her hair.

"You know a lot about...werewolves, Anne." There. She had said it. Out loud. Would she ever get comfortable with the word?

"Of course, dear. My family has served the d'Louncrais for centuries. I started my service as a young girl, helping in the kitchen. In this household, it is hard not to learn a lot about your kind." She sighed. "So many years, so many fond memories." She sniffed. "I assisted Elise through her turning, and Aimon as well. I was there when Gaharet was born, and his brother, D'Artagnon. All the d'Louncrais, dating back centuries, were born werewolves."

Kathryn bit into the side of her cheek, frowning at Anne's words as much as her manner of speech. Anne, it seemed, did not follow any of the rules of social status. Not a whisper of a Monsieur or Ma Dame as she talked. *They must do things differently here at the d'Louncrais keep.*

"It must have been a d'Louncrais who attacked me, then?"

Anne huffed. "A d'Louncrais would never attack a woman or a child. Dear girl, have you not listened to a word I have said?"

"But... Does that mean...? Are there others?"

"Of course there are. All Gaharet's men are werewolves."

Kathryn gasped and spun around to face Anne. "*All* of them?"

"Yes, all of them. Ulrik, Lance, Godfrey, Edmond, Aubert and Aimon. And most of their families were, too. God rest their eternal souls." She made a sign of the cross. "It is such a sorry business with all these lives lost of late. Has had Gaharet terribly worried." She sighed. "And now he is missing. What will the pack do without their alpha? They need him. For what my opinion is worth, he makes a good alpha." She turned Kathryn back around and began teasing a tangle from her hair. "Better than his father, and Jacques long had the respect of the pack."

"This alpha... It is an inherited position, then?"

"Not normally, no. The alpha is always the strongest wolf."

"And who decides that?"

"They must prove themselves the strongest, fight off those who think they deserve to be alpha."

Kathryn spun around again and stared up at Anne. "But I thought... You said they would not attack anyone."

"They do not. Unless someone wants to challenge the alpha for leadership. It is nothing to concern yourself about, child. It only seems frightening because you know so little about your kind." Anne pursed her lips, shaking her head. "'Tis such a shame. Had your father brought you to the pack the moment of your attack, you would know all this." She gently turned Kathryn's shoulders around again. "Keep still, child, so I can finish combing your hair. Now, where was I? Oh, yes. When Jacques died, Gaharet became the alpha. He had all but led the pack for the previous year as it was, with Jacques lost in his grief over Elise's death. And none saw fit to challenge him."

A knock on the door interrupted Anne, and a servant entered, setting a plate of food in front of Kathryn. Kathryn screwed up her nose at the chunks of meat, barely cooked, blood oozing out onto the platter. Then she caught the scent and she salivated, her stomach growling out her hunger.

"Not how I like it myself," said Anne, "but your kind seems to prefer it as fresh as it can get. Eat up. You will need your strength."

Kathryn, despite her initial aversion, ate every piece on the platter. She contemplated licking the plate but held the inclination in check. Rumors of her uncouth behavior abounded. She did not need to add to them. Although, to a cook who had served a family of werewolves most of her life, maybe nothing would come as a surprise to Anne.

She hid a yawn behind her hand.

"Come now, child." Anne turned down the covers on the bed. "Best you get a good night's sleep."

Dropping the damp linen, Kathryn slipped beneath the covers.

"Now, if I were you, I would be telling someone all that happened to you and your aunt the day of your attack. It is important for the pack to know."

Kathryn pulled the covers under her chin. "Who would I tell? Gaharet is the alpha, and he is not here. Do *you* know why he is not here?"

Anne's brow furrowed. "I do not, and I am a mite worried about him and his lovely mate, Erin. But, as he is not here, the handsome man downstairs is where I would start. He certainly has an eye for you."

Kathryn snorted and snuggled beneath the bedcovers. "If he ever did, I doubt he does still."

A bone-deep weariness settled over her and she stifled another yawn. She doubted she could stay awake much longer.

"Mmm. If you say so. Sleep well, Kathryn. You are safe here."

With that, she left Kathryn alone in her warm bed. Slinking into sleep, images of Aimon dancing behind her closed lids, an errant thought snagged in her mind. Who were all those lives lost? And why? But she could not hold on to her concern for long, and soon drifted off into a deep and dreamless sleep.

Anne closed the door on a sleeping Kathryn, and hurried down the stairs as fast as her old knees would take her. She needed to speak to Gascon. Elise attacked? Killed by one of her own kind? Something had to be done about that. Gascon would ensure Aimon knew, if he did not already.

Chapter Nine

Aimon settled into his saddle and cantered out the gate, away from the d'Louncrais keep. Worry about his decision to leave Kathryn behind pressed tight against his sternum. He had spoken with Gascon and Anne about Kathryn's safety, and they would do everything they could to protect her. They could use the training room and lock her in from the inside if the situation became dire. They would ensure she stayed within the safety of the walls until he returned. Still, he wondered if he should have brought her along with him.

Aimon had also spoken to Kathryn's father. Farren had not slept at all last night and had spent his time in the library drinking and castigating himself for the choices he had made on Kathryn's behalf. While Aimon did not agree with how Farren had handled things, they could not change the past. He saw no point in adding to Farren's guilt.

Farren had agreed to send word to Lothair of Aimon's arrival. Lothair's men would report his presence, anyway. While it could prompt a visit, or a summons from the comte, delaying it would not work in Farren's favor. Neither of them wanted Lothair anywhere near Kathryn, but disobeying a direct command from the comte would only provoke him. Nobody provoked Lothair. Not if they could help it. He had also enlightened Farren about the situation with Gaharet's other vassals. One more person to protect Kathryn in his absence.

The only person he did not speak with was Kathryn. As he had donned his mail and sword, she had slept on, a consequence of a stressful day, a complete transition from human to wolf and back again, and several mugs of Anne's chamomile brew. As Anne had predicted, he had spent most of the night slumped outside her bedchamber on the cold floor, leaning up against her door should she stir and need him.

She had slept well. He had not. Plagued by the memory of her in the forest, her hair tumbling about her shoulders, her feet bare and her werewolf scent spicing up the breeze, he had fought the temptation to slip into her bedchamber and into her bed. Much to his disquiet, he desired her. Fiercely. He craved the feel of her in his arms again, wanted to kiss her lips, caress every inch of her, stretch his naked body over hers and tease her to sublime release.

Her petite, flame-haired package contained this intriguing duality that taunted him. He wanted to kiss her, tumble between the sheets with her, but he also wanted to protect and comfort her. Her untamed wolf shone through, enhancing her spirited nature and giving her a fire that burned from within. Alongside it lived the frightened woman, unsure of her abilities, ill at ease with whom, and what, she was.

It was a powerful combination. It made him forget his purpose and forgo his common sense. Not good. That could get them both killed. He needed reminding that lust was no excuse to throw his conscience away in favor of sexual pleasure. He would not take an innocent for one night of bliss. Especially not one he was honor bound to protect. Perhaps a few days away from her would be a good thing.

As the first light of dawn crept across the sky, he cantered away from the d'Louncrais keep and turned his horse's head toward the rendezvous clearing near Langeais. A place they once had considered safe. A place where they had met many a time when summoned to Langeais. It had almost become their downfall. He had no need to go there to track Gaharet, but he had told the pack he would. Whoever had betrayed them may very well visit the clearing himself and would expect to find Aimon's fresh scent. And the clearing may yet have more to tell him.

He rode into the clearing as the sun beat down from its zenith. The bodies were gone, darkened blood stains and wilted sprigs of wolfsbane the only visible traces of what had transpired. He dismounted and tied his horse to a tree. Lance, Aubert and Edmond, so they had said, had all come here, while Godfrey had turned back when he caught sight of Lothair's mounted men. With the mild autumn weather of the last few days, he should be able to pick up everyone's scent, including his own. Except for Godfrey's.

He started where Ulrik had kneeled, weakened by wolfsbane and bound in silver. The power of the herb had dissipated as it had withered. Now it was but a minor distraction, a slight deadening of his senses. Not enough to make him as vulnerable as it had Ulrik, or to affect his ability in any considerable way. He picked up Ulrik's scent, faint but lingering, along with Erin's, Lothair's, Renaud's and a number of others belonging to mercenaries and keep guards.

Moving out from the scattered ring of wolfsbane, Aimon sought the residual traces of his own scent. From there he widened his search, finding where Gaharet, Erin and Ulrik had entered the clearing. A few steps further, he confirmed the spot Gaharet, cradling a wounded Erin in his arms, had revealed himself to Lothair before disappearing into the forest.

Closer to where he had hidden, he found Aubert's and Edmond's scents. Not surprising. They had chosen to stay downwind as he had. Had they seen what he saw? They made no mention of it, only that the wolfsbane had addled their senses. He kept searching.

Toward Langeais Keep, he found a confusion of scents where the mounted men had crossed the threshold from forest to clearing. What he could not detect was Godfrey or Lance. Puzzled, he retraced his steps around the clearing in ever-widening circles. The lack of Godfrey's scent confirmed his admission he had not approached the clearing at all. True to his word, on seeing the mounted men, he had avoided the area. Not detecting any trace of Lance bothered him.

Aimon tried again, backtracking everyone for a few meters. Still nothing.

Lance lied? Why?

Did he not think Aimon would discover his falsehood? He may not have the decades of experience the others could claim, but his wolf shared the same advantages. Did Lance regard him as inferior because of his turning? Did the others, too? The thought stung.

He stood and regarded the clearing. He could learn nothing more here.

He gathered his horse's reins and followed Gaharet's trail toward the witch's cottage. Staying on foot, leading his horse, he weaved across the path, trying his best to overlay Gaharet's older scent with his own. No one else had come this way yet. With any luck, the wind would pick up and disperse any trace of Gaharet before they did.

After a league or so, he remounted his horse and nudged him into a canter. As much as he loathed leaving Kathryn unguarded for so long, he had another task to complete. One which weighed heavily on him. He must talk to Gaharet. He did not want to be the one to open up old wounds, but he owed it to Gaharet. His alpha deserved to know the truth about his mother's death.

As Aimon neared the little cottage deep in the forest, he reined in his horse. Everything looked as he had left it. He dismounted and focused his senses, catching the hint of ash and old smoke from the fire, the bite of drying herbs and a familiar musky scent. Gaharet. He searched the surrounding gloom. Nothing. But his alpha was there.

"Aimon." Gaharet stepped into view. Dressed in his armor with his sword drawn, he scoured the forest behind Aimon. Finding no threat, he sheathed his sword. "You have news?"

Aimon nodded. "Some good, some bad."

Gaharet inclined his head. "Come inside. We will talk."

Aimon followed Gaharet into the cottage, stooping as he entered the doorway. It was a cozy space, with pots, scrolls and all manner of strange things lining the shelves. Bunches of herbs hung tethered to the rafters, and a large pot sat over the fire pit, the coals cold beneath it. A cloth covered an opening he presumed led to the sleeping nook of the strange woman who called this place home. Of her, he saw no sign. On a cot in the corner lay a sleeping Erin, her blonde hair splayed across the bed and her breathing soft and steady.

"How is she?"

Gaharet's face gentled at the mention of his betrothed. "She is well. Her turning is complete. The herbs Constance gave her made a significant difference to her pain." He looked over at Erin, his voice rough with emotion. "She would not be here if not for Ulrik. I have much to be grateful for."

"Constance? Is that the witch?"

"Yes. She knows all about us. It is unnerving. She tells me our ancestors turned to her people when they faced a similar plight as we do now, and her people created the amulets."

"Truly? I wonder what else she may assist us with."

"Precisely. We have been very lax with our lore and our history, to our detriment. I plan to remedy that as soon as Constance returns from the village." Gaharet removed his sword but kept it close as he took a seat at the table. Aimon joined him. "I am not certain how much sense we will make of what she can tell us. The woman speaks in riddles." He placed two mugs on the table, filling them with mead and handing one to Aimon. "What news do you have?"

Aimon took a sip from his mug, then filled Gaharet in on their summons from the comte.

When he finished, Gaharet shrugged. "So Lothair wants you all to re-pledge our allegiance? Not unexpected. We defied him. There were always going to be consequences. We should feel blessed that is all he asked for. Lance and the others, did they believe our deception?"

"They could not doubt it. Lothair has your amulet. Although, not all are convinced Ulrik is responsible for everything." Aimon raked his hands through his hair. "How am I supposed to ferret out this traitor, Gaharet? Aubert and Edmond's anger appears genuine. They are calling for Ulrik's blood. Godfrey does not believe Ulrik would betray us, and Lance is concerned for Erin's safety. But Godfrey thinks one of us should mate Erin now you are dead, and Lance lied about being in the clearing."

Gaharet glanced at his mate and growled low in his throat. "Wait, Lance *lied*?"

"Yes. He told us all he had gone there, but arrived too late, yet I found no scent of him anywhere near the clearing. And there is something else that bothers me. He planned to petition Lothair for your estate."

Gaharet raised his eyebrows.

"He claimed your estate is too important for the pack to lose." Aimon shrugged his shoulders. "It matters not. His plans are redundant now. Lothair bequeathed it all to your uncle, Farren Beauchene."

Aimon eyed his alpha, his maker, as Gaharet considered the news. How would he feel to lose everything his family had built up over centuries? His wealth, his title and his land?

Gaharet shifted his gaze to Erin.

Perhaps having her, having his mate, was enough. What would that feel like? Aimon's gaze sought the sleeping Erin. He remembered the bone aching weariness after his turning. He had slept for days.

"So, Lothair believes one of my vassals sold us out for wealth, land and power, and he set a trap. I wonder… Could Lothair have the right of it?" Gaharet tugged at his beard, his expression thoughtful.

"There is more. It complicates things."

At the thought of Kathryn, an unusual reluctance to divulge his discovery crept over Aimon, stilling his tongue. He flushed with a possessiveness, unfamiliar and disconcerting. What had happened last night—from his stolen kiss in the forest to Kathryn clinging to him, safe in his arms after her transformation—felt personal and was something he was not eager to share. Not even with his mated alpha. It confounded him.

"What is it, Aimon?"

He shook off his reticence. "I have fallen foul of Lothair's trap with the Beauchenes."

"Aimon?"

"I am sorry, Gaharet. There was no help for it."

Gaharet's lips twisted in a smirk. "Has our kind's compulsion to find a mate sunk its claws into you, Aimon? I cannot say I am surprised. We all feel it. You were bound to succumb to it eventually."

Aimon looked down at his hands. "No. That is not it. I had no choice but to visit the Beauchenes. If I could have sought confirmation another way, I would have, but I saw no other option."

"Confirmation?"

"Kathryn Beauchene is one of us."

Gaharet shook his head. "No, she is not. Of that, I am sure. Neither is her father. My father turned my mother, Kathryn's aunt, when she became his wife. He made the decision to leave the rest of her family alone."

"Farren is human," Aimon confirmed, "but Kathryn is most definitely a werewolf. I caught her scent at Langeais and followed her to your keep, to make certain."

Even here, a half day's journey from the d'Louncrais keep, Kathryn's spicy scent tugged at his awareness.

"You must be mistaken. You have had little experience with our females before they were all gone. The wolfsbane in the clearing could have confused your senses. Perhaps it has a prolonged effect."

"As I thought, too, at first," said Aimon. "But Gascon had his suspicions, and when I confronted Farren, he revealed the truth of it."

"How is this possible?" Gaharet's gaze darted about, his brow furrowing. "How did we not know? I do not recall the pack sanctioning her turning."

Aimon took in a deep breath, releasing it on a long sigh. "This was not a turning, sanctioned or otherwise, Gaharet. Kathryn was attacked. She was but a decade and two years old."

Gaharet recoiled. Attacking a child was not something the pack would take lightly. It crossed the unwritten laws of their kind, rules and traditions that had guided them for centuries.

"It gets worse."

Gaharet raised his eyebrows, and Aimon squirmed beneath his direct stare. "How much worse could it get, Aimon?"

Aimon spun his mug around in his hands, avoiding Gaharet's gaze. He had given Gaharet enough bad news, but this was personal. Aimon had never met Gaharet's mother—she had died long before his turning—but he had heard of the close relationship she had had with her sons. From all accounts, her death had devastated Gaharet.

"Aimon, what is it?"

His mouth went dry. He took a large swallow of mead and placed his mug down on the table. "Her Aunt Elise...your mother...she died in the attack."

Gaharet exploded from his seat, knocking it over, and rubbed his face with his hands. Erin stirred, moaning in her sleep, and Gaharet moved to sit by her side, brushing his hand across her forehead. Her eyes fluttered open, and she smiled at him before slipping back into a deep sleep. For a moment Gaharet remained there, quiet, looking down at his mate.

"One of our own attacked my mother? Killed her?" His voice cracked. "Are you sure?" Gaharet turned to him, his jaw clenched and his expression bleak.

"I am so sorry, Gaharet."

"My father always suspected something was amiss with the way she died, but...this!" He turned away from Aimon and focused on Erin, caressing her cheek. Her presence seemed to offer him comfort. "To be killed by one of our own. And to attack a child? Which one of us could have done that?" He stood and began to pace. "If Farren knew how my mother died, why did he not tell us? Why let us believe bandits killed her?"

"I guess he had his reasons — mistrust, fear he would lose his daughter. Right or wrong, he only wanted to protect her."

Gaharet's pacing came to an abrupt stop. "Farren must have trained her."

Aimon pursed his lips. "No, not really. He taught her to suppress it."

Gaharet snorted. "That is not possible. Our wolves are embedded in our psyche, linked to every thought and every emotion. It does not matter if you are born, turned or attacked, you simply cannot repress it. It is always there, clamoring to get out." Gaharet righted his seat and resumed his place at the table.

"As I told Farren, but Kathryn's control is phenomenal. *I* do not have that level of control. Certainly not in the beginning. Not now. I have never seen anything like it. Not in any of the others. Not even in you. For someone who has hidden it and never called on it... And she has had no training at all." He took another sip of mead. "But it all came undone the moment I revealed my wolf to her."

"I am not surprised."

"The poor woman believed herself cursed. I think, I hope, I have begun to convince her otherwise."

"Where is Kathryn now?"

"I left her in the care of Anne and Gascon. I made them aware of our situation."

"She will need training. We owe her that much." Gaharet's gaze slipped once more to his mate. "Erin's training will start any day now. Perhaps... Perhaps I should train them both."

"No!" Aimon burst out of his seat, growling, his canines extending and his jaw shifting. He leaned over Gaharet. A musky scent filled the room.

"Aimon! Control your wolf."

Gaharet's words slammed into him, the dominance of his alpha rolling over him.

Merde. I challenged my alpha. Why? What am I thinking?

Aimon slumped back in his seat and offered his neck in submission. "My apologies, Gaharet. I...I do not —" He shook his head. "I do not know what came over me. The thought of you with Kathryn...I... Forgive me."

Gaharet regarded him with no hint of anger or rebuke in his expression. He should be furious. Why had he not transformed and taken Aimon down, reminded him of his place in the pack? It was his right. Aimon deserved it. He had behaved no better than Ulrik, challenging his alpha.

"All is forgiven, Aimon." Gaharet studied him, no hint of anger in his scent, only curiosity. "You feel a certain protectiveness toward Kathryn?"

"Yes, I think I do. She is so...innocent, so frightened, and yet she faces every day with such courage. I want to help her through this. Show her the advantages of being a werewolf. That it is something she may come to embrace and not shun. Help her find joy and pride in what she is, as I have." Aimon rubbed his hand across the back of his neck. "I have found myself doing all manner of foolish things since I have met her. Challenging you, snapping at Anne."

Gaharet gave him a wry grin. "You are taking your life into your own hands there."

"Anne threatened to rap me over the knuckles," Aimon admitted.

Gaharet chuckled, and some of the tension left Aimon. "She would do it, too. She has given me a few sharp slaps across my snout over the years, especially when I was younger."

"No one messes with Anne," agreed Aimon.

Gaharet tapped his fingers on the table. "Given you have revealed yourself to Kathryn, and you understand how it feels to be turned, perhaps you should train Kathryn, not I. I will need to speak to her, though, about this attack."

"Of course. Do you want me to bring her here?"

"No. It is unsafe for us to remain here much longer. When you return to the keep, tell Gascon to prepare the farmer's cottage by the stream. It has lain empty for a few years now. I will cover our tracks from here as best as I can, and nobody, not even Lothair, would expect me to turn up on my own lands. Give me a sennight, then bring Kathryn to the farmer's cottage. Gascon will direct you. It may be helpful for both her and Erin to know they are not the only female among us."

"What about the others? If I am training Kathryn, how can I help uncover the traitor?"

"Right now, Kathryn's safety is more important. You may yet find answers by staying in the keep. If someone is after my estate, or my position, they may very well make an appearance."

"And Ulrik? We cannot leave him in that cell. Nor can we leave his rescue to the pack."

"We can do nothing until we have a way of counteracting the effect silver has on us. And wolfsbane. I will talk to Constance. She may know of something. Until then, there is little we can do."

Aimon nodded and drank down the last of his mead. He got to his feet and headed for the door. "Stay with Erin. I will keep watch tonight."

Gaharet watched Aimon leave the cottage, his heart heavy with renewed grief, but his mind alive with possibilities. Not so long ago, he had reacted as strongly as Aimon had at the mere suggestion of Erin in another wolf's company. Gaharet had not understood his own uncharacteristic reaction at the time, but he did now. His wolf had known Erin was his mate, though he had spent but a few moments in her presence. Listening to Aimon talk of Kathryn, watching his eyes dance with dark shadows and his voice full of admiration, Gaharet knew he was right. Aimon had found his mate. The question was, did Aimon realize it?

Chapter Ten

Kathryn awoke to sunlight streaming into the bedchamber and smooth linens cool against her skin. She stretched, a languid arching of her back, and a smile teased at the corners of her mouth.

"Good morning, child. How are you feeling?"

Kathryn's gaze followed Anne as she stirred up the coals in the brazier.

"I feel...good." When had she last woken feeling so rested?

"Are you planning on staying abed all day, or shall I help you dress?"

Kathryn rubbed her body against the linens—a quality of which she and her father could never have afforded—reveling in their silky slide against her skin. She *could* stay here all day, but she pushed aside the covers and clambered out of bed. She had questions. Anne had opened her eyes to a world she had not known existed, but there were things only another werewolf could answer. Aimon.

Nerves fluttered in her stomach, and she closed her eyes and inhaled deeply. Her eyelids snapped open. She could scent him. By the door. Yes. Not strong enough to indicate his presence, but he must have stood outside her door during the night, long enough for his scent to linger. The quivering in her stomach intensified. Did that mean she had not ruined any chance she had with him?

"Come, child. Let us get you dressed."

Anne slipped a chemise over Kathryn's head, then a linen under-dress, buttoning it up, and finally an over-dress of blue. Kathryn laced up her boots then, leaving Anne straightening up the bedcovers, slipped from the bedchamber and descended the stairs. Anticipating Aimon, or her father, in the hall, it surprised to her to find it deserted and silent. The large table she remembered from her childhood visits to her aunt sat empty. The only sound was the flutter of flame over the oil lamps and the crackle of a small fire in the central fire pit as it chased away the encroaching autumn chill.

As she stepped into the room, memories assaulted her. Memories of grand meals at the table with her aunt, her uncle and all the estate's staff. Of her cousins, Gaharet and D'Artagnon, racing through from the kitchen, laughing, with an angry servant on their heels. Of her aunt, pointing to the embroidered figures in the beautiful wall hanging and telling Kathryn its story. A second, newer wall hanging now hung beside it. Much had changed since those visits so many years ago. For her and for the d'Louncrais.

Kathryn skirted the fire pit and crossed the floor to stand before the familiar wall hanging. She picked out the figures of her aunt and uncle, taking in the scene — a hunt, a battle and a victory. As a child, her aunt's explanation had made no sense to her. Women did not go into battle. Now, looking at the figures dancing across the wall, understanding dawned.

This was not a battle over land or territory. Nor was it some hunt to bag the largest, most noble beast in the forest. It was the story of her aunt and uncle's courtship, and a testament to their love. Her aunt, as bold and as fiery as her red hair proclaimed, had tested her uncle, demanding he prove his worth. Uncle Jacques, had taken up her challenge, determined to make her his, and in the end, was victorious in his battle to claim her as his bride. Her father had the right of it. Jacques d'Louncrais had loved her aunt, and she him.

She leaned in, her eyes widening as she looked more closely at the figures. They rode horses. How was that possible? Since the day of her attack, no horse would bear her presence. Only the old plow horse, under sufferance, would allow her to sit behind him in a wagon. Was this evidence werewolves could ride? She rocked back on her heels. *Wait.* Her uncle, her cousins, they had all ridden horses. So did Aimon. So did all Gaharet's men.

Kathryn reached out and ran her fingers over the embroidered figure of her aunt on a horse. Oh, how she missed riding — galloping across the meadow, the pounding of hooves, the wind in her hair. *Is it possible? Could werewolves truly ride? Will I be able to ride again?* Another question for Aimon.

Kathryn turned to the other wall hanging, the more recent addition to the d'Louncrais keep. Chevaliers on horseback on a battleground. A real battle. She picked out Gaharet, black-haired, in a red surcoat with his sword raised. And there, two figures larger than the others, they must be Edmond and Aubert. A chevalier, his sword clashing with the enemy, might be Lance, and behind him, Godfrey. But it was the figure in blue, with long white hair, unhorsed and wounded, that drew her attention. Aimon.

"The battle of Montsoreau."

Kathryn spun around, startled, so engrossed in the scene she had not heard or scented anyone approaching.

"Good morning, Mademoiselle Kathryn. How are you feeling this morning?"

Kathryn flushed. "Well, thank you, Gascon." She turned back to the embroidered scene. "This is when Gaharet…"

"Yes. When Mon Seigneur Gaharet turned Monsieur Aimon."

Kathryn stared at the wall hanging, not really seeing it. It said something that one of only two wall hangings was of the injury that led to Aimon's turning. The other being her uncle's courtship of her aunt, which had also led to a turning.

"Is no one else awake yet, Gascon?"

"Seigneur Farren is in the library. I believe he has yet to sleep." A slight frown crossed his face but smoothed out in an instant. "He has asked not to be disturbed. Monsieur Aimon left at dawn."

"Oh." Her shoulders sagged. "Will he return? There were things… I wanted to talk to him. I thought he would be here this morning."

She rubbed absently at her chest, the sting of disappointment hard to swallow. He had left with nary a word. Was it wrong to feel so abandoned? She had, after all, rejected him. It seemed he had taken her words to heart.

"Monsieur Aimon had pressing business elsewhere. He wanted you to know he would return as soon as he could."

He is to return? Hope fluttered in her breast. "Well." She lifted her chin a little and pasted on a smile. "Of course, he has important things to do. I have no claim on Monsieur Aimon's time. Thank you, Gascon."

"Mademoiselle." Gascon gave her a half bow. "Monsieur Aimon did leave some instructions for you, that I might inform you of."

Kathryn's eyebrows rose. "Pardon?" *Instructions? Not a note or a message.* "And they are?"

"He has directed you not to leave the keep until he returns. You must not go into the forest without him."

Heat rose up her neck, and her hands clenched. "Directed? He did not ask? Or suggest?" If Gascon noted the tightness in her voice, he gave no indication of it.

"Directed, asked, suggested, whatever word you would like to choose, Mademoiselle. For your safety, you are not to leave the keep."

Kathryn snorted. "For my safety? I am perfectly capable of taking care of myself in the forest, Gascon. I have done so for years. Ask my father. Aimon is not master of this keep. He has no right to give orders to me or to anyone here, and I will not be abiding by them. I need the forest, the trees, the sun and the fresh air. I cannot, I will not, stay cooped up in here until he graces us with his presence once more."

Gascon stood unmoved by her protestations, meeting her eyes. "Monsieur Aimon does not wish you to leave the keep until he returns. I have informed the servants and the gate guards. You will not be able to leave the keep even if you so choose."

Kathryn heaved in a deep breath. First Anne and now Gascon. Did any of the servants in this keep abide by the social norms of class and status?

"Was there anything else I might assist you with, Mademoiselle?"

Kathryn fumed. So much for him feeling her rejection. Did Aimon think he could come into her life, issue orders, and she would simply obey? How *dare* he? She would see about this.

"That will be all, Gascon." Shoulders squared, her body vibrating her displeasure, she stalked past him into the corridor. She would see her father about this nonsense. Aimon could not keep her from the forest. She *needed* it.

Outside the library, her hand on the door, she paused. From Gascon's account, her father had not slept. And he did not wish to be disturbed. That did not sound like her father, but last night had been a shock. Perhaps her father needed time. She dropped her hand and eyed the heavy entrance doors. She could simply walk out, but chances were the gate guards would not let her pass. Not without someone to countermand Aimon's orders.

Kathryn smirked. *Anne.*

Kathryn found Anne in the kitchen, seasoning a large pot of stew hanging over the fire. Her face red from the heat, her apron speckled with sauce, she turned as Kathryn stormed in.

"It is a little early in the morning to be so flustered, child. Whatever is the matter?" Anne dipped the spoon into the pot, brought it to her mouth, and tasted the stew. "Mmm. Perhaps a little more rosemary." She added a sprinkle of chopped herb to the pot and stirred it in.

"Monsieur Aimon has gone." Kathryn crossed her arms across her chest, reining in her ire. She needed Anne as an ally. "And he has left orders he expects me to obey."

"Mmm-hmm. Those would be the directions you are not to leave the keep, I take it?"

"Yes. And Gascon said the gate guard would not let me pass. I know we have only arrived but yesterday, but Aimon is not the master of this keep. Why would the servants obey him? And the gall of him. He did not wait till I awoke. No good morrow, Kathryn. Not even a fare-thee-well, only directions. I thought he had left, never to return. I will not be able to contain myself if I cannot access the forest."

"What upsets you more, child? That he curtailed your freedoms, or he did not say goodbye?"

"Both." She gasped, covering her hand with her mouth.

The old cook chuckled, and her eyes sparkled. "He only has your best interests at heart."

Kathryn jutted out her chin. "Really? We shall see about that."

Anne brandished her spoon at her. "Do not go thinking about disobeying now. We do not want to have to send someone out to fetch you and bring you back."

Kathryn gaped at Anne. "You would not dare?"

Anne raised an eyebrow at her.

"Oooh." She stamped her foot and brushed past a startled young maid as she stomped out of the kitchen. Let the servants gossip about her temper. It would not be the first time someone had accused her of behavior unbecoming of a lady. When Aimon returned, she would tell *him* what she thought of his orders. That would really give them something to talk about.

The nerve of him. He was not her father, her husband or the comte. He had no authority to give her orders. On principle, she should defy him. From the look on Anne's face, though, the old cook would not hesitate to send someone to drag her back. By her hair if necessary. That indignity she could not, would not, bear.

Muttering to herself, Kathryn stalked the corridors of the keep, glowering at everything and everyone she encountered. Her new abode had luxuries she had only ever imagined, but she resented it. Wealth should grant greater freedoms, but for her it had all but curtailed them. First the comte, and now Aimon. Kathryn kicked out at a piece of furniture, hurting her toes and having no effect on the chair.

She was being childish. She had more fortitude than this. At the very least, it should please her he would be returning. That he had not forsaken her in search of a more amenable match. She resolved to bear the restrictions on her person with, if not good humor, at least a measure of grace befitting her station. Her future lay in this keep, with or without Aimon, and she need not give the servants any more reason to think her a shrew.

Kathryn's restraint lasted until the following morning. With no immediate need to be in the forest, her wolf, for once, was content. She was not. Aimon's edict chafed. Leaving her bedchamber and a bemused Anne, she sought out her father. He would support her.

She found him still secluded in the library, his face unshaven and his clothes rumpled, mumbling to himself as he sorted through the tomes and scrolls.

"Father?"

His head snapped up. "Kathryn." He swallowed, his gaze shifting away from her.

Dark circles ringed his eyes. *Has he not slept at all?*

"Father, is something wrong? This is not like you." The events of their first night here had been stressful, but... "Is this because I transformed again?"

His shoulders slumped. Was her father ashamed of her for her loss of control? Had *he* sent Aimon away, determined she should never shift again? Or worse, believing her claim she did not wish to marry Aimon?

"Come, Kathryn. Come sit down." He motioned her to a chair, pulled another close then sat, his gaze on his hands, his fingers clasped tight. "I want you to know, Kathryn, whatever you may think of me, I never meant to hurt you. What I did..." He paused, taking a deep, tremulous breath. "What I did, I did because I thought it the best for you. For us. I did what I did to protect you." He reached out and grasped her hands. He looked up at her, pleading.

"Father, what do you speak of? What is it you have done?"

"I...I knew."

She stared at him, puzzled. "You knew what, exactly?"

He dragged in a deep breath. "I knew about the d'Louncrais. About your aunt. I have always known what they were." He hung his head.

Kathryn shook her head, frowning. "What? You — ?"

He cut her off. "I thought the two of us, we could handle things. Work it out together. I did not want you drawn into that world. My sister was, and she died because of it. I had lost your mother, my sister... I could not bear losing you, too."

The air rushed out of her lungs and the room closed in. What was he saying? She pulled her hands out of her father's grasp. "You...you knew? All along you have known? That I was not alone? That there were others like me?" She stared at her father, eyes brimming with tears. "Why would you keep that from me?"

"I am so sorry, Kathryn."

"*How* could you keep that from me?"

"I thought it for the best. I really did."

"But..." Her bottom lip trembled. "I believed I was cursed. You let me think I was a monster."

"No." His arms reached out for her, but she shrunk away. "Never a monster. You are my daughter and I love you. All I could think about was you being discovered. That they would take you away." He dropped his arms, deep pain shimmering in his eyes.

Kathryn pushed out of her chair and blinked back tears. One slipped out, rolling down her cheek, and she brushed it away. Her one and only ally in this world had betrayed her, had kept this knowledge from her.

"Do you know how difficult it has been for me? Do you have *any* idea of the struggle I have faced? Every. Damn. Day?" Her father shrunk before her eyes. "The *hell* I have lived with when there was an answer? All along, help was nearby, and you have denied me that." A sob escaped her throat.

"I know now I should have taken you to the d'Louncrais. That they could have helped you. I was wrong, Kathryn. I know *now* I was wrong. That my decision to keep you away from them has hurt you. Can you find it in your heart to forgive me? *Please*?"

Kathryn turned away and pressed her hand against her chest. How could her own father have kept something so important from her? It hurt. *L'enfer*, it burned. How different her life would have been. How much pain, fear and self-doubt she would have avoided had her father made another choice? Forgiveness was beyond her right now.

"I cannot change what I have done, but perhaps I can make it right by you. Aimon says you need training. If that is what you wish, I will not stand in your way."

She looked at him then, nodding her head, her tears spilling down her face. "I *need* it, father. I needed it years ago."

"Oh, Kathryn," he said, getting out of his chair and standing before her. "I am so sorry."

She backed away from him, her hands out fending him off. "No." She sobbed. "I cannot."

He halted. "Kathryn…"

He looked at her with such heartbreaking anguish. He truly was sorry, but Kathryn could not accept it. Not now. Not yet. Maybe not ever.

"I need…I need some space." Sobbing, she turned her back on him and made for the door. "I need the forest."

"No, Kathryn. You cannot. It is not safe." He strode to the door and blocked her retreat.

"Do not tell me what I cannot do. You have made enough choices for me."

Her father stood his ground. She needed to get away, needed to be alone.

"Aimon does not want you in the forest alone. You are not safe. Please, Kathryn, stay in the keep. Do not make me confine you to your chamber."

"Leave me be."

"Promise me you will not leave the keep. Promise me, Kathryn."

She eyed him through her tears. "I promise," she whispered. She would not break a promise. Not to her father. Not even after what he had done.

Her father moved out of her way, opened the door and Kathryn fled down the hall, up the stairs, to where she did not know. Somewhere dark and somewhere quiet. Somewhere she could be alone with her pain.

Chapter Eleven

Ulrik sat in the dark, propped up against the stone wall of a small underground cell. The chill from the damp, cold floor seeped into his bones, his torn tunic doing little to keep him warm. Where the silver shackles touched his neck and wrists, his skin was blistered and raw. At least he no longer felt the effect of that damned herb, wolfsbane. Instead, trapped in human form, he was shackled to the wall.

Five days. Five long, solitary days since they had dragged him down into this godforsaken hole, and not a soul had come to see him save for the guard bringing him meager rations and water. Even in here with no light, and no sound, he could feel the passing of the days and the rising and setting of the moon. As each day came and went, his unease grew. What did Lothair wait for? Why did he not come to demand he turn his chevaliers into werewolves? Did he think to wear him down with darkened isolation and little sustenance? Ulrik had to concede such a plan had merit.

The rattle of keys, a clang and the screech of iron as the grate above opened, had him on his feet. Flickering light preceded footsteps down the steep, narrow stairs chiseled from the rock. He caught a scent on the air. Renaud. He growled low in his throat.

Archeveque Renaud stalked toward him in a swish of ecclesiastical robes, a self-satisfied smile on his face.

"Ulrik Voclain. Not exactly the man, or werewolf, that I wanted to see in here, but I have to say, I could not have planned things better myself."

Ulrik snarled. *Why is Renaud here? Alone? Does Lothair know?*

The archeveque paced in front of him, keeping some distance between the two of them, sizing Ulrik up and down.

Come closer, old man.

"Gaharet d'Louncrais is dead, no longer a thorn in my side. Thank *you* very much." He gave Ulrik a nod of appreciation. "And the comte has a werewolf in chains to help him create his new and improved army."

Ulrik remained silent—watching, waiting.

Renaud edged closer, continuing to pace.

Nearly there.

"Do you know what *I* want?" Renaud asked. When he did not answer, Renaud grinned. "I suspect you would really like to know."

Ulrik inclined his head to the side, indicating he was listening.

Close. Only another step or two.

"I shall tell you." He leaned in and whispered, "I want Lothair."

Now.

Ulrik lunged. His chains snapped tight, and Renaud danced out of reach, more agile than was right for a man of his years. Ulrik snarled and jerked on his chains.

Renaud cackled. "Nice try, young wolf." He turned his back on him. "With those chains, the silver... You are not going anywhere."

Ulrik growled low in his throat. What he would not give for a moment alone with the archeveque, unfettered. He would tear his throat out. Panting from exertion, the pain in his wrists and his neck almost unbearable, Ulrik let his head drop forward and his hair fall across his face.

"But *I* could help you escape from here."

Ulrik grunted. "And why would you do that? Why would I *believe* you would do that?" His throat was so dry, his voice was a mere whisper of sound.

"Because I have a proposition for you." Renaud moved in, careful not to get too close. "I want to take Lothair to Rome. As a werewolf. Bound in silver. To achieve that end, I will offer you release from this hole in the ground. All *you* have to do for me is bite him."

Ulrik's head snapped up. Renaud may be a clergyman, but right now he was the devil sent to tempt him.

"I know you want to. I remember what Lothair did to your family. Why he did it." A knowing smile hovered on Renaud's lips. "You want revenge. D'Louncrais would not let you have it. You have killed him. Now is your chance for retribution against Lothair."

No. Ulrik backed away from Renaud. *I could not, could I?* He dropped his gaze to the floor. *Why not?*

Lothair would want him to bite someone, several someones, to create his supernatural army. Why not bite Lothair and let Renaud bind him? Punish the man who had killed his family? Chances were, he would die here, with or without a deal from Renaud.

Renaud retreated, the room dimming as he moved toward the stairs. "Think about it, Voclain. I am giving you the chance to avenge your family. Bite Lothair and in return, I will set you free."

Renaud's words echoed through the cell, ringing in his ears, taunting him long after the archeveque had gone and the grate above had clanged shut. Thumping his fist against the stone wall, he threw his head back and roared. Renaud's offer tempted him beyond all measure, and he was uncertain if he would be able to resist it.

Chapter Twelve

With the afternoon sun sitting low on the horizon, Aimon cantered into the bailey. He had spent the morning discussing plans with Gaharet for Ulrik's rescue, but loath to leave Kathryn unprotected any longer, he had set out for the d'Louncrais keep at midday. He dismounted and handed his reins to a stable boy, a troubled Farren meeting him at the door.

"Farren, is something wrong?" His chest squeezed tight. "Kathryn? Where is she?" Had she slipped past them all and snuck out into the forest? In her position, he would have tried to do the same.

Farren grimaced. "I am glad you have returned so soon, Aimon. She is in the armory."

"The *armory*?"

Farren gave him a sad little smile. "She came to me this morning, and I told her everything." Farren looked down at his feet. "I told her I knew about the d'Louncrais, about you, and have done for years. She... She did not take it well."

"Kathryn tried to leave the keep?"

"She wanted to, but I made her promise not to."

Aimon raised an eyebrow. A promise would not stop a determined wolf.

"She will not break a promise. She never has," said Farren, a hint of pride in his voice.

The man loved his daughter, he had no doubt of that. If only he had consulted the d'Louncrais years ago.

"She has sequestered herself in the armory. Has not left it all day. We have kept an eye on her."

Kathryn had taken her father's deception hard. That he could empathize with. Who knew what state he would find Kathryn in? Tears, recriminations, perhaps one very angry auburn wolf. He nodded at Farren and headed inside.

"Be gentle with her, Aimon. These last two days have been difficult for her. Mostly because of me," Farren called after him.

Aimon paused in the doorway. "Mostly?"

"She was not happy with your orders to remain in the keep. Some of her ire may also be directed at you."

Aimon grunted. Steeling himself, he mounted the stairs to the armory. He had not expected Kathryn to like her new restrictions. In his own experience, he had chafed at his initial loss of freedom, had resented it and had not comprehended the reason for the imposition. Now he understood the wisdom of Gaharet's edict. And during his early days as a wolf, he had not faced treachery within the pack, or a comte determined to use him as bait.

He halted in the doorway of the armory and peered in, the darkened room no challenge to his enhanced eyesight. Within the room full of hauberks, hunting bows, sheaths of arrows, lances and shields, stood Kathryn. Before her, shelves lined with cloth wrapped swords and daggers. Her back to him, with a sword gripped in her hand, she stiffened. Tilting her head, she sniffed the air. At least he had found her in human form.

Wary of the tension radiating from her, Aimon approached her with slow, measured treads. She did not turn to face him.

"Kathryn." He kept his voice soft, not wanting to precipitate an uncontrolled shift. "I have spoken with your father."

She growled and her grip tightened around the sword's pommel.

He halted and opened his senses. Beneath the heat of her anger was a sorrow so deep it took his breath away. His heart ached for her.

"Kathryn, I do not agree with the decision your father made for you, but it is done. We cannot change it."

She spun around and leveled the sword at his chest. She was a sight to behold. Her dark auburn hair hung loose and disheveled. Anger burned in hazel eyes puffy and red from crying, her cheeks tear-stained and flushed. It awakened in him conflicting needs to gather her in his arms to comfort her or to kiss her anger into submission.

"My father is not the only one to make decisions on my behalf. You are equally guilty, are you not?"

He inclined his head in agreement. "For your own safety." Did she know how to wield a sword? Had her father taught her?

She snorted. "Not unlike my father's reasoning."

"I suppose it would seem that way to you." His gaze locked on hers.

"Yes, it does," she said, pushing the tip of the sword against his armor.

He looked down at the sword, then back at her. "Do you plan on using that? Assuaging your anger at me, and at your father, by taking my life?"

Uncertainty shimmered in her eyes. "Maybe." She pushed the tip a little harder against his mail, thrust her chin out and glared at him.

Her defiance did nothing to ease the burgeoning constriction of his breeches. With a shifting of weight, he sidestepped the sword, closed the gap between them and disarmed her in seconds. He brought the flat of the blade up against her throat. Kathryn gasped, and his gaze fixed on her pretty, parted lips.

"Be careful picking up a sword, Kathryn. Or any weapon. Make sure you are prepared to use it. If you are not, it will most assuredly be used against you."

Her pulse throbbed in her neck, and dark shadows flitted in her hazel eyes as her wolf rushed to the surface. But it was not fear he scented. His cock roared to attention, and his own wolf pushed against his mind. Two days away from her had done nothing to quell his desire for her. Rather, the separation had intensified it.

He backed away from her, her body so close to his more dangerous than the sword she had held against his chest. He re-wrapped the weapon in its protective oil cloth and returned it to the shelf. There was nothing he could do about his raging erection.

"I would not know how to use it anyway," she muttered behind him. "Yet another choice taken from me."

Her words tugged at his heart. The path her father had chosen for her could have done enormous damage. Perhaps he could give her back some small amount of control over her life. "If you wish to learn how to use a sword, then I will teach you."

"You would?"

He suppressed a smile at her surprise. "Yes. There are other things you need training in first, but I see no harm in teaching you whatever wish to learn." He turned to face her, letting her see the truth of his words. "I will help you in any way I can."

Her eyes glittered in the darkness. "And will you let me go out into the forest? By myself?"

"No." He held her stare. On this he would not be moved, any more than Gaharet had been when *he* had been in training and had demanded to be let out.

Her lips thinned, and her eyes flashed. "Of course not. You left orders you expected me to follow, coerced the staff into supporting your ridiculous demands, and all without having the decency to relay them to me in person. Now you return, thinking I will absolve you because you tell me you are willing to help me? I *needed* the forest today." She brushed past him and made for the door.

"I am surprised you did not attempt to sneak out. I tried it three times when Gaharet confined me to the keep."

She stopped short of the doorway and spun to face him. "But Anne said they would send someone to fetch me back!"

Aimon inclined his head. "She would have, too. The first two times I escaped, Gaharet and Ulrik dragged me back. And believe me, they had to drag me, because I did not go willingly. The third time, Anne assisted

Gaharet. I think Anne scared me more than Gaharet and Ulrik combined, because I never tried it again."

She bit down on her lip, a smile threatening to turn up the corner of her mouth. He ventured toward her, stopping a few feet away. The urge to cup her face, to run his fingers through her hair would be too much should he get any closer.

"I understand your need to be in the forest, Kathryn. I really do. I have been where you are," he said, his feet propelling him forward against the direct commands from his brain. He brushed his hand against her cheek, reveling in the softness of her skin. All manner of body parts were refusing his command to keep his distance, to remain unaffected. "But it is not safe for you out there, not alone and not untrained."

She frowned. "I have often gone into the forest alone. No harm has ever come of it."

"That was before you came here, before the comte made a target of you."

Her shoulders sagged.

He cupped her chin, lifting her gaze to meet his. "Let me help you, Kathryn. Let me train you."

Her breathing hitched, and the scent of her arousal swirled around them. "Will you teach me everything I want to know?" Her voice was a breathless whisper.

Everything? His nostrils flared at her innocent question, and his own breathing became erratic. She swayed toward him.

Merde.

He pulled away and put some much-needed space between them. His wolf howled, but he reined it in. Gaharet had charged him with training her, and not in the bedchamber. As the more experienced wolf of the two, he had a responsibility to show restraint.

"We will start tomorrow. For now, you need to eat and get a decent night's sleep." The flare of disappointment in her eyes nearly undid him. "Training will require all your concentration. It will not be easy. That I can promise you." He headed for the door. "Come, Kathryn."

"Once I am trained, I can go into the forest on my own, yes?"

"We shall see."

She moved past him into the corridor, brushing her body against him. As she did so, her gaze met his, a hint of challenge in their hazel depths. He stilled the growl in his throat before it could form. *Little vixen.* Untrained she may be, but her senses were as sharp as his. Had she caught the scent of his arousal?

"When Gascon informed me you had left, I thought you were gone for good. Why did you return, Aimon?"

Aimon schooled his features into a blank mask. "You need a teacher. Someone to show you what it means to be a wolf. I have returned to teach you." And that was all he would do. Training her would test the strength of his morals, but he owed it to her to do right by her. He would not fail.

Chapter Thirteen

The following morning, with her stomach a jumble of nerves and excitement, Kathryn went in search of Aimon. She had barely slept, anticipation of this moment making it impossible for her mind to relax. What would her training entail? How hard would it be? Could she finally put her fears of turning into a ravening beast, of savaging anything or anyone in her path to rest?

She found Aimon in the hall with his broad back to her, staring at the scene of the battle of Montsoreau. She rubbed her hands together and cleared her throat. He turned.

"Are you ready, Kathryn?"

She licked her lips, her mouth dry. "I am."

He smiled. "Then let us begin."

He walked toward her, lithe and silent, and brushed past her into the corridor. She inhaled his scent, and her wolf stirred in response. How was it possible for a man to smell so divine? She turned and followed him, taking two steps to his one. What would he look like as a wolf? Rangy and lean, or big and muscled? Would his fur be as pale as his hair, and his eyes the same piercing blue?

She halted at the foot of the stairwell as he ascended the stairs. "Are we not going into the forest?"

"Patience, Kathryn. I will take you there when you are ready. Not before."

"Oh." She raced to catch up to him. What could he possibly teach her within the walls of the d'Louncrais keep? He did not stop at the next floor, instead taking another set of stairs. And on the top floor, no less? Perhaps he planned to teach her how to use a sword first. She bit back her disappointment.

But upon reaching the top floor, he continued past the armory and stopped in front of a substantial door with two huge, iron bolts. Cut into the timber was a peephole. Casting a bewildered glance at Aimon, she leaned forward and peered through the slot. Lit oil lamps threw light and shadows across the room, revealing a table, a chair, a cot with a few blankets and no windows. Ice settled in her veins, and she took a step away from Aimon.

"Remember I told you I got caught sneaking out of the keep?" he asked, leaning against the door. "This is where Gaharet and Ulrik locked me away for a few days. They thought it would convince me to stay within the keep as ordered." He gave her a wry smile. "It did not. I escaped a further two times. I needed a little more convincing." He chuckled. "Anne threatened to lock me in here for the entire length of my training."

Kathryn sucked in a breath. "The entire length of your—" She glared at him. "Are you threatening to lock *me* in there?"

"Are you going to give me a reason to?"

Kathryn eyed the door and its sturdy bolts, the thought of being confined filling her with dread. She shook her head. No, she would not try to leave, not if this would be her punishment.

"Then, no. I wanted to show you I understand how frustrating it is to be locked away from the forest. Even after I had escaped twice, Gaharet balked at locking me in here for too long. He understood my need to roam, to feel the earth beneath my paws, but Anne would not relent. Her resolve persuaded me to stay put. The consequences of escaping again were too high."

He slid the bolts across, unlocking the door, and swung it open. "We also use this room for training." He stood aside so she could enter.

She hesitated. "After you."

Aimon chuckled at her distrust, but he entered the room first. Cautiously, taking small, reluctant steps, Kathryn followed him. He closed the door behind them with a resounding thud. She jumped, startled.

"There are bolts on the inside, too," said Aimon, sliding them across locking them in.

Kathryn's heart faltered.

"In this room, I had my first transformation." His gaze shifted to the cot, a tense stillness settling about him. "I also went through the turning here."

Kathryn followed his gaze. Her memories of her turning were the thing of nightmares — a blur of pain and terror. She had screamed a lot. *That* she could remember. Moving to the cot, she fingered the leather restraints attached to the frame. They were broken. They had tried to strap him down and failed.

"Not a pleasant time." His blue eyes were shuttered, and his face was a blank mask.

Aimon really did understand. That thought saddened her, but it also comforted her.

"Why are there bolts on the inside of the door?" she asked, turning the conversation away from the pain of their past to her more present concerns.

"Our first few transformations are often a little uncontrolled, so we lock ourselves in here. It is a little difficult to slide the bolts back with paws. That is why training starts here and not in the forest. For you too, Kathryn. Your first few changes will happen in this room. It is safer that way. For you, for me, for everybody."

Kathryn stared at the heavy bolts, at the solidness of the door, and the peephole that was their only connection with the outside world. As jittery as it made her feel to be locked in, it made perfect sense. Nobody else could get hurt if she could not restrain her wolf.

"Have you ever called forth your wolf, Kathryn? Deliberately? Asking for the change and embracing it?"

She clutched her dress with sweaty palms and gave him a sharp shake of her head.

"Today you will, and we will see if you can master your darker half, your wolf. You have repressed it for years, so I know you can hold it back, but the first few times you release it, you may not have command over it."

Her mouth was suddenly as parched as any desert. Her greatest fear—losing control. Conversely, Aimon seemed unconcerned, despite not wearing the added protection of his armor.

"What if…?" She licked her lips. "What if I cannot rein it in? What if I cannot change back? What if I get it all wrong and I get stuck as a wolf forever?"

He placed a comforting hand on her shoulder and squeezed. "You can do this, Kathryn. I will be here with you, talking you through it. As I did the night we met. We will do this together."

"Has anyone ever struggled to shift back?" persisted Kathryn.

Aimon shrugged. "Not that I am aware of. I once stayed in wolf form for an entire week, and I had no problems changing back." He looked thoughtful. "I suppose it could happen if you stayed wolf for an extended period. But I do not think it would be that you could not change back, but you would not want to."

Despite his reassurances, Kathryn wanted to unbolt the door and escape into the sanctuary of the forest. She repressed the urge to flee. She could do this. Kathryn clenched her hands into fists. She *needed* to do this.

"How do I begin? Do I just think I want to be a wolf? Do I command it to come forth? Every other time it has rushed up on me, uncalled for." Her voice wavered.

He pulled at his tunic, and the hem rose to reveal a bare, muscled abdomen. "First, we will need to remove all our clothes."

Kathryn gaped at him. He could not mean... She clasped her hands across her chest, her face heating. No man had ever seen her naked. She could not undress. Not here. Not in front of Aimon. Not with him standing there as naked as she.

Aimon dropped his tunic, covering the tantalizing glimpse of bare flesh. He cleared his throat. "Shifting form is not compatible with clothing." He paused, his gaze darting about, settling on anything but her. "Remember what happened to your dress the other night?"

She gulped. She remembered.

He rubbed his hand against the back of his neck. "My apologies, Kathryn. I have grown accustomed to some aspects of our existence, and I did not consider this may be uncomfortable for you."

"You are shifting, too? I did not expect that."

Heat flooded her body, and an awareness crept over her that had little to do with embarrassment or modesty. Her wolf pressed forward. She looked Aimon up and down. Lean and muscled, he was a grown man. Seeing him naked would be far different from those village boys she had spied on so many years ago. Would she *dare* look? Would she be able to stop herself?

Aimon's nostrils flared, and his eyes darkened. He took a step back, his Adam's apple bobbing, and a slow flush crept up his throat. He tugged at the neckline of his tunic as though the room had suddenly become too warm. She was not the only one discomfited at the idea of them locked in a room together naked.

"I will wait until you have completed your transformation so I can talk you through it. If I need to shift to bring you under control, I will. So, I will also need to be unclothed." He searched the room, his gaze landing on the cot. He strode over to it and snatched up a blanket. "I will cover myself until the need to change arises." His brow furrowed. "Normally, under these circumstances, you would undertake your training with a woman or your mate, your husband. Those options are not available to us. I am sorry, Kathryn. There is no other way."

"Can you turn around? Please?"

Aimon paused, then nodded. "Very well," he said, turning his back to her.

"No peeking."

"Of course not." He sounded offended she would think he would.

"Are there no other women like me?" she asked, as she turned to face the wall.

The silence hung between them, broken only by the rustle of his tunic hitting the floor. The fine hairs on the back of her neck rose, and she itched to turn around, to catch a glimpse of him.

When Aimon spoke, his tone was subdued. "There has not been a female amongst us for some time."

Aimon's boots hit the floor, and the slide of fabric as he shucked his breeches had her inner thighs clenching.

"Oh." What had happened to all the females? Is that what Anne meant when she had spoken about all those lives lost?

"Kathryn, if we are going to train today, you will need to undress."

"Yes... I... Yes, of course."

She unlaced her boots and set them aside. Grabbing the hem of her over-dress, she removed it and dropped it to the floor. With trembling fingers, she fumbled with the first few buttons on her under-dress, but no matter how hard she tried, she could not reach the rest.

"Aimon?"

"Yes?"

"I might need some help with my buttons."

Chapter Fourteen

Buttons. Aimon closed his eyes and let his head drop forward. Her dress had buttons. And she needed his help with them. He looked down at his naked body. It had no problem with her request, rising to the occasion. What had he done so wrong God sought to punish him like this? Tempting him with something he could not, should not have? He sighed. There was no help for it. Steeling himself, he turned, his cock pointing unerringly at the object of his desire.

She stood with her back to him, the buttons of her under-dress running from her neck down to the curve of her bottom. He swallowed hard, forcing himself to pad over to her, praying she would not turn and see him thus. With trembling fingers and a throbbing groin, he started on the buttons.

Each one he undid parted the material further, with only her thin chemise a barrier between his hands and her bare skin. His knuckles brushed against her near naked back, and he gritted his teeth on the groan threatening to spill from his lips. His fingers stalled halfway down her back, and he shut his eyes against temptation.

"Aimon? Is something wrong?"

There were more than half of the cursed things still to undo, and he could not undo them with his eyes closed.

"No." Did his voice sound as hoarse to her as it did to him?

Opening his eyes, he continued, focusing on the tiny buttons, not the slender patch of barely covered skin that grew larger with each one he undid. By the time he had them all undone, his body was flushed, the cool air of the training room doing nothing to diminish his ardor.

He stepped back, and turned to face the wall, grateful her enticing body no longer filled his vision. His mind's eye saw it clear enough. Material rustled and fell to the floor. His mouth went dry. Knowing she stood mere steps away, wearing nothing but the skin she was born in, her coppery locks spilling over her naked shoulders, set his heart pounding. He wrapped the scratchy blanket around his own nakedness and calmed his ragged breathing. Hanging on to the threads of his control, he clung to his principles. He had told her he would not look. He would keep his word.

"Do not turn around, but I am ready to shift to my wolf now," she called out.

Oh, thank the Lord. He could not bear it much longer.

"Let us begin." His words came out a little choked, and he cleared his throat. "The first thing you need to do is find your center. If you are not secure within it, when you change, your wolf may take control."

"What?"

He caught the note of panic in her voice.

"I will not let anything happen to you, Kathryn. Now, once you have found your center, encourage your wolf to the surface and let it take over your body, but only your body, not your mind, and it will do the rest. Stay in your center. That is the most important thing. All I want from you right now is for you to shift form and keep command of your wolf. Do not panic if you do not succeed at first. If you do, *when* you do, sit down on your haunches facing me, so I know. Do you understand what I am asking you to do?"

"Yes."

"Very well. When you are ready, Kathryn. Take your time. There is no rush."

Kathryn inhaled several unsteady breaths, and Aimon listened for the telltale signs of transformation. Cracking and popping sounds broke the silence as bones melded and rearranged. He clenched his fists in the blanket. In a few moments, she would no longer be naked. He offered a silent prayer of thanks.

Before she had completed her transformation, he turned around. He could not risk having his back to an untrained wolf. To do so risked damage to them both.

Kathryn was almost all wolf. There was little visible of her human form, but his pulse pounded at the hint of bare skin and his cock responded. The damn thing had a mind of its own, refusing to respond to the entreaties of his conscience.

"Stay in your center, Kathryn. You are nearly there." He tried to keep his voice steady — *think of the forest* — but it cracked and wavered.

Kathryn paid him no heed. Her wolf roared to the surface, a force not to be denied. Too long kept at bay, it knocked her out of her center. She spun around, no hint of Kathryn in the eyes of the large auburn wolf, banishing his desire in a beat of his heart. He tensed, preparing to shift. She snarled at him—her canines bared.

"Take control, Kathryn. Get back into your center. Find that quiet place and show your wolf who is in charge."

With a toss of her large head, she turned away from him and threw herself at the door, hitting it hard. It did not budge. She snarled at it and raked it with her claws, biting down on the cold metal bolts.

"You can do this, Kathryn. You are in charge. Go to your quiet place. Feel secure in it. Feel your wolf around you, but do not let it control you. Only from there can you guide it, master it, and be both Kathryn and your wolf at the same time. Do it. Now."

Her wolf abandoned the door and crouched, preparing to launch at him. He stood his ground. Aimon believed she could do this. He must give her the chance.

"Kathryn. Master. Your. Wolf."

Her ears pricked forward, and she hesitated. Shadows flickered in her eyes, and her snarl wavered. The battle for dominance had begun—wolf against Kathryn. Hazel wolf's eyes fixed on him. With a slow easing of tension in her wolf's body, her hackles smoothed out, and she sat on her haunches.

Aimon let out his breath. Kathryn had won. She had done it. On the first try.

"Well done, Kathryn." He grabbed another blanket from the cot and deposited it next to her. "Now turn around and reverse the change." He averted his gaze as she shifted back.

She wrapped the blanket around her naked body and beamed at him. "I did it?"

He smiled at her astonishment.

"I did it," she said again. Firmer this time.

"Yes, you did."

"My wolf wanted to attack you, and I would not let it. I made it do what I wanted. Made it sit like you asked me to." Her smile lit up her face. "I did it."

Her joy was infectious, and he grinned at her exuberance. She had done it. And quicker by far than he had. *Well done, Kathryn.*

His first transformation had been a disaster, and Gaharet had had to shift and take him down, Gaharet's teeth buried around the scruff of his neck until his wolf had submitted. Not for one moment had Aimon felt the need to take such measures with Kathryn. She had fought for supremacy in her mind and succeeded. Living with it, repressing it for over a decade, had taught her ways of keeping her darker half in check. He could not be more proud of her.

"You have done very well, Kathryn. Congratulations on your first intentional shift. How did it feel?"

Her eyes lit up. "Wonderful. Powerful. Not at all what I expected." Her face turned serious, and she placed a hand on his chest. "Thank you, Aimon. This means so much to me."

Clutched about her with only one hand, the blanket slipped, revealing a pale, bare shoulder. Aimon's gaze dipped, following the line of her throat, and slid across her collarbone. He ripped his gaze back to her face and stepped back lest he reach for her.

"Can we do it again? I want to do it again."

Aimon nodded, gripping his own blanket tighter should it slip from his nerveless fingers.

"We will go through the process a few more times. I will ask you to do things — walk around the room, fetch items. Once I am confident you can shift and not lose control, not for a moment, then I will take you out into the forest."

Kathryn gaped at him. "Are you certain?"

"Yes, I am certain."

Things were progressing faster than he had expected. It would be good to be out in the forest. He eyed the cot. There were too many memories in here for him. The blanket around Kathryn's shoulders slipped further. And too much temptation. He wanted out of this room, too.

Chapter Fifteen

"Do you trust me, Kathryn?" Aimon asked, exiting the keep and leading Kathryn down the hill to the bailey. So dogged was she in her determination to be out in the forest, she had pushed herself hard. In no time at all, Aimon had concluded her capable enough to continue beyond the training room. He, too, relished being free of that room, breathing the fresh air.

"I suppose I do. Why?"

He untied a strip of cloth from around his wrist. "Because it is time for your next lesson."

Kathryn scrunched her freckled nose up at the material. "What is that for? I thought you were taking me for a run."

"Not yet."

"But you said…"

"I said I would take you out into the forest, not that we would go for a run. There is more to being a werewolf than shifting and running. You must become proficient with every aspect of your wolf before I will take you for a run. Small steps first."

She huffed her disappointment.

"I am going to blindfold you, and I am going to test your senses. I want to see how well you can use them."

Kathryn scowled, but she let him fix the material over her eyes. She pushed at it with her fingers. "I feel silly."

"No more than I did when Gaharet blindfolded me. And it took me much longer to get to this stage of my training than you have."

"Really? How long did it take you?"

"Weeks."

"*Weeks*?"

He suppressed a laugh at her horrified expression. Had Gaharet told him it would take him so long he would have felt much the same.

"How long until I am fully trained? Until I can change one part of my body like you did in the library?"

"Well, it took me three months before Gaharet would allow me into the forest on my own."

"*Three months!*" She subsided into a dejected silence.

"Do not despair, Kathryn. I do not think it will take you as long as it took me. You have lived over a decade with your wolf. When I began my training, I had been a werewolf for only a week. Everything was new to me. Come."

He took her elbow and guided her through the gate into the bailey. *L'enfer,* was he pleased to be doing this part of her training. He could not have borne another minute longer in the training room. Not with her naked between shifts.

"Now, without allowing the change, I want you to open your senses. What can you smell? What can you hear?"

"Will the servants not think this a little odd? Me, blindfolded, wandering about the bailey?"

Aimon chuckled. She did present as a strange sight and would cause concern on any other estate. Not this one.

"I think those who work here will have seen far stranger things than this. Besides, all who live on this estate come from one very large extended family. A family that has served the d'Louncrais for centuries."

"Anne and Gascon are related?"

"Mmm-hmm. Brother and sister, in fact."

"Oh. Well, that explains why they are both so bossy. It must be a family trait."

Aimon laughed. "Possibly. Though, I would not mention to Gascon you think him like his sister. Even he is wary of her at times."

Kathryn grinned. "I like her, though."

"The keep would not be the same without Anne," he agreed. "So, you have no need to worry about the servants. They will not talk, no matter what they see."

Kathryn's expression sobered, and her hands fiddled with her dress. "The other night, when I transitioned, Anne said I should tell you about..." Her breathe hitched. "...tell you about how I..."

Her voice trailed off, and a tendril of anguish, bitter and acrid teased his nostrils.

"All is well, Kathryn. Your father has informed me of the particulars of your turning. You need not relive it now for my benefit. Now concentrate, open your senses and tell me what you hear, what you smell."

Kathryn's scent sweetened, her shoulders relaxed and she tilted her head to the breeze and sniffed the air. She jerked in his direction. She inhaled another deep breath, her mouth parting on a soft sigh. The sweet change in her scent carried to him, coating the back of his throat. He raked his hand through his hair. *Mon Dieu.* Even fully clothed, she tempted him.

"Focus, Kathryn, beyond me."

"I cannot help it. Your scent is so distracting." Her face flushed at her admission.

"It is difficult, I know, but you can do this." *He* could do this.

Her top lip curled, but she took a deep breath, and tried again.

"Argh." She waved her arms around and stamped her foot. "All I can smell is you. I will never be able to do this."

"You are reaching out with your human senses, Kathryn. They are enhanced, but your wolf's senses are much stronger. You need to bring your wolf to the surface."

"But…if I bring my wolf to the surface, will I not transform?"

"Remember what we did in the training room? Finding your quiet place, your center? Find it again, feel secure in it, *then* let your wolf reach out. Take it slow and let it out only enough so your wolf is present, but not too much that you bring forth the change. Remember, you are in charge. You can command it, guide it and be both Kathryn *and* your wolf. In time, it will be seamless. For now, it will take practice. This is why we train, so it will become as natural as breathing for you." The scent of her doubt hovered between them. "I despaired of ever mastering my wolf, but I did. Through practice. As will you."

She pouted. "I would much rather go for a run."

So would he. "Concentrate, Kathryn."

She groaned, but she did as he asked. Her scent deepened, musky and thick, and he readied himself should her wolf take over. Then her brow smoothed out, and a smile tilted up the corners of her mouth. The tension in his muscles eased. "What do you sense?"

"I can hear people moving about." She tilted her head to the side. "A baby's cry. His mother is pacing. There are two men ahead of us. They are talking. Can I...? Yes, I can hear what they are saying. They are discussing a horse. He is lame again and they want to shoe him."

"Very good. What else? What can you smell?"

"Smoke. Cooking fires. A stew. And over there" — she pointed toward the stables — "horses, hay, manure and leather."

"See if you can reach a little further?"

She tilted her chin, inhaling a deep breath in through her nose. "Some type of grain. Lots of it. The storerooms? And the scratching of mice. No. Wait." She screwed up her face and raised her hand to cover her mouth. "I think a cat ate the mouse. It crunched."

He shrugged. "It will please Gascon the cat is keeping the stores free of vermin. Let us move on."

He guided her forward until they came to the gatehouse. He held a finger to his lips, silencing the guard before he could greet them.

She clutched at his arm. "There is another man here."

His body reacted as though she had touched a different part of his body, *not* his arm. "There is. What can you tell me about him?"

"He smells of soap and...and steel. He is wearing armor."

"Emotions give off a scent, too. This can help you decide if someone, or something, means you harm. Can you sense a threat? Is he friend or foe?"

"Friend? Is it the gate guard?" She turned to him, seeking reassurance, her face tilted in his direction, her lips parted. She had no clue how vulnerable, how inviting she looked, with the blindfold on.

"Friend," he confirmed. "No hint of anger or aggression."

He nodded to the guard, and they passed through the gate. The closer to the forest he took her, the faster she walked. By the time they reached the tree line, she was tugging on his arm, urging him on. Once beneath the canopy of trees, the tension slipped from her slight frame. Her head tilted up to the leafy canopy, her copper locks cascading down her back, and the dappled sunlight played across her freckled nose. Aimon's breathing faltered. He would challenge any man, any werewolf, to not be affected by Kathryn.

Aimon released her arm, letting the coolness of the forest wash over him. He never felt so alive than when he could immerse himself in its depths. It called to him, it calmed him and it energized him. Right now, he wanted nothing more than to shed his clothes, shift and run through its shaded depths until exhausted. Until his mind cleared, and he could think of Kathryn without imagining her writhing beneath him, crying out his name. He had a task far more important than his own needs.

"Are we going for a run now?"

Kathryn leaned toward him, eager, and he loathed disappointing her. She reached up to remove the blindfold, and he caught her hand.

"Leave the blindfold on. We are not going for a run today."

Her shoulders slumped.

"You are not ready. Today has been challenging enough. I will not push you so hard you collapse from fatigue."

"But I am not tired."

"You do not feel it now, but you will soon. Shifting takes energy. Your body has yet to accustom itself to the extra demands you are placing on it. As with mastering your wolf, so, too, will this take time and training. One more lesson and we will conclude for the day. Then you will rest."

She placed her hands on her hips and scowled at him. "I do not need to rest."

"Come, Kathryn. Push your senses out into the forest and tell me what you can hear, what you can smell?"

She held her pose for a moment, then dropped her hands to her side with a sigh. "Pine needles, wildflowers, chirping crickets. The wind in the treetops and the bees buzzing." She rattled them off at him in a flat voice.

"Is that all? Perhaps you are more in need of a rest than I thought."

Her glare bored through the blindfold. "I am *not* tired."

He grinned. Her disposition was as fiery as her hair. She turned her ire on the forest, jutting out her chin. She sniffed—large, loud sniffs.

"Eww." She screwed up her face and covered her nose. "That smells awful. I think something has died." She rounded on him. "You did that on purpose. You *knew* that was out there. What is it?"

"A rabbit. Not too fresh. I would guess it died a few days ago. Not everything we smell will be pleasant, but we still need to know it is there."

"Langeais Keep smells awful. I think I would rather not know what makes it smell so bad."

Aimon chuckled. "You make a fair point. I confess I do not enjoy my visits there overly much. The rankness of it is legendary amongst our kind."

Kathryn giggled. "I do not like going there much either. At least you only have the horrible smells to contend with. I must spend my day embroidering with a room full of gossiping women who coat themselves in any number of potent floral unguents."

He bit back a grin. "Do you not like embroidering?"

Even blindfolded, the horror on her face told him everything. He laughed. "No, I suppose you would much rather be out here in the forest."

"Oh my, yes."

She smiled at him again, and his heart warmed. He cleared his throat. "Let us focus back on the forest. There is something you have missed."

"I did? What is it? A bird? An animal?"

"Knowing what is in your immediate surroundings is important, but knowing what has been here in the recent past can also be useful. Try again. See if you can scent it."

She turned her attention back to the forest and raised her nose to the air. "I think... Yes, there is something else. It is very faint, like the scent is not fresh, and there are layers of it heading out in different directions. It smells almost like you, but…different."

"And what do you think it was?"

"Was it…? Could it be…another werewolf?"

"Very good. Gaharet patrolled his demesne frequently. The last time would have been a week at most, before…" Aimon stopped himself before he revealed too much. "What you smell is the residue of his scent." He stepped closer and slipped the blindfold from her eyes. "You have done well today, Kathryn." She beamed at his praise. He would praise her often to have her smile at him. "We will continue again tomorrow."

"But—"

"Tomorrow, and the next day, and the day after that. You have waited eleven years for this, I know, but training takes time. We all make mistakes when we are tired. Your safety, and the safety of all those who live on this estate, is paramount." He inclined his head toward the keep. "Come. Anne will have a hot bath and a good meal waiting for you."

She would come to look forward to those as her training continued and be grateful of Anne's ministrations. While Kathryn would not admit it, her energy was flagging, her feet all but dragging on the ground by the time he handed her over into Anne's care.

As he watched her weary body climb the stairs, disappearing around the curve, his thoughts already skipping ahead to tomorrow's training, Farren appeared at his side.

"All went well?"

Aimon nodded. "Very well. She is progressing much faster than I had imagined."

"She has nightmares. Has had them regularly since her turning. Do you think they will stop now?"

Aimon stared at the empty stairwell, unwilling to look at Farren. "I imagine so."

Farren's sigh was steeped in regret. "I hope one day she can forgive me. Perhaps then I can forgive myself."

Farren shuffled back to the library, a dejected cast to his shoulders. Aimon stared after him. Whatever the future held for Kathryn, she needed Farren in it. Until the truth had come out, they had shared a bond far stronger than Aimon had with his father. It would be a travesty if she gained her wolf, only to lose the father she loved.

Chapter Sixteen

Kathryn stepped into the bath and eased her aching body into the heated water. She would not admit it to Aimon, but she was tired. Shifting so many times had taken its toll on her body, and a headache was forming behind her eyes. She rubbed her temples. Would it always be this way? Did Aimon feel as fatigued as she did? She should heed Aimon's advice and rest. After all, he had experience in this.

Three months it had taken him. Three whole months. She had much to catch up on. If only her father... A lump lodged in her throat. Well, he had not, and nothing could change that now. But she would learn everything she could from Aimon and be thankful for the opportunity. It did not bear thinking she might never have had the chance, never have understood she was not cursed, had events played out differently.

Kathryn rested her head against the rim of the barrel and closed her eyes. She should be grateful Aimon had shown her the truth, shown her what he was, forcing her transition. *Wait. Why did he do that?* She opened her eyes and sat up, splashing water over the rim of the barrel. Why *had* he done that? He must have known, or suspected, she was a werewolf, for he would never have revealed himself to her otherwise.

She cast her mind back over the past few months. When had he caught her scent? She had not spoken a word to him, nor been in his direct company. Not once, only admiring him from afar, along with every other woman at court. And the smells of Langeais Keep affected him as much as they did her. He had admitted so today. So how... Oh. She remembered. She had bumped into him at Langeais Keep the day Comte Lothair had bequeathed them Gaharet's estate. Aimon had not come to the d'Louncrais Keep because of her change in fortune. He had not come here to marry her at all.

Kathryn slumped back into the water. She had made a fool of herself. No wonder her rejection had not perturbed him.

What about that kiss in the forest? Had she imagined his interest? She reached for a lock of her hair, sliding her fingers through the copper strands. No. She did not think so. Kathryn rubbed her face with her hand. How she wished she had a mother to talk to, to ask questions about men.

The door swung open, and Anne shuffled in, a plate of undercooked meat, bread and cheese in her hands. She eyed the old cook. Anne had a motherly, if somewhat forceful way about her. Did she dare ask her? Kathryn blushed. No. She would figure this out for herself.

Anne hustled her from the bath. "Dry yourself, child, and eat up. You must be hungry."

Surprised to find she was, Kathryn ate everything on the platter as Anne combed the tangles from her hair.

When she had finished, Anne whisked the empty plate away. "Now pop yourself into bed. A good sleep will ease the ache in your bones. You have more training tomorrow and you need to be well rested."

It seemed decadent to be in bed while the sun still shone, but her eyes were drooping, so she did not protest, snuggling under the covers. Before long, her eyelids fluttered closed, her worries about Aimon the last thing on her mind as she slipped into a deep sleep.

Kathryn slept away the remainder of the day, only waking when Anne roused her to dress for the evening meal. She entered the hall to a low hum of chatter, the servants and farmers seated along the large oak table. Her father glanced up, his expression hollow and dark shadows under his eyes. He was still not sleeping well. She could ease his pain. A simple word or two would do. She remained silent.

A place beside him sat empty, and he looked hopeful she would take it. Her gaze darted to Aimon. If she wanted to sit near Aimon, and she did, she must sit beside her father. She stood for a moment, weighing her options, then chose a space on the opposite side of the table. Her father's shoulders sagged, but he said nothing. Aimon's lips thinned, and his eyes narrowed. Oh dear, had she offended Aimon? Perhaps... She made to stand, but a young servant girl slipped into the vacant place between Aimon and her father, and she resigned herself to her chosen seat.

A grizzled farmer slumped onto the bench beside her, and she turned her attention to him, smiling a greeting. He scowled.

"Humph. Another new woman." He grumbled under his breath. "More changes. I dislike changes. It is a bad omen."

Startled, she leaned away from him, her wolf pulsing to the surface.

"Do not mind Old Tumas," said the farmer to her right. "He is always grumpy. My name is Brenton. I farm pigs for the estate."

"I am Kathryn."

"Welcome, Mademoiselle Kathryn. You know" — he leaned in with a conspiratorial twinkle in his eye — "not too long ago, old Tumas chased me around with his pitchfork because my pigs got into his cabbages."

Tumas grunted. "If you had made better fences, your pigs would have stayed in their own paddock."

Brenton chuckled. "My pigs were a little too smart for their own good."

Kathryn glanced between the two men. Brenton had an amiable smile and laughing eyes, while Tumas glared past her at the friendly pig farmer.

"Best mind your pigs." Tumas pointed his knife at her father. "He might not be as kind to you as Seigneur Gaharet."

"Tumas." Gascon's steely gaze pinned the surly old man from the far end of the table. The conversation around the table quietened. "This is Seigneur Beauchene's estate now. As decreed by Comte Lothair. Both he and his daughter are to be accorded the same respect and courtesy as Seigneur Gaharet. Is that understood?"

He looked at each person at the table, seeking their acknowledgment. When he reached Tumas, his gaze lingered. No one made a sound, save for a baby gurgling in his mother's arms.

Her father cleared his throat. "Thank you, Gascon. And thank you to all of you for helping myself and Kathryn with this difficult transition. I do not know how Seigneur Gaharet ran the estate, but I will work with Gascon to make it as smooth as possible. I thank you all for your ongoing support."

Nods and nervous smiles came from everyone around the table, except for Tumas.

"I still do not like changes."

Servants entering with the food saved Tumas from a rebuke from Gascon. They placed steaming platters of meat, salted fish, crusty bread, freshly churned butter and large bowls of stewed meat and vegetables on the table. Kathryn's mouth watered. They had not wanted for food in their previous home in the Langeais village, but they had not eaten this well.

"Tuck in, Kathryn," said Anne, placing her considerable girth next to the lady with the baby. Anne tickled the baby under his chin. "Georges, you get more beautiful every day." Georges gurgled, and his mother beamed.

Brenton passed her a platter of meat. She hesitated over the portions more raw than cooked before slipping them onto her plate.

Tumas' appraising gaze followed her actions. "So that is the way of it, is it? Like Seigneur Gaharet?"

Kathryn froze, waiting for the horror, the recriminations.

With a brief nod, he turned back to his own meal. "Good enough for me."

Kathryn breathed out a breath, her nerveless fingers almost dropping her knife.

Anne passed her a platter of bread. "Kathryn, this is Eleonore and her baby, Georges."

Kathryn took a few pieces of bread, smiling her greeting at the young woman and her baby.

"And this is her husband, Henri." Anne pointed to the man next to Eleonore.

He smiled, ducking his head in deference. "Mademoiselle Kathryn."

"Henri is the stable master. If you like to ride, you can get him to arrange a horse for you. Elise loved to ride."

A lightness bloomed in Kathryn's chest. The wall hanging had not deceived her. "I can ride?"

"Well, of course, dear. The d'Louncrais are excellent horse trainers. Either Gaharet or his father trained all the horses in the stables. And the horses Gaharet's vassals ride as well."

That explained how they could ride, and she could not. Kathryn flicked her gaze to her father, and he had the decency to look ashamed. She rubbed at her chest. For all her satisfaction at his discomfort, it saddened her to see him this way.

"I would like that very much. Perhaps I will visit you in the stables tomorrow, if that is suitable for you, Henri?"

"No." Aimon's voice cut across Henri's smiling agreement.

Kathryn raised her eyebrows at him. "No?"

"No."

Kathryn's cheeks heated.

"Not yet." He softened the denial.

Kathryn stabbed at a piece of meat. "When?"

Aimon leaned his elbow on the table, resting his chin on his hand. "When I think you are ready."

She opened her mouth to protest.

"And not before. Small steps, Kathryn. Remember?"

Kathryn shoved a piece of meat in her mouth, chewing on it with ferocious intensity. Her father ducked his head, rubbing at his neck. Aimon remained unfazed.

"Come now, love. No point getting worked up over naught," said Anne. "There is time enough. The horses are not going anywhere. Now Henri knows you are keen to ride, he can ensure there is a horse for you when you are ready."

"Of course, Mademoiselle Kathryn," said Henri. "Have you ridden much?"

Kathryn swallowed her anger, her disappointment. "I used to ride all the time, but it has been some years since I have been on horseback."

"I think I have just the horse for you. Josephine is a lovely mare. I will have her out in the yard tomorrow and start working her. She will be ready for when you need her."

"Thank you, Henri." She smiled at the stable master and cut a glare in her father and Aimon's direction. Aimon shrugged it off. Her father dropped his gaze to his meal, his shoulders hunched over.

Not since her turning had so many options been open to her, and yet her freedoms were more confined and controlled than ever. She glanced at Aimon through her lashes. He talked to the people around him, smiling, eating and drinking his wine. He laughed at something someone said, relaxed, as though he belonged amongst them, as though he were as human as they were. To be a werewolf and to be so carefree. To have the freedom to come and go as he pleased. Make his own choices. To not hide away or restrain himself lest someone discover what he had become. She envied him.

Kathryn scowled at her meal, no longer hungry. She glanced back at Aimon. The pretty servant girl next to him had her hand on his arm, smiling up at him. The fluttering of her eyelashes would make Manette Chapet proud. A gentle laugh, a pretty compliment, and Aimon smiled down at the serving wench.

Kathryn's lip curled in a snarl, and a low growl reverberated in her chest. Aimon's blue eyes pinned her with a warning look, and he shook his head. She dipped her head and pushed uneaten food around on her plate.

Is that what Aimon preferred? Coy glances and simpering adulation? The servant girl played the part of the gentile, besotted lady better than she ever could. Could he find her behavior too bold? Had the rumors of her wild ways gone beyond the women of the court? He would not be the first person to disapprove of her. Was it any wonder Aimon had returned only to be her teacher?

The sense of someone's regard lifted her head. Her father studied her, tight lines around his eyes. His gaze flicked to Aimon, then back to her. His eyebrows rose, questioning. Kathryn gave him a half-hearted shrug and stared glumly at her unfinished meal. Tomorrow she would try harder. She would keep her temper in check and behave as any lady of her station should behave. Then, maybe, Aimon might see her as more than his student. As someone he might wish to take as his wife.

Chapter Seventeen

"Are you going to tell me what all this is for?" Anne asked, wrapping a loaf of bread in a cloth and placing it with the other larder items Gascon had asked her to prepare. All the other servants had gone to bed — the fire banked down to coals, and the kitchen cleared and ready for the morrow. She stared at her brother, awaiting a response. Something was afoot, and she would know of it.

She eyed the items — fresh loaves of bread, rounds of hard cheese, salted fish, cured meats, boiled fruit and pots of wine. None of the estate retainers were in dire need. She would know if they were. Who did he intend to feed? And in secret, too, for he had asked her to prepare the items once all the servants had dispersed for the evening.

Gascon ran his hand through his graying hair. "I know I should not, but you will hound me until I do."

"I can help you better, brother, if I know what it is I am helping you with."

He wagged his finger at her. "You are not to tell a soul, Anne."

"Of course not. Do you take me for a fool?"

Gascon sighed. "The goods are to go to the old farmer's cottage by the stream."

Anne narrowed her eyes at him. "No one has lived there for years. I hope you are going to prepare it beyond delivering food for whomever you are hiding there."

Gascon pinched the bridge of his nose. "Yes, yes. I plan to go myself."

"Tsk, tsk, tsk." She shook her head at him. "Not wise, brother. Your absence will be noted. Mine, however, I can easily explain away." She patted his arm. "I will take care of it. I told you I would look after that boy, and I meant it."

"Who told you it was for Seigneur Gaharet?"

She chuckled. "You just did. And I am glad. I have been so worried about him since he failed to return from Langeais Keep. Both he and his lovely mate. Why would you keep this from me? We are family."

Gascon huffed. "We are all family of some degree here, Anne, and I am trying to protect Seigneur Gaharet. He wants his men to think he is dead. It would not do if his entire estate believed him living." He sighed. "I should have known keeping anything from you would be impossible. Any wonder my hair is turning gray." He pointed his finger at her. "You are the cause of it."

"You should know better than to hide something from me, especially something this important. I will always ferret it out."

She added a few more items to the pile of goods—a pot of Gaharet's favorite honey, a knob of butter she had churned this morning and some chamomile flowers to make her brew. She also added a cake of soap. Not for Gaharet, but for Erin, should she be with him.

"I will take some fresh breeches and tunics with me as well." She raised an eyebrow at him. "And a few dresses, too?"

Gascon rolled his eyes to the ceiling. "Can I keep anything from you?" He sighed. "Yes, I think the dresses will be most appreciated."

"Good. Then it is settled. In the morning, I will take the cart and head off toward the village. Once I am out of sight, I will change direction. I must say, it is a relief to know he is safe, and his mate is with him. I shall rest easier tonight. And with Aimon here, Kathryn is safe, too."

Gascon nodded. "I am rather glad Monsieur Aimon arrived when he did, what with Kathryn being untrained as she is. Imagine if we had sent for one of the others. Imagine if we had sent for the wrong one."

"It is a sorry business, the lot of it. We can only pray Gaharet can find out who is behind all this, and why. The poor lad. Losing his mother all but broke his heart. To learn one of his men killed her... Well, it is shocking. What is to be done about it?"

Gascon fixed her with a stern stare. "That is not our concern. We will do what we can to assist Seigneur Gaharet, but right now our responsibility is Mademoiselle Kathryn."

Anne bustled to the door. "I can do more than one thing at a time, Gascon. If it is all the same to you, I shall worry about Gaharet as much as I do Kathryn. And nothing you can say will make me do otherwise."

"Worry all you like, Anne," he called after her as she mounted the stairs. "But make sure that is all you do."

She kept trudging up the stairs. "Good night, Gascon."

"Good night, Anne. Sleep well."

Oh, she would. Now she knew Gaharet to be alive and soon to be safe on his own lands. And his mate with him, no less. She smiled in the darkness of the corridor. Things were changing fast in the d'Louncrais keep. For so many years, Gaharet had rattled around its halls alone and lonely. Until Erin had come along. Then overnight they were gone. Now the Beauchenes had arrived, and Anne had a new charge. Kathryn.

Anne started up the stairs to the third floor, her knees protesting. If ever a child needed her, it was Kathryn. Cresting the top, she rounded the corner and almost collided with Aimon. His fists clenched, he pressed his forehead against Kathryn's bedchamber door.

"Well, well, young man."

Aimon looked up, startled at the sound of her voice. To have surprised him and his werewolf senses told Anne everything she needed to know.

He pushed himself away from the door. "I was not going in, Anne, I promise you that."

"Oh, I know. You are an honorable one, that is for certain." She patted him on the shoulder, a smile twitching at the corners of her mouth. "When Erin first arrived here, Gaharet spent almost every night in the forest. Seemed to help him. Maybe you might need to do the same."

Aimon looked thoughtful. "Yes. Some fresh air and a long run. That is exactly what I need." He moved toward the stairs. "Good night, Anne," he called over his shoulder.

"Good night, Aimon."

Anne waited until Aimon rounded the corner before she moved to Kathryn's door and cracked it open a sliver. Kathryn slept soundly—her face relaxed in repose. Anne smiled. Two of her young men had found their mates. Happier times were on the horizon. She could feel it in her old bones. With any luck, in less than a year, there would be the sound of crying babies in these halls once again. Just what this place needed.

Chapter Eighteen

Kathryn made her way to the training room, as she had the last few mornings, to meet Aimon and continue her lessons. Three days of training, and each time when she had asked if they would go for a run that day, he had replied *"you are not ready"*. Three days of practicing her shifts. Hours spent familiarizing herself with the full scope of her senses, sometimes blindfolded, sometimes not. And throughout it all, she had maintained her decorum and kept her countenance agreeable. Not a single hint of dissension escaped her lips.

Three days of training with Aimon the consummate teacher—patient, competent and thoroughly detached. But when he thought her attention elsewhere, his eyes followed her, the heat in his stare burning through her clothing and setting her body on fire. He wanted her. She may be unversed in the ways of the bedchamber, but she could not mistake his desire. The scent of it, which she had come to recognize, bloomed thick in the air between them. So, why did he not act on it? Why did he keep her at such a chaste distance?

With a dejected sigh, she pushed open the door to the training room only to find it dark and empty. Her stomach lurched. Had he left her without so much as a word? Would she once more be confined to the keep until he returned? Not again. She spun on her heel and raced down the stairs.

The thudding of her heart slowed when she poked her head into the hall and found him staring at the wall hanging of the battle at Montsoreau. He had not left. She leaned against the door frame until her pulse returned to normal and her knees ceased to wobble. What she would have done had he truly left the keep she did not know.

He did not turn as she approached him, his eyes fixed on the embroidered figures in front of him, but a squaring of his shoulders told her he knew she was there. She sampled the air, teasing out his emotions as he had taught her. Deep sorrow washed over her, and a longing so intense it took her breath away. She stood beside him and stared at the scene depicted in embroidered thread.

"Do you regret becoming a werewolf?" she asked.

He took in a deep breath before releasing it with a long, drawn-out sigh. "No. If Gaharet had not turned me, I would have died that day, one more chevalier killed on the battlefield. I love being a wolf. The joy of running on all fours through the forest, allowing my wolf free rein… It is indescribable."

"I would not know," she muttered, but he did not respond. They stood in silence for a moment, side by side, staring at the wall hanging. "If you love being a wolf so much, then why do I sense sadness? What is it you are yearning for?"

Aimon chuckled. "You are progressing well." He turned and headed for the door. "Are you ready to begin your training today?"

"Of course." She followed him. "But why are you sad?"

He slowed, allowing her to catch up to him, heading not for the training room, but the large entryway doors. Were they going to the forest? Could he possibly be taking her for a run? Her breath quickened, but she said not a word, afraid to voice her hope should he quash it with a firm 'no'.

"When I awoke after my turning, Gaharet gave me a choice — tell my family what I had become and ensure they did not betray me or keep my secret and distance myself from them."

"Oh."

Aimon opened the large doors and stepped into the sunshine. Kathryn quelled her burgeoning excitement. Today's lesson would most likely focus on more scent work.

"I chose not to tell them."

She stopped, staring after Aimon, before hurrying to catch up. "Why? Were you not close to your family?"

"My parents and my brother and I were as close as any family, I guess, although werewolves seem to have a stronger connection with their kin than humans. But telling them would put them in danger. As you well know, it is hard enough as a werewolf to keep our secret, but to expect others to, those who do not truly comprehend what it means..." He gave her a rueful smile. "It is a lot of responsibility. And I was not entirely certain how my mother would take it. There was a very real possibility she would inform the local abbot in an attempt to save my soul. That would have ended badly for both of us."

He led her down the hill, past the guard and out through the gate. The forest beckoned her, and her wolf pressed close. She did her best to ignore it.

"Do you still see them? Spend time with them?"

"On rare occasions. I spend much more time with Gaharet and the rest of the pack now."

"Do you miss them? Your family, I mean."

He rubbed a hand across his chin. "We are more distant now than we ever were. I have little to say to them. My life has taken such a different path from theirs."

Kathryn's heart ached for him, and she laid a comforting hand on his arm. "But you have the pack— Gaharet and his other vassals."

Aimon nodded. "I do, but it is not the same. And Gaharet and the others have had a lifetime together. All of them born into the pack, it in itself like a large, extended family. They were raised together, grew up together and have hunted together. I am but a recent addition, and while they accept me without question, I do not have the years of shared experiences that they all have." He halted them on the edge of the forest, turning to her. "You have the opportunity to have both, Kathryn. Your family and the pack. That is no small thing."

He paused. She dropped her hand, retreating. Was this just another part of her training? *Aimon reveals his own sorrow in order to teach me a lesson?*

"I know what your father did hurt you. You have every right to be angry. In your place, I would feel the same." Aimon's stare bored into her, earnest and heartfelt. "But he did what he did because he loves you, and he believed it the best way to protect you. I imagine he has regretted his decision many times over in these last few days."

Kathryn turned away, folding her arms across her chest. She did not want to talk about her father. Or *to* her father. Not yet. The wound was still too raw.

"Do not cast away what you have because he made one mistake."

Kathryn stared at the ground, toeing the earth with her boot. She missed her father, felt the absence of his calming presence, his sage advice, but the anger at his betrayal still churned inside her.

"Think about what I have said. Things are…complicated in the pack at the moment. Having someone who solely thinks of what is best for you, someone beyond the pack, someone you can trust, is to your advantage. You may need him in the coming months."

She cut a sharp glance at Aimon. What did he mean by that? She opened her mouth to ask, but he strode off into the forest.

"Come, Kathryn. It is time to continue your education."

With his words ringing in her mind, and the possibility of a run slipping further away, Kathryn trudged after him into the forest.

Chapter Nineteen

Aimon stopped in a small clearing not far from the keep, waiting for Kathryn to join him. He did not know if she would take his advice to heart, but he hoped she would at least consider it. She stopped in front of him, her arms still folded across her chest and her expression shuttered. With a huff of discontent, she closed her eyes and raised her nose, sniffing the air.

"Open your eyes, Kathryn. We are doing something different today."

Her eyes snapped open and stared at him, eager.

He could not help but smile. "Yes, Kathryn. I am taking you for a run today."

Her mouth dropped open, her arms uncrossed and she took a step toward him. She pulled herself up short and clenched her hands by her side. Had she been about to throw her arms around him? Press her soft body against him?

He nearly groaned. *You are but her teacher, Aimon, nothing more.* And that role was temporary at best, bestowed on him because he had the good fortune to be the first to discover her. Once she became part of the pack, as the only available female werewolf, she could have her pick of instructors, of werewolves, to continue her education. As the least experienced, certainly not the strongest, chances were, she would not choose him. It was for the best she did not thank him with an embrace.

"Before we get started, there are a few things you must understand. This will be more difficult than our exercises in the training room. Shifting out here is different. The pull of the forest is strong, and there are no locked doors to contain you. I cannot turn my back on you this time."

Her eyes widened, her mouth forming an unspoken 'oh'. The uplift of her chin and the set of her jaw, all signs he had come to recognize over the last few days, told him nothing would deter her. She wanted this and she would face it head on. *Such courage, such determination.* Her inner fire called to his wolf. He shook his head, brushing aside his primal impulses. Focus on her training, nothing more.

"I will shift first, so I am ready should you need me. I will avert my gaze," he hastened to add. "Your modesty is safe with me, I promise you."

A frown pinched at her brow. "Can you help with my buttons again?"

L'enfer. These infernal buttons. He had asked Anne to dress Kathryn in garments without buttons or laces. Ones she could remove without his help. And for the past few days, she had. Why not today? *Of all the days…*

Her hazel eyes implored him. He swallowed the hard lump in his throat, conscious of the hardening further down his body, in his groin.

"Very well."

She removed her over-dress and turned her back to him, waiting. Fingers fumbling her buttons undone, he hastened away from her lest he be tempted to touch, as she slipped the garment off her shoulders. He looked away, but not before he glimpsed a slim waist and the curve of her hip outlined beneath her thin chemise.

Merde.

Divesting himself of his own clothes, forcing his breeches down over his erection, he quickly called forth the change. Standing on all fours, he kept his gaze fixed on the forest floor. What he could not see, his imagination taunted him with. It took everything he had to not raise his head and look his fill.

He waited, his body thrumming. Her chemise rustled as it fell about her feet, and her discarded boots hit the ground. She took a quick, apprehensive breath, then the unmistakable sound of bones shifting as she transformed filled the clearing. He tensed, ready to pounce.

Silence.

Aimon tore his gaze from the ground and looked into the eyes of Kathryn's wolf. She stood, the dark copper of her fur like fire in the morning sun, ears pricked forward and eyes alight with curiosity. She had achieved the unthinkable. Twice now, she had mastered that which had taken him weeks.

He remained still as she approached, stalking around him, sniffing him and looking him all over. Her first friendly encounter with another werewolf. The first time seeing him as a wolf. He let her take her time, let her familiarize herself with his form. Would she admire his fur as he did hers? She paused on his right side, near his rib cage, and touched her nose to the thin ribbon of flesh where no fur would grow. Tension rippled through him.

His scar.

The pain of the enemy's ax biting deep still haunted him. Blurred memories of clashing swords, a ring of men around him, arguing, and Gaharet's face morphing into a black wolf's snout leaning over him. Kathryn's cold nose brushed his scar again, and she whined. He touched his nose to her foreleg, a similar pink patch in her own fur. Some injuries, even werewolf blood could not erase completely. She seemed satisfied with his response, and he turned toward the forest. Being the focus of her intense scrutiny had not helped ease his arousal.

L'enfer, he needed this run.

He set off at a slow trot, giving Kathryn time to adjust to running on four legs instead of two. When he was sure she could manage, he opened up into a run. He modified his pace to hers, keeping a keen eye on her should she falter. For Aimon, being alive, when not so long ago he had faced his own death, he saw each day as a gift. Living his life changed, as more than human, was extraordinary. There was nothing like the sense of freedom, the pure exhilaration, that came with running as a wolf. This is what he wanted for Kathryn. To experience this joy for herself.

With an expression of extreme concentration, she bounded over a log and landed on all fours. She skidded to a halt, her eyes wide and her jaw dropping open. He halted. Was she hurt? Had she landed awkwardly? Kathryn turned to him, a semblance of a grin forming. She tilted her head back and howled, a song full of exultation and triumph. She had found it.

What it meant to be a wolf. He lifted his own muzzle and howled with her.

He yipped at her to follow him, and he turned, starting off again. He traversed game trails as he led her through the forest, down ravines and across small creeks, weaving through the trees. She did not falter, keeping pace with him, the breeze ruffling through her fur and sheer joy shining in her eyes. When he reached a small meadow, he stopped. He could run for leagues yet, but Kathryn would need to rest. If he pushed her too hard, her human body, unaccustomed to such physical activity, would suffer. He settled himself on the grass and Kathryn flopped down beside him, panting, but happy.

A cricket hopped in front of her, and she tracked it, ears pricked. It landed on her paw. She jumped up, and the cricket leaped away. She bounded off after it, pouncing about the meadow in a fruitless attempt to catch it. Another jumped across her nose, then another, and she darted about, chasing them all, catching none.

Aimon rested his nose on his paws. Had he looked as young to Gaharet when he had first come into the forest? Playing like a pup, full of energy and enthusiasm, his attention so easily distracted? Had Gaharet found his antics as amusing as he found Kathryn's? *Most likely.*

Abandoning the crickets in favor of chasing her tail, Kathryn spun herself in ever smaller circles. She had no more success catching her tail than she had with the crickets, falling over and rolling amongst the wildflowers. His tongue lolling out, he grinned at her. She mock growled and leaped at him, pouncing on *his* tail. Springing to his feet, spurred on by her playfulness, he threw his shoulder into her, knocking her off balance, and grabbed her tail. She yipped and bounded away. He followed, chasing her around the meadow and nipping at her heels. She rounded on him, pounced again, and they rolled about in the grass.

Larger than her, he gained the upper hand and pinned her down. His teeth gently gripped the scruff of her neck, trapping her beautiful auburn wolf beneath him. His blood heated. It roared through his veins, his body trembling with his need to shift, to return to his human form. He would claim her, mate her. It felt right, natural, and there was no other place he would rather be, no other woman he would rather have beneath him than her. He raised his head and howled his triumph.

The lick of her tongue against his muzzle broke his thoughts. He stiffened.

What am I doing?

He looked down at her. Her hazel eyes stared at him, but not with fear. The haze in his vision shifted, and he lifted himself off her, backing away. He turned his back to her, flushed with shame at the thoughts rolling through his head. Thoughts of his body wedged between her thighs, plunging deep. He shook his big, furry head and slunk away to the edge of the meadow.

He kept his head down, and his focus on the forest, refusing to look at Kathryn's beautiful auburn wolf. If he did, he knew damn well he would shift and take her right here on the forest floor. Not the smartest thing he would have ever done. Certainly not the most considerate either. He wanted to, more than anything, but he could not. She tempted him beyond measure, testing every ounce of his control. Perhaps Gaharet should be Kathryn's teacher, not him.

With a quick glance over his shoulder, urging Kathryn to follow him, he trotted from the clearing and headed back toward the keep. Training Kathryn was proving to be his own personal hell.

Chapter Twenty

They were leaving? Had she done something wrong? Had he not enjoyed their playful romp across the meadow? Kathryn scowled after the retreating white wolf. Were all men as confusing as Aimon? She had played the demure lady, kept her temper in check and worked hard. She had pleased him with her progress. He had said so. And yet still, he wished to keep his distance.

She hastened after him, following him as he retraced their steps through the forest. Did he not see them as a good match? Their days together had only convinced her. His longing to find his place, to belong somewhere — emotions she had touched briefly in the hall — echoed her own insecurities. He understood her like no one else could. And she liked him. A lot.

For a man trained to kill with a sword, there was a gentleness about him, a kindness. The more time she spent with him, the more he impressed her with his calm confidence, his patience, even his honorable dedication to protecting her modesty. Aimon Proulx was a good man. And the way he stirred within her unfamiliar desires gave her hope that, with him, she might find the kind of marriage her father had had. She might find love.

Not so long ago, such a thing had seemed beyond her reach. Something few would ever find, least of all her. But with Aimon... She could not let this chance slip her by.

They entered the clearing, their discarded clothing awaiting them. She trotted over to her dress and chemise and glanced over at him. His shoulders stiff, Aimon resolutely faced away from her. She narrowed her eyes at his back. What would it take for him to cross the line from being her teacher to something more intimate?

She turned her back to him, closed her eyes, calmed her mind and willed herself human. With a sigh and a cracking of bones, her wolf's fur receded, her spine elongated, her snout shrank, and she shifted.

The light breeze brushed against her naked skin. She looked down at her hands. Human. She wiggled her fingers and smiled. She had done it. She had become her wolf and run through the forest and frolicked in the meadow, and none of her fears had materialized. She had not been stuck as a wolf unable to return to human form, her transition no more difficult than those in the training room. She was still, and had at all times been, Kathryn. And, oh, the joy of running as a wolf and allowing the darker half free rein... Nothing in her life would ever compare.

The cracking and popping of bones as Aimon shifted filled her awareness. Maybe one thing could compare... Her body tingled, heat blooming between her thighs and her nipples pebbling. No other man had ever had this effect on her.

Kathryn hastened to dress, doing up the buttons she could reach, and turned to face Aimon. Breeches on, his broad back bare, he bent to retrieve his tunic, his muscles flexing as he moved. Her stomach fluttered. Her gaze lingered. No more playing at being a lady.

She sidled up to him, admiring the play of muscles across his back that bunched the closer she came. Her gaze fell to the jagged pink scar below his right shoulder blade. Reaching out, she traced her fingers across the puckered skin. A shiver rippled across his torso. She curled her fingers into her palm.

"I am…" Was she sorry she had touched him? Run her hands across his golden skin? No, she was not. She itched to touch him again. Would he think her too bold? Kathryn no longer cared.

"Thank you." She uncurled her fingers and placed her palm against his warm skin, trailing a path down his spine. His muscles twitched beneath her fingers. "For everything. For today." She licked her lips. "For taking me for a run, as you promised. For teaching me." Her hand reached the band of his breeches. An eerie stillness settled about his body, and his musky scent deepened. "For showing me that being a werewolf is not all bad."

"Being a werewolf is nothing to fear. I am pleased I could show you this." His voice was gruff, and it rumbled through her, tweaking her nipples and her sex. Her own pheromones filled the air. He coughed and cleared his throat, the muscles in his shoulders tightening even more.

She ran her hand over his tense muscles, wanting to break through his stoic reserve. "I am glad you came to the keep. I wanted you to come…for whatever reason." Kathryn hesitated. Talking to his broad back, not seeing if she reached him at all, made continuing difficult. She plowed on. "I want you to know… When I said what I did in the library, I…I was not angry with you. I did not want you to leave. In truth I…I wanted you to stay, but…" She swallowed. "You have this effect on me, and I…I struggled to hold my werewolf in, to keep it hidden." She took a deep breath. "I thought I was protecting you." She caressed his back, enjoying the way his muscles quivered beneath her fingers. She blew out a breath. For all her good breeding, her words lacked eloquence.

Aimon dropped his tunic to the ground and spun to face her. Kathryn wanted to continue touching him, run her hand across his glorious chest, but face to face, she did not dare.

"I know, Kathryn. I understood."

She tilted her head up to meet his gaze. Dark indigo swirled in the depths of his eyes, and his musky scent intensified, but his shoulders remained stiff and unyielding. Must she say it? Give him permission to court her?

She gathered her courage, reached up, brought his face down to hers, and pressed her lips against his. His eyes widened, and he stiffened further, reaching for her hands. Then he moaned against her mouth, a sound of raw need and surrender that sent shivers right to her toes.

She released him, giddy laughter bubbling up inside. She bit her lip to prevent the smile that threatened and turned to leave. Aimon's arm snaked out, grasping her wrist, and he pulled her into his arms.

Kathryn's breath whooshed out as he crushed her against his bare chest.

"You want a kiss?" he growled, holding her body firm against the length of his.

The feel of him, muscular and strong against her, had her quivering all over. With her lips parted and her eyes wide, she nodded.

"Then I am going to damn well kiss you good and proper."

His mouth descended, all reticence disappearing as he took her mouth in his. No light touching of lips, no gentle pressure. This kiss claimed, demanded and took. It spoke of carnal pleasure, of an intimacy so deep she had never dared dream existed. She opened her mouth to him, and his tongue slipped between her lips, plunging into her mouth. Oh. He tasted…amazing. She followed his lead, meeting him stroke for stroke, clinging to him, need bursting over her and threatening to consume her.

She swooned against him, and her wolf roared to the surface, a prickling under her skin, coarse hair threatening to cover her hands. She held it in check. Barely. He drew away from her, his release as sudden as his embrace. Dazed, her chest heaving, she tried to catch her breath. *Oh my.* Now she knew what it felt like to be kissed, really kissed. Never had she thought to experience such…such passion. She wanted to do it again. She reached for him, but he stepped away and scooped up his tunic. He jerked it over his head, avoiding her eyes.

He pressed his lips into a thin line. "I am sorry, Kathryn. I forgot myself. It will not happen again. I promise."

Without a backward glance, Aimon stalked off to the keep, leaving Kathryn staring after him, her lips still tingling.

What if she wanted it to happen again? Her eyes narrowed on his retreating back. She may not be as conniving as Manette and her malevolent little posse, but if he thought she would let him kiss her like that and forget it ever happened... Because of some misguided idea about her modesty... She lifted her skirts and dashed after Aimon. It was high time people stopped making decisions on her behalf and let her make her own.

Chapter Twenty-One

Renaud stared across the bailey at the two hulking chevaliers, Edmond and Aubert Montagne. No doubt the brutish twins were here for him. To spy on him, or to intimidate him perhaps. It mattered not. Their continued presence was only a minor inconvenience, nothing more. Some days it was both twins. Others only one.

"Will you join us for mass, Votre Excellence?"

Renaud turned to see Amonier Touissant standing in the sacristy's doorway. A mild-mannered man half his age, Touissant had come to the profession through a 'call from God'. He cared for his congregation, ministered to their souls and listened to their petty sins, attempting to ease the burden of their wretched lives with a dedication Renaud had never felt, nor fostered, within himself. He supposed there were bound to be those in the church motivated by a desire to do God's will.

"Thank you, Amonier Touissant, not this morning. You may perform the service. I am not here to intrude on your good work."

"As you wish, Votre Excellence."

Touissant bowed and retreated from the sacristy. Renaud returned his gaze to the bailey. One of the brutish twins had vanished, Aubert or Edmond, he could not tell which. Most likely the absent brother sat in the chapel awaiting his appearance, preparing to glower at him through mass. He smirked. He had slipped past them before. They were not taking any chances he would do so again.

He pulled a piece of parchment from within the folds of his robe, unfurled it, and stared at the two images scratched out in ink — one of a howling wolf's head, the other of a stone. Both set in a round disc, an amulet. Beneath them, four incomplete lines of a rhyme he had yet to discern the meaning of. A rhyme engraved onto the amulets of those godforsaken creatures, the werewolves. A spell. Blood magic, he suspected, that made them disappear.

His gaze flicked back to the lone twin leaning against the palisade. No doubt he wore one around his neck. What Renaud would not give to know the words of the verse. Better yet, to have one of those amulets in his possession.

He frowned at the words on the parchment. He could guess at a few of the words, had heard the spoken rhyme when he had had many a werewolf trapped, but the spell would not work without the precise incantation. Or the amulet, he suspected. He had tried it. Many times.

And what of the amulet with the stone? It had no inscription on it he had seen. Only a howling wolf's head on one side and the blood-red stone on the other. He fingered the parchment. Perhaps he should be grateful the spell had not worked for him. He suspected this bloodstone was the key to the werewolves' disappearances. He may not have liked where the spell propelled him to had he been successful.

At a rap on the door, Renaud thrust the parchment back beneath the folds of his robe, concealing it.

"Eveque Faucher." Renaud raised his eyebrows at the young man standing in the doorway. "What a...pleasant surprise." He frowned. "I do not recall giving you leave to depart your jurisdiction." Nor to join him here in Langeais. The last thing he needed, or wanted, was the prying eyes of this pretentious whelp.

"Votre Excellence."

Renaud held out his hand, forcing Faucher to kneel and kiss his ring. Renaud's gaze narrowed. Faucher's genuflection was perfunctory at best.

"My orders came from above."

Renaud's nostrils flared. From the Cardinal or the Pontiff, himself? He fixed a smile on his face. "Well then, I trust your journey from Tours was satisfactory." He chose a chair, indicating Faucher should also sit. "Is there something I can assist you with?"

Eveque Faucher smiled, giving his face an almost angelic cast. He did not fool Renaud.

"Yes. You are the very reason I am here."

Of all the conceited... Renaud gritted his teeth. He took a deep breath and calmed himself. He had known from the moment of his appointment into the clergy the young priest would be trouble and had tried to stem his rapid ascension through the church ranks. But Faucher had powerful connections.

"I am at your disposal." Renaud clasped his hands in his lap and relaxed his shoulders. He would not let this ambitious git rile him. "What is so urgent you had need to travel all this way to see me?"

"We hope nothing."

We?

"You have spent quite some time here in Langeais of late, Votre Excellence. Why is that?"

Renaud studied Faucher—the hint of a smug smile on his lips, the arrogant tilt of his chin. He thought himself so cunning, did this young eveque, daring to question him, his superior. As soon as Renaud made Cardinal, he would reassign this impudent upstart to some far-flung county and keep him there indefinitely. There, anyone of importance would soon forget about him.

"I go where I am needed, and that is not for you to question. Your appointment as eveque at such a young age is an achievement," if one considered benefiting from nepotism an achievement, "but you lack experience."

Faucher's gaze turned flinty. "I am not the only one concerned with your long absence from Tours." Faucher cocked his head. "Is there some trouble brewing here, some threat to the church?"

Renaud snorted. "The Comte de Anjou has always been a threat to the church. It behooves us to keep watch over him from time to time, do you not think?"

"Hmm."

"You have not met our *beloved* comte, have you, Faucher?" Renaud smirked. Perhaps he should take the eveque to the keep. Show him the man who used fear to keep his county in line. Put him at the mercy of Comte Lothair. "He is a rather unpleasant man who I am not entirely certain has all his wits about him. Why only the other day, he drove his sword through the throat of the capitaine of the keep guard. I believe the capitaine had lost something belonging to the comte. Deserving of a demotion, yes. But death? I think not."

"What about the disappearance of his adviser? D'Louncrais?"

Renaud's eyes narrowed on Faucher. For someone only just arrived in Langeais, he was remarkably well informed.

"Mm, yes, it is a little concerning. D'Louncrais had a lot of influence over the comte. He tempered many of his decisions. Given the circumstances, I may need to stay in Langeais a little longer yet. Perhaps..." He tapped his chin. "Perhaps there is an opportunity here. An opening, if you will, to become part of the comte's council."

Faucher's eyes lit up. Renaud almost chuckled. Too easy to read, the young eveque had much to learn. Faucher's ambitions were irrelevant. Soon Renaud's plans would come to fruition and the problem of Comte Lothair resolved. And he would be in a position to rid himself of an annoyance — Faucher.

"Perhaps I should meet Comte Lothair."

Renaud's lips curled, unable to contain his mirth. "If — and the chances are slim — you *were* to secure an audience with Comte Lothair," Renaud's smile turned to a sneer, "you would soon discover you are no match for him. Very few are. Leave Lothair to me. I am sure Amonier Touissant could use your assistance in administering to his flock."

Faucher's face reddened, and he scowled. He thrust his hands into his robes and produced a piece of parchment, unfolding it.

"If you have such a connection with the comte, then perhaps you know of his interest in this, *Votre Excellence*?"

Renaud snatched up the parchment. A drawing of a howling wolf's head, and four lines of strange script, indecipherable, but complete. There was only one place, indeed one person, he could have received such information from.

Faucher leaned back in his chair with exaggerated casualness and crossed his arms over his chest.

Renaud dismissed the parchment with a sniff. "What is this? A family crest? A wolf is a common motif in these parts."

"And the writing?"

"Nothing more than the scratchings of an illiterate peasant."

Faucher's eyes gleamed. "I assure you, Votre Excellence, it is not. It is witchcraft."

Renaud snorted. "Witchcraft?"

"Indeed. It is understandable you do not recognize it. You have not studied the darker arts as I have."

Renaud looked down his nose at Faucher. "This obsession you have with these matters is clouding your judgment. It is time for you to put such...unseemly and un-godlike pursuits behind you. You could have a great future in the church. This"—Renaud waved about the parchment—"will not aid you. I suggest you take some time in prayer and quiet reflection. Consider how you wish to proceed." Renaud held up the parchment. "I will see this nonsense destroyed. Dismissed."

Renaud waited until Faucher, jaw clenched tight and his back rigid, stalked from the sacristy before he turned his attention to the parchment. He stared at the four lines of script. His informant had not been idle after their last confrontation. Clever move, seeking out Eveque Faucher. Word of his fervor in routing out witchcraft had reached even this backwater village. Renaud had worked too hard and invested too much in his plans to have them commandeered. Not by Faucher. He would take whatever steps necessary to keep him far away from the werewolves of Langeais.

Chapter Twenty-Two

After another two days of training, and Aimon resolutely keeping his promise not to touch her again, Kathryn flounced into the keep and stomped up the stairs. Damn that man. She would be an old maid before he ever kissed her again. Not a look, or a touch on the arm, barely a smile for her. And no matter how hard she tried to maneuver herself into his space, into his arms, he always managed to slip away and keep his distance.

She stormed into her bedchamber and slammed the door so hard it shook on its hinges.

"Oh, deary me, Kathryn! Whatever is the matter?" Anne frowned. "Do I need to take that boy in hand?"

Kathryn flushed. "Are all men so difficult to understand?"

Anne chuckled as she stepped in to help her undress. "They can be at that."

Kathryn groaned and slid into the waiting bath. She sighed, welcoming the hot scented water. It soothed her aching muscles, though it did nothing for her temper.

"Come now, love, tell old Anne. What has that boy done? I am sure it is nothing a good clip across the ears cannot solve."

Kathryn's lip curled in a snarl. "Aimon has done nothing."

"Oh, I think he has done something to have you in such a mood."

Kathryn's shoulders slumped. "No, Anne. He has done *nothing*." She pouted. "I kissed him. And he kissed me back. It was..." She touched her fingers to her lips. "Wonderful." She dropped her hand back into the water. "Then he apologized and promised it would never happen again. As though he had done something wrong. As if *we* had done something wrong. Ever since then, he trains me and I learn. We talk werewolf things, and that is all."

"Ah." Anne stoked up the coals in the brazier.

"I thought he liked me and wanted to kiss me. Enjoyed kissing me. I was certain of it, but..." She rested her hands on the edge of the barrel, her chin on her hands. "Maybe he prefers the attentions of that servant girl. The one who sat next to him one night at the evening meal. You know, the blonde one who helps you in the kitchen."

Anne snorted. "Cosette? She has as much chance of snaring Aimon's affections as I have."

"Then why? Is there something wrong with me?"

"Tsk, tsk, tsk. There is naught wrong with you, Kathryn. Now you get that idea out of your pretty, little head."

Kathryn leaned back against the barrel and stared at the ceiling. "Ever since he kissed me, all I can think about is how much I want to kiss him again. That cannot be normal."

"Oh, I think it is. At your age, if I had a handsome, young chevalier like Aimon Proulx parading around in front of me, I would think of naught but kissing him, too."

"It is not only kissing him I think about." She flushed. "It fills my every thought. So much so, I am struggling to keep my mind focused. I almost lost control of my form out there today. And I had yet to undress. A fine thing that would have been. Could you imagine it? Me walking through the bailey half naked. The servants would gossip about it for months."

Anne chuckled. "The staff would have paid you no mind. You would not have been the first to struggle with that predicament."

"Really?"

"When Elise trained with Jacques, not long after her turning, she had many a mishap with her dresses. I cannot say Jacques seemed to mind too much. And the servants knew better than to say a word."

"Humph."

"Never you mind what the staff think. You are not the first werewolf to struggle with those urges. It is all the more difficult for you to resist them because your kind feels them much stronger than any of us mere humans do."

"We do?" asked Kathryn as she stepped out of the bath and took the proffered cloth from Anne to dry herself.

"Yes, dear. Jacques, Elise, Gaharet. You *and* Aimon. If you are finding it difficult, do you not think it would be the same for him?"

Kathryn scowled. "He seems to have no difficulty controlling his form."

"Of course not, child. He has had lots of practice. Besides, I would imagine the moonlit runs he takes at night help him a bit."

Kathryn spun to stare at Anne. "He does *what*?"

Anne's smile was sly. "You did not hear it from me, child. I cannot have those boys thinking I tell tales about them, or they will never trust old Anne again. But yes, Aimon goes for a run every night once you are soundly sleeping. Gaharet did much the same with Erin. It takes the edge off."

"That is not fair."

Anne guided Kathryn to the chair. "Whatever made you think life was fair, child?"

"What can I do, Anne? I have tried everything to get his attention. Nothing seems to work."

"Hmm." Anne ran a comb through her hair. "You know, moonlight has a strange effect on werewolves. It amplifies whatever they are feeling."

Kathryn's ears pricked. "It does?"

"Yes, and I believe it is almost a full moon, too. The closer to the full moon, the more powerful the effect."

Kathryn leaned back in the chair, crossing her arms over her chest. "Really? How interesting."

"Mmm-hmm. Aimon has not told you that?"

"No. He has not. It appears there are a few things he has neglected to mention."

"Oh, he must have forgotten. Good thing old Anne is here to ensure you have all the information. There now," she said, finishing Kathryn's hair. "Into bed with you."

Kathryn crawled beneath the bedcovers, no longer tired, her mind full of possibilities.

Clutching the blankets to her body, her gaze narrowed on the old cook. "What would *you* suggest I do, Anne?"

"Oh Lordy. I am too old to know what shenanigans you young folk get up to."

"But," Kathryn persisted, "if you were me, what would you do?"

"Mmm. Now let me think."

Anne tapped her chin as though considering her reply, but she did not fool Kathryn. If she had not asked, for certain Anne would tell her all the same and she was not averse to taking advantage of Anne's meddling.

"If I were in your situation—not that I ever have been—but if I were, I think I would turn the tables on Aimon Proulx. We cannot let those boys think they are in control all the time."

"And how would I go about doing that?"

Anne raised an eyebrow. "Why, offer him something he wants, something he cannot possibly refuse."

Kathryn frowned.

Anne chuckled. "Oh, my dear child. What he wants is you. Any half-wit can see that. He cannot keep his eyes off you."

Kathryn's heart fluttered. Could Anne be right? Were Aimon's feelings so obvious? An idea formed in her mind. Would she have the courage to follow it through?

"He goes for a run every night, you say?"

"Mmm-hmm. Without fail."

Kathryn worried the inside of her cheek. "He has forbidden me from entering the forest on my own."

"True, but if you go at night, you will not be alone. Not for long. Aimon will soon join you."

"What of the guards? They will not let me through the gate."

Anne winked at her, moving to the door. "You leave the guards to me. Now, get some rest, and I will wake you for the evening meal."

Her thoughts racing, Kathryn snuggled under the covers, sleep now the furthest thing from her mind.

Chapter Twenty-Three

Aimon needed his run tonight more than ever. Keeping his distance from Kathryn, enticing, innocent Kathryn, tested him beyond all measure. Her hazel eyes watched him, stared at him with the same longing that clawed at his own mind. The pout of her pretty mouth that begged for his attention. The curve of her hip beneath her chemise, the light touch of her hand on his arm. He swallowed. Her flush of pleasure when he praised her for her successes. The scent of her arousal when he let himself get too close to her, and the force of her frustration when he moved away. Each day of training proved more difficult than the one before.

He eyed the moon, slung low in the sky, as he headed for the forest. Almost full. It called to him, stirring his lust to a fever pitch. He wanted to admit defeat. Beg Gaharet to take over her training. It warred with his selfish desire to keep her to himself. To have her smile at only him, laugh with him, and gaze at no other with such undisguised longing like she did when she thought his attention elsewhere.

In the back of his mind hung the threat of another pack member discovering what Kathryn was. Of her being at the mercy of the one who had betrayed them. A heavy weight settled in his chest. In four days hence, he must meet with the pack and update them on his progress with the tasks assigned to him. Kathryn's scent on him would be difficult to disguise, and her existence would no longer be his secret. She would need all he could teach her and more. His determination to protect her burned as strong as his desire.

He slipped into the forest. Beams of moonlight pierced the leafy canopy and lit up the gloom. Two steps beyond the tree line, he caught her scent. Not the remaining trace from earlier, but the full power of her presence. Kathryn was here. In the forest. Alone.

His footsteps quickened. His fear for her safety, matched only by his lust, burst forth with a power that nearly drove him to his knees.

Damn the moon to hell.

His heart racing, he came to an abrupt halt at the edge of the clearing.

Merde.

Desire punched him in the gut, stealing his breath and momentarily stopping his heart. His nostrils flared, and his gaze devoured every inch of her. Whether by design or accident, she stood in a halo of soft moonlight, her hair tumbling loose in dark copper waves about her shoulders. The filmy chemise she wore billowed in the night breeze, hiding neither her shape, the hard points of her nipples, nor the hint of auburn curls at the crux of her thighs. Did she realize she was all but bare to his hungry eyes?

Hands clenched by his side, he planted his feet firmly on the ground. He would not, could not, go to her and scoop her into his arms. As much as he wanted to. As much as he *needed* to. Taking a deep breath, he reminded his heart to beat and his lungs to breathe.

"Kathryn." He growled, his grip on his wolf treacherously thin. "It is not safe for you to be beyond the walls by yourself, especially at night."

"I am no longer alone, am I?" A hint of a smile teased at her lips.

If she had planned on sneaking out, waiting for him in the clearing would have been counterproductive. No, Kathryn had something else on her mind.

"I thought I might join you this evening for a moonlit run. It does not seem fair that I should miss a chance to run as a wolf because you have been remiss in asking me to join you."

Aimon's eyes narrowed. Anne. She had divulged his little secret. He pressed his lips together. Kathryn stood there, too arousing for words, her eyes wide and her eyebrows arched in feigned innocence. Untouched and virginal, yes, but innocent? Right now, she was playing him. She had schemed with Anne.

It did not matter what her plans were. Aimon could not skip his run. Not after seeing her here like this. Not with the moon so close to full. He doubted she would go back to the keep if he asked, even ordered, her to. Dragging her back there and locking her in the training room was not an option, either. Anne would box his ears. He had no other choice than to take her with him.

Aimon gritted his teeth. He would keep his emotions leashed tight, take her with him, run her ragged, and leave her so exhausted she would not resist when he took her back to the keep. He could then return to the forest and run some more, burn away every shred of his pent-up lust until his body ached and begged for rest.

"Very well," he said, struggling to maintain his composure. "We will go for a run together tonight. But from now on, you must promise me never to leave the keep on your own again, night or day."

"Thank you." Kathryn shot him a coy smile, a mischievous gleam in her eyes. What *was* she up to?

She reached down, grabbed the hem of her chemise and, in one fluid, unexpected movement, she pulled it over her head and dropped it to the ground beside her.

Merde.

He should look away. He should close his eyes, but he could not. He stared. At her pert breasts, with their dark areolas and pebble hard nipples. At the soft swell of her stomach, at the flare of her hips, and at the dark auburn curls that hid her sex. He licked his lips, his cock standing to immediate attention, and he strained against the impulse to move toward her.

She looked shocked at her own audacity. Her gaze settled on his erection, barely contained by his breeches. Panic flashed in her eyes, then she shifted from human to wolf, the fastest he had seen. As quick as she had revealed her naked flesh to him, it was gone, and he was left staring at her auburn-furred wolf. She spun away from him and ran. Kathryn had lost control. Her wolf was in charge.

"*Merde.*"

His wolf burst forth, clothes tearing and falling to the forest floor. He gnashed his teeth and stretched out his legs, racing through the trees to catch up with her. He had promised to take care of her, be ready if something went wrong. When it had, blinded by the vision of her naked body, he had reacted too slow. A poor excuse for a teacher, he was.

He caught up with her not far from the clearing. She did not try to outrun him and make him chase her, and some of the tension eased from his body. Kathryn had regained control. *Thank the Lord.*

When he fell in step beside her, she refused to look at him or acknowledge him. Her wolf had taken them both by surprise. His lips curled into a snarl. He would have a long talk with Anne when he returned. She would not take well to his reproach, would even berate him for challenging her so, but he could not have her jeopardizing Kathryn's safety. The old cook's meddling could have proven disastrous.

Aimon set a grueling pace — as much to wear himself out as Kathryn. He did not stop at the meadow as he did during training. He did not slow at ravines, at felled trees or at creeks. Aimon kept running, taking them several leagues from the keep before circling back. Not once did Kathryn leave his side. Had her loss of control frightened her? He hoped it would give her pause, lest she attempt something so foolhardy again.

And he would take the memory of her naked body with him, though it would be sure to plague his empty, lonely nights once her training had concluded. He doubted he would ever forget how she looked, her body bare, her pale skin flushed in the moonlight. It would be his blessing and his curse to have seen that which he would never have.

Entering the clearing, he found a spot away from her discarded chemise and sat down on his haunches, his back to her. If Kathryn were to leave the forest tonight with her innocence intact, he could not risk another look. The telltale sounds of her shifting reached his ears, then the rustle of fabric as she picked up her chemise. Good. Her common sense had prevailed. Perhaps now she would return to the keep without protest.

"Aimon," she called out to him.

His ears twitched, and the fur bristled on the back of his neck, but he kept his gaze fixed on the forest in front of him.

"Please look at me."

He shook his large, furry head in negation. To turn around would be a mistake.

"Please."

The pleading in her voice cut through his determination, and Aimon had turned around before he could stop himself. Her thin chemise clasped to her body, her breathing uneven and her cheeks flushed, she stood her ground. His gaze slid to the rise and fall of her chest. He would not shift back. He did not dare. Being in wolf form was the only thing stopping him from wrapping Kathryn in his embrace, laying her down on the forest floor, and covering her with his body.

"I am sorry. What I did was stupid and irresponsible. I thought...I did not expect..." She lowered her eyes, her hands twisting in the material of her chemise. She lifted her head, meeting his gaze. "I wanted you to see me as more than your student. To see me as a woman."

He sat on his haunches, not moving a muscle, wanting her with every fiber of his being. How could she think he did not see her as a woman? When she stood before him like this? He was doing his best to do right by her, and she poked at his resolve with every word, every glance and every determined thrust of her chin.

She let go of her chemise, and it fell to the ground. "Make love to me, Aimon."

The air rushed from his lungs.

Merde. The right thing be damned.

His body shifted before he could stop it, and he stalked to her, pulled her into his arms and crushed her to him. Slanting his mouth across hers, he gave in to the call of his body, and the demands of his wolf.

Kathryn's body molded to his, skin against skin, her erotic wolf scent enveloping him. His wolf's howl of triumph echoed in his mind, blasting away any residual restraint. She had taunted him, offered herself to him. That he would take her if she let him was no longer in question.

He parted her lips, and thrust his tongue into her mouth, and she clung to him like she needed this as much as he. He could no longer deny her. Perhaps, from the moment he had first brushed against her at Langeais Keep, they were destined to arrive at this point. That she should end up in his arms, inevitable.

She arched her back, pressing against him, and he groaned.

"Kathryn," he murmured, making one last effort to reinstate reason. "We should stop. While we still can." His ragged breathing belied the words spilling from his mouth.

Her hands tightened in his hair. "Do you want to stop?"

"No, but..." Of course he did not want to stop. Knowing Kathryn in the most intimate way a man could know a woman was all he had thought of for the past ten days.

"I want this. I want you."

Aimon closed his eyes, blocking out the vision of her, her face tilted up at him and her lips moist from his kiss. So trusting. Would she still want him when she realized she had others to choose from? When he introduced her to the rest of the pack?

He clasped her face in his hands and stared into her eyes. "Do not do something you may come to regret, Kathryn."

He would let her go, take her back to the keep if that was what she asked of him. Though his body, his mind and his wolf would scream at the loss, at being denied what he wanted from the tips of his toes to the depths of his soul, he would do it. For her.

Kathryn's hands slipped from his hair, down his chest, fingering his amulet. "I have dreamed of this, of us, since before you came to the d'Louncrais Keep."

His breath hitched. *She has?* "I am your teacher."

"But I want more."

Kathryn took his hand and placed it over the swell of her breast, and Aimon lost the battle to his all-consuming need to make her his.

Chapter Twenty-Four

Kathryn met Aimon's gaze. His warm palm cupped her breast and her lower body pressed flush against the evidence of his arousal. Uncertainty simmered in his eyes. For a moment, she thought he would deny her, would hold firm to some misguided sense of duty he seemed to have placed on their relationship. Another person, another man, making decisions he believed best for her. But then his blue eyes blazed bright, and he scooped her up in his arms.

Kathryn sighed, and she gave herself over to the anticipation of what she hoped was to come. Laying her down on a soft, grassy patch of ground, he covered her body with his, his knee parting her thighs, pressing against her. Her womb clenched and her mouth dropped open in a breathless sigh. Would it be all she dreamed of? An explosion of passion, heat and need that consumed them both and filled the ache inside her? Or would it leave her disappointed, confused and wanting as many women at court had experienced before her?

Aimon dipped his head, and dropped soft kisses along her collarbone, the night breeze licking across her skin, a cooling breath following the trail of fire he ignited. His hand brushed across her body, raising goose bumps in its wake. Her nipples hardened, seeking his touch, and, as if he had read her body and her mind, he covered her breast with his warm palm again and gave a gentle squeeze.

He rolled her nipple between his thumb and forefinger, and she gasped at this new, intense and unexpected sensation. It was almost too much — the feel of his body against hers, his hand at her breast, his thigh against her core. His arousal, hot, hard and thick, pressed into her hip.

Panic flared, and she squirmed beneath him. He was so big. Would it hurt?

"I will be gentle, Kathryn, I promise," he whispered, taking her mouth in his again, plunging his tongue deep, giving her no room to think of anything else but the thrust of his tongue and his lips on hers. He rubbed his thigh against her, and she moaned into his mouth. Her body was tinder and he the spark. She all but burst into flames.

His mouth left hers, shifting lower, sucking and teasing at her greedy skin. His lips closed over her nipple.

Oh. Have I died and gone to heaven?

She arched her back against him, craving more, seeking something indefinable. His teeth scraped against her sensitized skin, and her body quivered.

A prickle of heat was all the warning she got. With a roar, her wolf burst forth in her mind, making its presence felt.

"*Mon Dieu*, Aimon, I am shifting."

Not now!

He released her nipple with a soft plop to stare into her eyes, a gentle hand cupping her face.

"Take a deep breath," he said, his voice calm. "Will it away."

Coarse hair crept up her forearm, and a bone cracked in her wrist.

No.

Her thoughts scattered, unable to find a focal point. Her jaw clicked, her canines extended, and her wolf claimed more ground. She whimpered.

"Close your eyes." He stared at her, with his blue eyes boring into her soul. "Trust me, Kathryn."

Kathryn let her eyelids flutter closed.

"Now take a deep breath and focus within."

She did as he asked, attempting to center herself as he had taught her, but her senses were full of Aimon — his scent, the feel of his strong, naked body, his lips mere inches from hers. Her ankle popped. Fingernails became claws.

"It is not *working!*"

"Listen to me. You can do this." His warm breath whispered against her face, and she moaned, quivering beneath him. She searched for things to fill her mind with. Things other than Aimon. Things that helped to calm her in times of stress. She followed the scent of the forest, the pine, the damp earth and the wildflowers at the edge of the clearing.

The roaring began to subside. An owl returned to its hollow, a polecat followed the scent of rabbits looking for their burrow and a pine marten scurried into hiding. With each breath, her wolf retreated, her fur receded and her canines retracted. With a final crack of her wrist, her body relaxed back into her human form. She lay still, holding her wolf firmly in place. Would Aimon retreat now? Deem her not ready because she could not control her wolf? She opened her eyes to Aimon smiling down at her.

"You did it."

He planted a kiss on her nose, her cheek, her mouth—soft and gentle. Chaste. She swallowed her disappointment. He would push away from her now, her chance lost.

Aimon caressed her face with his fingers, his gaze locked on hers. "I am not leaving you, *ma belle renarde*. I am too far gone to back away now."

He claimed her mouth again and his tongue slipped past her lips. A poker to the burning coals of her need, he stoked her desire. Her wolf rumbled in the back of her mind but remained dormant. No sprouting fur or cracking bones. It wanted Aimon, too.

Emboldened, she let her hands wander, caressing the soft skin over the hard packed muscle of his shoulders and his back. Lower still over the rounded globes of his cheeks. He nipped at her lip and her fingers clenched, clasping his muscular buttocks. He ground his hips against her core, and an unfamiliar ache settled deep in her womb. She held on tight, urging him to do it again. When he did, she tilted her hips, thrusting herself against his thick erection.

He groaned. "Oh, Kathryn. You are testing my control. Have tested it since the day I first kissed you."

He nuzzled at her neck, the hollow of her throat, then across her chest to first one nipple then the other, nipping and licking a fiery trail across her skin. Further still, his velvety mouth continued down, her stomach quivering with each touch. His hands clasping her hips, his mouth dipped lower until his tongue licked a path along the seam of her core.

Kathryn's eyes flew open. *No one in the women's circle had ever mentioned this.*

"Aimon," she rasped, her breathing heavy. Wetness dampened between her legs, and not from his tongue. Mortified, she attempted to push him away, but he grasped her hands, stilling her protests.

"Let me look at you."

Kathryn squirmed beneath his intense stare.

"So wet for me." He pressed his nose against her and inhaled. "You smell divine."

More dampness. Her face heated, her cheeks burning hot. With gentle hands, he spread her thighs, opening her up to his covetous gaze. He growled.

With that one look, her embarrassment fled, replaced by a need so strong she almost forgot to breathe. She let her legs flop open, reveling in Aimon's fixed attention. To be so desired, to elicit such longing, made her feel powerful. She arched her spine, her nipples taut and engorged, thrust out, presenting herself to him.

He growled again and buried his face between her thighs, lathing her with his tongue. Her eyes fluttered closed, and her head dropped back. It was sinful, decadent and more than she could ever have imagined.

Aimon's tongue circled the little nub at the top of her sex, and her hips jerked. He chuckled against her and did it again.

"Do you like it when I do that?"

"Mnh." Her tongue stuck to the roof of her mouth, making it impossible to verbalize her feelings. Her whole body shook with sensation. Aimon did it once more, this time sliding his finger through her wet folds.

Kathryn moaned. His finger pressed at her entrance, and as he sucked her nub into his mouth, he slid his finger in. A stream of nonsense words fell from her mouth.

With a gentle hand and a firm tongue, he set up a slow rhythm, and Kathryn flung her arms out clutching at the grass for something to hold, something to ground her. Her head rolled from side to side, her body flushed and tensed in expectation. Then Aimon curled his finger inside her and stars exploded behind her eyes. Her body arched, and a cry tore from her throat, as wave after wave of intense pleasure rolled over her body.

Kathryn's orgasm ripped through her. He had given her that, the only man to have done so.

Aimon growled low in his throat. *Merde*, he needed her, wanted to be buried in her wet heat to the hilt and thrusting inside of her. Arms flung out, eyes closed, her hair spread like flames of fire across the forest floor — he had never seen a more beautiful sight. His nostrils flared. His wolf was now the one threatening to take over. Somehow, he maintained his form.

He slid his body over hers and positioned himself between her thighs. She was wet and ready for him, and he was more than ready for her, but he would need to take this slowly. He dipped his head into the curve of her neck and inhaled her scent. Her body quivered beneath him, and she clung to him. He slid his cock through her slippery folds, then paused at her entrance. Her eyes flew open, her pupils wide and uncertain.

"This may hurt a little at first," he whispered against her cheek.

Her breath hitched, but her hands pulled him closer. Steeling himself, he sank slowly into her warm, wet heat. He groaned. *Mon Dieu*, she was tight, and the clench of her channel around him almost had him spill his seed as if it were *his* first time, not hers.

This, this bliss, was what he had hungered for from the moment he had seen her in the forest. No, from the moment he had caught her scent at Langeais Keep. Why he had denied himself this for so long, he could no longer recall.

She whimpered, and he stilled, though his body demanded he fulfill the act to completion. Holding his control together by the barest of threads, his cock buried deep, he waited and watched for a sign that she was ready. He would wait all night if need be, but he sent a fervent prayer to God, to the moon, to anyone who would listen, that it would not take that long.

With an impatient mewl, she shifted her hips, driving him deeper. He moaned, leaned down, nipping her bottom lip with his teeth and began to move, a slow rhythm of withdraw and thrust. His body shook with the effort to maintain his sedate pace, her breath puffing against his cheek and her hips undulating to meet his.

"Aimon," she gasped. "I need...I need more."

Her plea, and the insistent urging of her hands, were a testament to the fire inside of her that intrigued and excited him so much. He could deny her nothing. Relaxing his restraint, he gave them both what they wanted, what they needed, pounding into her, and she met his thrusts with reckless abandon. A tingle started in his balls, racing up his spine, and as she clenched around him, reaching her peak, she sent him over the edge.

"Aimon!"

His hoarse shout mingled with hers, as his whole body went rigid, and he emptied his seed inside her.

As his body ceased its shuddering, he collapsed beside Kathryn, spent, but sated. For now. Aimon turned his face toward her, looking at her through hooded lids, and found her staring at him — beautiful hazel eyes and a nose full of freckles. He leaned in and dropped a kiss on her forehead. He let his gaze run over her body, her nipples still pert and skin flushed from their lovemaking. It would only be a matter of time before he would want Kathryn again.

She smiled at him and reached out to lay a hand on his chest. "Thank you for my moonlit run. We should do this every night."

He raised his eyebrows at her, grinning. "You are very bold, Kathryn Beauchene."

She frowned. "I guess I do not behave the way other women do," she said, looking away from him.

"No, you do not, *ma belle renarde.*"

He reached out and turned her to face him. He took her mouth in his, letting her know just how much he liked that. Aimon released her, and she snuggled into him, her soft, feminine body curved against him. The moonlight filtered through the trees, casting a gentle light about the clearing. He wished they could stay this way all night, basking in the afterglow of their lovemaking, but they would need to return to the keep soon or Anne would send out a search party.

With the old cook sure to gloat at the outcome of her scheming, Aimon had no wish for a confrontation. As it was, with his clothes torn during his hurried transition, they would have to sneak back into the keep through the kitchen. Anne was not the only person they would need to avoid. The guilt would hit him soon enough. That he had taken Kathryn at all, much less in the middle of the night on the forest floor, already pinched at him. Meeting Farren in the halls while naked, in the company of his scantily clad daughter, was something his conscience was not yet ready to face.

Beyond the clearing, careful to remain downwind, belly flat to the grass, lay a brown wolf. His lip curled in a vicious, silent snarl, he stared at the reclining lovers before slipping away, unseen, into the forest.

Chapter Twenty-Five

With his hand tucked in hers, Kathryn and Aimon snuck in through the kitchen, tiptoeing along the halls to her bedchamber, giggling like a pair of naughty children. A bath of steaming hot, scented water awaited them and coals, freshly stoked, glowed in the brazier. She grinned.

Thank you, Anne. For everything.

She ran her gaze over Aimon, every glorious inch of him available for her eyes to feast on.

"Shall we?" Aimon asked, inclining his head to the tub.

Kathryn's breath hitched at the heat in his gaze. "Oh, yes."

She doffed her chemise and climbed in. Water sloshed over the rim as Aimon settled his muscular frame in behind her. He drew her back against his chest, his thighs bracketing her hips, and proceeded to wash her down with gentle hands. He started at her neck, working his way across her shoulders and down her arms, easing the tightness in her muscles.

Kathryn rested her head back against his shoulder, lost in his tender ministrations. Nothing she had heard from the women of the court had prepared her for such tenderness, or such passion. Her instincts, her careful weighing of her options, had not led her astray. Aimon would make her a good match, a good husband.

Tilting her head to look at him, she met his gaze, and her heart swelled, the intensity of emotion overwhelming. Was this what her father had experienced with her mother? Her aunt with her Uncle Jacques?

Aimon touched his lips to her forehead, his hands shifting to her stomach, then her breasts. Desire flared, and her exhaustion dissipated. Again? So soon? His hands slipped lower, gently washing her inner thighs and cleansing her folds with soft strokes. She arched her back, all but lost to sensation. His hard length pressed into her bottom. She was not alone in being aroused. Could her hands on him elicit a similar response, as his did on her?

Twisting herself around to face him, she straddled his long legs and planted her bottom on his thighs. She wanted to see him, touch him, have him lost in her caresses as she had been in his. She placed her palms on his chest. His blue eyes darkened. Emboldened, she rubbed her thumbs against his nipples. He gasped, and she stilled, her hands poised over him. He leaned back against the tub and placed his arms along the rim.

"Touch me all you want, *ma belle renarde*."

A shiver quivered down her spine. *Ma belle renarde.* My beautiful vixen. His. He had said it before in the forest, but caught up in his kisses, in the way he had awakened her body with his touch, she had paid it no mind.

She flicked her fingers across his nipples once more, reveling in the flair of his nostrils. She dipped her hands beneath the water, trailing them across his stomach. His muscles rippled under her touch. Lower still, until her hands connected with his hardened shaft. As hard as steel, yet supple. She wrapped a hand around him. He uttered a tortured groan, and his cock twitched beneath her palm. Alarmed, she snatched her hand away. Had she hurt him? She did not think she had squeezed him too hard.

Aimon grasped her hand and moved it back to his cock. Hesitant, she wrapped her fingers around him again, opening her mind and calling on her wolf to read him. His pleasure battered her senses, and the scent of his arousal drenched her. Her sex clenched. With his hand still covering hers, he tightened her grip, guiding her in smooth strokes up and down his length. He closed his eyes, a look of pure rapture on his face. A look *she* had put there.

Braver now, Kathryn swiped her thumb across the tip of his cock. He growled. A shiver rippled through her body, and her vision glazed. The power she had over him was intoxicating. Adjusting her hand, she slowed her strokes, experimenting, taking him from the tip to the base. He groaned, his breathing erratic. She changed her pace again, faster this time, and his hands dipped beneath the water, gripping her hips. She pressed against him, her core flush to his muscular thigh.

"Kathryn." He groaned again, and she relished his guttural response.

Strong hands lifted her by the waist and her hands slipped free of him. He held her against his chest for a moment, holding her above him, and her breath caught in anticipation. Then, ever so slowly, he lowered her onto his cock.

The sensation of being filled overwhelmed any residual tenderness. Kathryn flung her hands around his neck. It was all-encompassing, negating reason and restraint. Spying on those boys by the pond all those years ago, watching them frolic naked, envious of the girls they brought with them, girls they kissed, she had pictured what it would be like to be intimate with a man. Never in her wildest dreams had she imagined this.

"Ride me, *ma belle renarde*. Take your pleasure."

And she did, sliding up and down his length, seeking her release. His hips bucked in time with hers, water sloshing onto the floor, but she spared it not a thought. All she had room for was Aimon. Her world narrowed down to him, to his strong hands, his muscular body and his thick cock deep inside her. His hand slipped between them, swiping against her nub, and her climax hit her with the force of an autumn storm. Her body clenched around him, and she cried out, unable to contain the pleasure rippling through her. With a grip like steel, he held her in place, slamming up into her, prolonging her bliss. She screamed again, her head dropping back, her body quivering with the onslaught. His body stiffened, and he thrust one last time, deep, as though reaching for her womb, and he roared out his release.

Breathless, she collapsed against his chest, and he held her close, nuzzling her neck, their wet bodies clinging to each other until the last tingles of their orgasms had faded away.

"Is it always like this?" she mumbled into his neck, her body pleasantly limp.

Aimon palmed the back of her head, stroking her hair. He swallowed, his Adam's apple bobbing, his chest still heaving. "No."

"Is it a werewolf thing?"

He took a moment to respond. "Perhaps."

Kathryn closed her eyes and let herself float away on the residual euphoria, sated, content, cocooned in Aimon's arms.

The cooling of the water roused them, and Aimon helped her from the tub, toweling her down with infinite tenderness. He led her to the bed, tucking her in against his warm body, and pulled the covers over them both.

As Kathryn drifted off to sleep, wrapped in Aimon's arms, her heart beat a troubled rhythm. She had given more than her body to Aimon this night. There was every chance she was losing her heart to her angelic warrior, but would he lose his to her, too?

As dawn approached, Aimon slipped from the bed, tucking the covers beneath a still sleeping Kathryn. Though Anne would suspect where he had spent the night, he did not wish for it to become common knowledge. He paused in the doorway and looked back at her, her crowning glory of auburn locks spread across the pale linens. *Ma belle renarde* he had called her, but was she truly his? Never had he felt such a connection with a woman before, nor experienced such protectiveness, such need to be with her, close to her and touching her, as he did with Kathryn. What they had done would make it even more difficult when she chose another.

The ache in his heart pounded in sync with the throb in his groin. He should not have taken her, not in the forest, not ever, but he could not bring himself to regret it. And he could not bring himself to never let it happen again. He would take whatever stolen moments he could, and treasure them, for they would keep him company in the empty years ahead that were sure to come.

He slipped from the room, careful not to wake her, and went in search of fresh clothes. It was time to introduce her to her alpha. Time to make her one of the pack. He gritted his teeth. Gaharet would scent him on Kathryn in an instant, and he would take whatever recriminations Gaharet leveled at him. He deserved every one. He had failed as a teacher and failed in his duty, for he had been unable to keep her safe from himself.

Chapter Twenty-Six

Kathryn's eyes fluttered open to a cold, bare space beside her. She looked around the room. It was empty, save for her. Her heart dropped to her stomach. After the intimacy they had shared, he had left her? When had he retreated from her bedchamber? In the early hours of the morn, or the moment she had fallen asleep? Her throat tightened, and she tucked the covers up under her chin. Her bottom lip trembled. How naïve of her to assume one night in each other's arms would mean as much to him as it did to her.

The door swung open, and Anne bustled in, a dress slung over her arm. "Up and out of bed, my dear. You have a big day ahead of you."

Kathryn rolled herself into a ball and buried herself in the bedcovers. How could she face Aimon if last night had been nothing more than the result of moonlit madness? How could she spend another day with him pretending last night had not happened, had not changed everything? Had not meant everything? For her, at least.

"Now do not be like that, child. A little more excitement on your behalf is warranted, I should think," said Anne. "Aimon tells me you are going riding today."

Kathryn's heart stuttered. He was taking her riding? Was that why he had left? To prepare for the day?

"Come. I have the perfect thing for you to wear."

Kathryn peered over the bedcovers. Anne held up an under-dress unlike any other she had ever seen before.

"It belonged to Elise. Your aunt simply refused to ride sidesaddle, or on a pillion box, so she had these made so she could ride astride. I thought you might have a similar preference."

Kathryn roused herself from the bed to examine the dress. Someone had split the bottom half and sewn it into two halves, one for each leg. Like men's breeches and yet not, allowing for the legs to be held apart, like when riding astride. The volume of the skirt remained, so when not riding, it would appear like any other dress. Having the chance to ride again was beyond anything she had hoped for. Riding astride as she used to, without censure, enabled by this altered dress, made her eyes sting with unshed tears.

"Oh, come now, lass. No time for crying. That man of yours is already awaiting you at the stables."

That man of mine? Her heart fluttered like a thousand butterflies. Could this be what falling in love felt like? Careening from one emotion to another at every thought, every mention of the object of one's desire? Could Aimon be experiencing the same?

Anne held out the modified under-dress for Kathryn to step into, then pulled it up over her shoulders, buttoning it up. She slipped the over-dress on after it. It, too, had undergone alteration, with large splits up the center and the side.

"Thank you, Anne."

Anne patted her cheek. "You are most welcome, child. Now go. If I keep you too long, Aimon may well come looking for you. I imagine it is difficult for him to have you out of his sight after last night."

Anne propelled her toward the door. Her cheeks heating, Kathryn ducked her head and descended the stairs, eager to ride again and impatient to see Aimon, the unfamiliar feel of her dress swishing between her legs. She passed the library, its door ajar and the soft glow from the oil lamps spilling into the corridor. A rustle of parchment and the scrape of a chair on the floor gave her pause. Pressure built in her chest. She had never gone so long without speaking to her father. Before she could change her mind, Kathryn pushed the door open.

Her father looked up from his book as she entered the room, regarding her with sad eyes. Kathryn closed the door behind her, unsure of what to say or where to begin.

"Kathryn? Are you unwell? Is there a problem?"

Kathryn smoothed down the skirts of her dress. "Can we...can we talk?"

Marking his page, her father snapped his book shut and placed it aside. "Of course." He motioned for her to come sit with him. She shifted from one foot to the other, then moved to a chair by the brazier and sat. The last time they had sat thus, things had not gone well.

He smiled at her, and Kathryn dropped her gaze to her hands.

"Kathryn, I know I hurt you, though believe me, it was not my intention. If you need to rail at me, curse me, then do so, but *please*, talk to me."

She fidgeted in her seat.

"I have missed you," he said.

Her shoulders slumped. "I have missed you too, Father." She looked at his familiar face, the regret shining in eyes so like her own.

Her father exhaled a long, low breath. Coals shifted in the brazier. Flames sputtered in the oil lamps. Kathryn picked at her fingernails.

"How is your training with Aimon going? Is he teaching you all you need to know?"

Kathryn blushed. "It is going well. I am learning many things." Her eyes dipped to her hands in her lap. "Father…"

Talking to her father never used to be this hard. She had always talked to him with openness and honesty, no matter the subject. Had they lost that?

Her father reached out and took her hand in his. "What troubles you, Kathryn?"

Kathryn stared at her hands, resting in her father's larger ones. "How did you know you loved my mother?"

He raised his eyebrows at her. "Is this about Aimon? I thought you did not want to marry him. If I recall, you told him you were 'not for sale'."

She released a nervous chuckle. "Yes, well, that was before I knew he was a werewolf."

"And now?"

Kathryn looked away, fixing her gaze on the glowing coals in the brazier, worrying the inside of her cheek.

"What if...? What happens if I do, and...?" Her tongue stuck to the roof of her mouth. "How do I know if he feels the same?"

A smile crept across her father's face. "Are you developing feelings for him, Kathryn?"

Heat suffused her neck and spread across her cheeks. She did not dare tell her father what she had done—what she and Aimon had done. In the forest, and again in the bath.

Her father leaned back in his chair, a satisfied gleam in his eyes. "I am pleased. Aimon is a good man. It horrified him the decisions I made on your behalf. The way he held you when you shifted, protected you, kept you safe in a way I could never do—" He broke off. "He would make you a fine husband."

"But how do I know if he wants to be my husband? Has he said anything to you?"

Her father shook his head. "No. Not yet."

Kathryn's hopes fell. "Does Aimon have no interest in me or the d'Louncrais estate? Apart from training me?"

He had said as much, when he had first returned. Being intimate with her had meant nothing? Of course he had wanted to bed her. She had all but thrown herself at him, begged him. What man would refuse something offered so freely?

Her father shook his head. "I did not say that." He smiled and squeezed her hand. "Give it time, Kathryn. He is very protective of you—"

She snorted. "That is a werewolf thing."

"He spends all his time with you—"

She rolled her eyes. "Of course he does. He is training me."

"And I have seen the way he looks at you."

Kathryn's breath stalled in her lungs, and she stared at her father. "How does he look at me?"

Her father's gaze softened. "Like he cannot take his eyes off you."

Kathryn's heart fluttered. "Are you sure?"

"I might be getting on in years, but I know what I see." He smiled and patted her hands. "Trust your old father. Like you once used to. That young man wants to be more than your teacher. Now, I believe he is waiting for you in the stables."

On impulse, she leaned over and gave her father a hug. "Thank you, Father."

He held her tight before releasing her. "I want you to enjoy yourself today, hmm? If Aimon is a smart man, and I believe he is, he will not let something so precious slip from his grasp. Now go."

With a spring in her step and a lightness in her heart, Kathryn left the library. As she approached the stables, Aimon appeared, leading his stallion. Her steps faltered, and her hand tugged at the neck of her dress. How did one act after what they had shared?

He turned to her, a smile on his lips and heat in his eyes. "Good morning, Kathryn." He adjusted the girth on the saddle, patting the stallion's nose away as it turned to nip him. "Are you ready to reclaim a part of the life you lost?"

Kathryn hurried over. "Yes. Yes, I am ready."

Henri emerged from the stables with a chestnut mare in tow. "Good morning, Mademoiselle Kathryn. I have your horse ready for you." Smiling, he held the reins out to her. "This is the mare I spoke of. Josephine."

Kathryn's stomach lurched, and her eagerness fled. She eyed the horse warily. The chestnut mare stood patient and calm, but Kathryn still hesitated. Since her attack, Kathryn's experiences with horses had been equal parts terrifying and heartbreaking. The first of many hard realizations her life had forever changed.

"She is well trained, Kathryn," said Aimon, coming to stand beside her. "She will not react to you."

Her hands itched to take up the reins and to know once again the feel of being on a horse. The wind in her hair, the pounding of hooves beneath her and the exhilaration of galloping across fields. As a child, she had been obsessed with horses, brushing them and braiding their tails, spending as much time in the stables as she did in the forest. Half the time she had spent in the forest had been on horseback.

Becoming a werewolf had ended all that. Months after her attack, she had snuck out to the stables, eager to see the horses and to taste the freedom of a ride in the forest. She had barely set foot in the door when the horses started reacting—whinnying, snorting and stamping their hooves. With every step she had taken inside the building, the horses' distress had escalated. The stable hands had gone from stall to stall trying to soothe the troubled animals, at a loss as to what stirred the mounts.

The head groom had warned her to stay out of the way. Standing near the hooks of hanging tack and saddles, her back to the stable door, she had not seen the approaching stable boy with the reins of a large bay stallion in his hand. The agitated horse had balked at entering the stable, fighting his handler's grip. Kathryn had gone to help him. The horse had screamed, reared up and had struck the young man, knocking him to the ground, leaving him wounded and prone beneath trampling hooves.

The ruckus had brought villagers running, her father amongst them. Taking in the chaos, the agitated horses, the injured and bleeding boy on the ground, her father had scooped her up and had raced her from the building. That was the last time Kathryn had set foot in a stable. She had never ridden a horse again, and a much-loved part of her life had slipped away to a faded memory.

Aimon took the reins from Henri, placing his hand on her lower back, urging her forward. His comforting touch gave her the courage to step toward the mare. Other than worrying the bridle bit between her teeth, Josephine remained unmoved. Her hand shaking, Kathryn ran her fingers over the mare's head, tracing the white blaze down her velvety nose. Josephine nickered and nuzzled at her hand.

Tears threatened to form, and Kathryn touched her forehead to Josephine's, stroking her neck and breathed in her horsey smell. After all these years, she would ride again. She took the reins from Aimon's outstretched hand and flicked them over Josephine's head.

Aimon stepped in close to assist her to mount. He smiled down at her, touching her cheek with the back of his hand. "Today, you are one step closer to regaining your life."

She tilted her head up and leaned in, her lips parting. Would he kiss her? In front of Henri?

His lips touched hers, light and brief, but Kathryn's heart beat a triumphant rhythm.

"Shall we go?" he asked, moving to assist her to mount.

With his hands on her waist, Kathryn swung into the saddle and settled onto Josephine's back with ease. She rubbed the mare's neck. She had missed this. She had not forgotten how good it felt.

Aimon's hand rested on her knee. Nor had she forgotten the feel of his hands on her. She placed her hand on top of his and squeezed. "Thank you, Aimon."

"You are most welcome."

He met her gaze and something different, something gentler, shone in his eyes. Not the heat that made her pulse race and her stomach flutter, but something softer that spoke of a deeper emotion. Was this the look her father had talked of?

Aimon mounted his stallion and turned its head toward the gate. Kathryn nudged Josephine into a trot, allowing Aimon the lead, and followed him out the gate and into the forest.

Chapter Twenty-Seven

Henri had spoken true. Josephine was a gentle mare, with a responsive mouth and a smooth gait. With her modified dress flowing about her legs, Kathryn rode with all the freedom and abandon she had as a child. No more riding in a cart for her. She breathed in the air, gloried in the kiss of the sun on her face and relished the feel of once again being on horseback. As the forest opened up into a meadow, Aimon spurred his horse into a canter. Kathryn followed, urging Josephine on, laughter bubbling up in her chest and her spirit soaring.

Rounding a patch of trees, she eyed the green grass stretching out in front of them. *Perfect.* She kicked Josephine into a gallop. The mare bounded forward, streaking past Aimon. He muttered a curse, and the pounding of hooves behind her told her he gave chase. Leaning into her horse, standing in the stirrups, her knees pressed against the horse's sides, she gave Josephine her head.

The mare took the bit in her mouth and increased her speed. Josephine liked to run, too. Wind whipped through Kathryn's hair and stung her eyes as they galloped across the meadow with Aimon in close pursuit. She had not felt so alive in years.

As the forest loomed, Kathryn reined Josephine in. Panting and out of breath, Kathryn's smile was so wide her face hurt.

Oh, how I have missed this.

As the mare slowed to a walk, she dropped her reins, and Josephine stretched her neck, snorting and lowering her head to pick at the grass. Kathryn patted the mare's neck and received a nicker of acknowledgment. They would make a good team.

Aimon reined in beside her, positioning his horse against hers, knee to knee, blue eyes dark and stormy.

"Have a care for the danger, Kathryn."

She rolled her eyes at him. "I have not forgotten how to ride, Aimon."

"*That* is not what I speak of."

She took up her reins and steered Josephine away, spinning her around, giving Aimon her back.

"Here is where I get a lecture about not racing off on my own," she called out over her shoulder. "That it is not safe for me in the forest without you. That I must be coddled and protected and watched." She sighed and turned Josephine back around so she could face him, but at a distance. "You dangle freedom in front of my nose, Aimon, and when I grab it with both hands, you want to stop me. What is so wrong with a gallop across a meadow?"

Aimon pressed his lips together. "There are dangers you know nothing of. I do not like you so far from me. I cannot protect you."

"I have lived eleven years, eleven long years, afraid of what I am, hiding myself away and giving up many of the things I loved. You have shown me it does not need to be that way. That my life can be different. I no longer wish to live in fear, Aimon. I want to be me again. To do the things I used to do. Can you not understand that?"

Aimon huffed out a breath. "My aim is not to take anything away from you, Kathryn. I am trying to give it back to you. Why do you think I am training you so hard?" He raked his fingers through his hair. "Unfortunately, your discovery could not have come at a more inopportune time."

"What do you mean?"

"Things..." He tilted his head back, released a heavy sigh. "Archeveque Renaud and Comte Lothair know of our existence and have formed an alliance against us."

Kathryn recoiled. *L'enfer*. When she had stood before him in the hall of Langeais Keep, had Comte Lothair known then?

"Does he...? Does the comte know about me?"

Aimon shook his head. "*We* did not know about you, Kathryn, so it is unlikely. That your existence was unknown is, perhaps, the only reason they spared you."

"Spared? Whatever do you —? Oh." All those lives lost Anne had spoken of. "What happened?"

Aimon stared off into the forest. "One of our own betrayed us. Sold our secrets to Archeveque Renaud. And Renaud used that information to trap and murder our kind. His scheming has forced Gaharet to lie to the pack, to let them think he is dead, when in truth he is alive and well and in hiding. You are not safe. None of us are, but you are in danger more than most."

"Because I am untrained?"

He inclined his head. "Partly."

Kathryn remained silent, waiting for him to explain.

"When I became a werewolf, after the battle of Montsoreau, there were over one hundred werewolves in the pack, including children. Not so long ago, Renaud and this…this *traitor* started targeting us. Seasoned female werewolves, born werewolves, trapped and killed, one by one. Then the children, the weak and the elderly. But he did not stop there. Hardened, battle tested chevaliers in their prime fell victim until only seven of us remained. And one of those seven has betrayed us."

Kathryn did the sums. Gaharet, Aimon, Lance, Godfrey, Ulrik, Edmond and Aubert. Seven. "I am the only female?"

"If not for Gaharet's betrothed's recent turning, you would have been. Like me, a mortal wound made it necessary for her to be turned. Can you now understand why I cannot let you go beyond the keep walls alone? Gaharet will not want Erin out of his sight either. It will be hard for you both, but it is the best way to keep you safe, to keep you alive."

Aimon moved his horse in close.

"I know how frustrating it is to be confined, Kathryn. I had three long months of it, and I hated every damn day. But there will come a time, God willing, where there will be no need for such measures, and you will be free to do whatever you choose."

She considered him for a moment. "And I could take a run in the forest on my own? Go for a ride on my own?"

"Yes, if that is what you wish. You could swim in the pond in naught but your chemise if it takes your fancy."

She gaped at him. Had one of their servants gossiped? Had someone spied on *her* in the millpond?

"How did you know about that?"

"There have been rumors." Mirth and something else, something heated, danced in his eyes.

Her stomach fluttered. "You do not think my behavior uncouth? You would not stop me?"

He gave her an incredulous look. "You? In the stream? In naught but your chemise? Wet?" His irises darkened, and he shifted in his saddle. "*L'enfer* no. I would not stop you. I would *join* you." He bit his bottom lip between his teeth and released it. "In naught but my skin."

Air whooshed from Kathryn's lungs, and her thighs clenched against Josephine.

Aimon broke the moment, turning his horse away, guiding it toward a faint trail leading into the forest. "Until then, until I can ensure your safety, I will endeavor to give you as much freedom as I can. Like today. Although we do have some business to attend to as well."

"Business?"

"I am taking you to meet the pack alpha."

"Gaharet?"

"Yes, Gaharet is our alpha. It is time you swore your allegiance to him, to the pack."

Kathryn's skin prickled, and her hands tightened on the reins. "I have to swear allegiance?"

Aimon nodded. "We all do. He is our alpha. We must submit to his will for the good of the pack."

The hairs on the back of Kathryn's neck bristled, and her wolf rose to the surface. Josephine danced beneath her, unsettled.

Aimon swiveled in his saddle and stared at her, his nostrils flaring. "Kathryn, control your wolf."

The command in his voice rippled across her mind. Her wolf growled, in tune with Kathryn's resistance to allowing, nay swearing, to let yet another man have the right to make decisions on her behalf. Would she ever have a say in her own life?

Aimon vaulted from his saddle and grasped Josephine's bridle. "Kathryn, you must take control. As well trained as she is, the mare will not stand for you shifting."

Inhaling deep breaths of pine and oak, Kathryn forced her wolf to recede, a sullen, prowling presence in her mind.

Aimon relaxed his hold on the reins. "All will be well, Kathryn." He patted her knee. "Gaharet is a good and fair alpha. Come. Talk to him. See for yourself."

She stared at Aimon, wanting to trust him. Aimon remounted and set off again at a trot. Kathryn sat unmoving, watching his retreating back. Josephine nickered, not wanting to be left behind. She gathered her reins. She would talk to Gaharet. He was, after all, her cousin. He had not seemed so bad at the family gatherings she had attended as a child. Tall and lanky, full of mischief, but not unfriendly. Not at all obnoxious like Jean-Luc Cadieux.

She kicked Josephine into a trot and followed Aimon along the trail. Where would this new life take her? She could not turn back. Not now her wolf knew the taste of freedom. Her life had changed again, through no fault of her own, no conscious decision she had made. Mayhap this time, it would lead to a better, happier path. One which, she hoped, would include Aimon by her side.

Chapter Twenty-Eight

Lothair eyed the man seated in his chambers. Again. His third visit in as many days. "Did something slip your mind when last we spoke?"

Lance Vautour smiled, deference feigned in the bowing of his head. Lothair curbed his disdain. The man sought to replace Gaharet as his council, yet he would never be the man Gaharet was. Too willing to flatter him with pretty words, telling him what he wanted to hear, not what needed to be said.

As one of his men, that suited Lothair fine. As an advisor, Lothair had no use for him. Gaharet had never hesitated to give his opinion, or to disagree with him. He had always spoken his mind, and Lothair had relied on his advice. Not so with Lance.

"Mon Seigneur Comte, I wish to speak to you about a rather delicate matter."

Lothair smiled. "Go on." Lance's attempts to maneuver into his confidence were entertaining.

Lance cleared his throat. "I...hmm... I find it is long past the time where perhaps I should consider taking a wife."

Lothair raised an eyebrow and leaned forward in his chair. Interesting indeed. "Marriage can be quite an advantageous pursuit. You have a young lady in mind?"

"I do. As you say, marriage can be advantageous. I would think such a union as I am about to propose would serve many, including you."

"Mm. How so?"

"You have my allegiance. Without question. If I were to marry Kathryn Beauchene, I would secure not only the largest estate in your county, but also the surety of Gaharet's vassals."

Well, well, well. His plan was producing results. Lothair leaned back in his chair and crossed his arms over his chest.

"Gaharet's vassals will fall in line, regardless, and they will soon reinvest themselves to me. Have you not assured me of this yourself?"

"I have, and they will, but the d'Louncrais estate was the seat of the pack's power. Do you not wish for it to stay with someone you can trust, rather than it fall in the hands of some ambitious, status climbing family?"

Lothair resisted a smirk. Unlike Lance's own? Lance came not from a long lineage of titled chevaliers.

"Tell me, Lance. Why would I wish to give the pack back its power? Its wealth?"

"Because I can guarantee that power and wealth will remain under your absolute control. Through me."

"Hmm, but what of your alpha? Ulrik?"

The corners of Lance's mouth dipped, but the expression in his eyes never changed. The chevalier's regret only ran skin deep. Did Lance think he could fool him? He who had survived his childhood because he could read people and sense their deepest, darkest intentions? Lance overestimated his abilities.

"I fear Ulrik is lost to us. He has always been hot tempered and impulsive, but of late he has fought against the restrictions of the pack and been at odds with Gaharet. At odds with the world."

Lothair tapped his finger against his chin. In this, Lance spoke true. Ulrik had ever been a thorn in his side. In more recent years, his discontent had grown. More worrisome, Ulrik had ceased trying to hide it. Not a barrel of wine existed in the county he had not drunk from, and nary a woman of Langeais, of common or noble birth, had he not bedded. Had his behavior created dissension among the pack? Enough they would leave him to rot? And yet... Ulrik knew of Gaharet's survival, while Lance did not.

He tugged at his bottom lip. "The estate in question is extensive and comes with a myriad of obligations. Are you prepared to take on the responsibilities Gaharet's death has left void?"

"I will serve you in any way you deem fit, Mon Seigneur Comte. As I always have."

Yes, he would, and it would not be in Gaharet's stead. Nor as Kathryn's husband.

Lothair nodded, pretending to consider Lance's proposal. "I will think on this. Dismissed."

As Lance departed, Lothair rose and poured himself a drink, then dropped back into his chair. He kicked his feet up on his desk and leaned back, pondering this new turn of events. He now had three of Gaharet's vassals vying for Kathryn, but only one of them had dared turn up at the estate. As of today, two men had petitioned him for Kathryn Beauchene's hand in marriage. Both Gaharet's men. Neither of them Aimon Proulx.

Lothair had expected a reaction, but not from Aimon. It made no sense. If Aimon knew Gaharet to be alive, and Lothair was certain he did, why would he call on the d'Louncrais estate? *What are you up to, Aimon?*

He took a sip of wine. He did not believe Aimon had betrayed Gaharet. The young man did not possess the guile. He never had. A fine warrior on the battlefield, he lacked the ruthlessness one needed for court politics, to deal with the likes of consummate players like Renaud. And yet, for one not well suited to cutthroat intrigue, he was holding his own, keeping secrets from Gaharet's other vassals. Lothair had never erred when judging a man's character. He did not believe he had misread Aimon.

And what of the other petitioner? Godfrey Lagarde? Quiet and scholarly, but a solid warrior, his request for Kathryn's hand in marriage, and by extension the d'Louncrais estate, had surprised Lothair. He had always thought Godfrey's interests lay elsewhere. Perhaps Godfrey had more than one secret.

Lothair drank down his wine. Werewolf pack politics, it seemed, were as convoluted as those of the court. But which one of them had aligned with Renaud?

"Robert," he called to the guard stationed outside his door. "Inform the stables to have my mount ready first thing tomorrow morning. And tell the capitaine of the guard to have a score of men ready to ride to the d'Louncrais keep."

"It shall be as you command, Mon Seigneur Comte."

The time had come for him to have a talk with Aimon. Lothair swung his legs down and refilled his wine. He would need more fortification to deal with his next appointment.

"Send in the archeveque."

Lothair made himself comfortable behind the wide expanse of his desk. He wanted something solid between them and his sword within easy reach. He had never trusted Archeveque Renaud. The man was a diabolical schemer, but knowing he could entrap and kill a werewolf had Lothair taking more precautions than usual. Renaud might use mercenaries to do his killing, but it did not mean he would not attempt something on his own.

The door swung open. Archeveque Renaud swished into the room using his ecclesiastical robes like a pass granting him all access. His ring of office glinted on his aged and wrinkled fingers, and, in his hands, he held a clay pot from which sprouted a plant. He placed it on the desk, taking a seat Lothair had not granted him.

Lothair scowled. *Do not get too comfortable, old man.*

It mattered not how many times Lothair excluded him, ignored him or rebuked him. Renaud took it all in his stride. He had lost count of the myriad of Renaud's schemes he had foiled, and how many he had refused to sanction. He could not dissuade Renaud. The man continued to approach him with yet another idea, petition or, as Renaud liked to put it, opportunity. Until now, Gaharet had been at his side, a formidable barrier, cutting Renaud down with a sneer or a well-chosen barb. He wished Gaharet were here now.

Renaud bobbed his head in a semblance of a bow. "Mon Seigneur Comte."

"What is this?" Lothair asked, pointing at the plant.

He had no intention of giving Renaud any cause to think they were co-conspirators. For certain, Renaud had brought him the knowledge of werewolves. Should he be grateful? Perhaps. Should he reward Renaud for it? Absolutely not. Renaud had overplayed his hand on this one. He had put Lothair at odds with Gaharet, his closest advisor, and the only man he had ever thought of as his friend. He suspected Renaud had planned that all along, in order to bring him, Comte of Anjou, down. How did Renaud think he could succeed when Lothair's own brothers had failed?

"The plant is a safeguard, Mon Seigneur."

Lothair's scowl darkened.

"Wolfsbane," said Renaud. "It never hurts to be prepared. One never knows when one might need it."

Lothair narrowed his eyes. Renaud giving him something for protection? Unrequested? Out of character for Renaud. No. The wolfsbane served a purpose. For Renaud's benefit, no doubt.

"How goes it with our captive werewolf? Have you made any progress?" asked Renaud, ignoring Lothair's lack of appreciation for the gift.

Lothair waved his hand dismissively. "I have yet to speak to him. For all I know, he is dead."

Ulrik was not dead. Lothair had spoken to the guards stationed at the grate to his cell that very morning to see how Ulrik fared. Not well, but he was not dead. A week or two in the dark, dank cell, alone, weak and on meager rations might make Ulrik more amenable to his plan. Perhaps not. Perhaps it would only make Ulrik's anger and hunger for revenge burn hotter, but Lothair was in no rush. Not with Renaud salivating at the prospect. Not until he determined how this fit with the archeveque's plan.

Renaud grinned, a joyless smile all teeth and jutting cheekbones. "You think he may be more agreeable to your demands once he has had time to enjoy your hospitality? Ulrik has ever been hot tempered. Time in that miserable hole should dampen his enthusiasm a little."

Renaud's smile, all cruel intent, would have chilled a lesser man to the bone. Age brought wisdom, so the saying went. In Renaud's case, it brought him cunning and, if the lines on Renaud's face were anything to go by, he had an endless supply.

Renaud steepled his fingers, settling into his chair. "Have you given any thought to who you might turn first? A loyal chevalier? A servant?"

Or perhaps himself? Is this where Renaud's scheme led? Lothair took several sips of his wine, letting Renaud wait for his answer.

Two can play this game, old man.

He placed his goblet down and leaned forward, his arms resting on his desk.

"Do you know anything about the process, Renaud? I cannot imagine being bitten would be pleasant."

Renaud frowned and adjusted his pectoral cross. "I imagine once a werewolf, the bite itself would be irrelevant. Werewolves heal fast, I am told. The benefits — speed, agility, strength, heightened senses — would outweigh any discomfort. Why, were I not a man of God, I might be tempted to offer myself up."

Lothair eyed Renaud up and down. *I should get Ulrik to bite Renaud.* The thought amused him, though he would have no use for a werewolf priest. Other than as a sacrificial victim. Tempting, but likely to bring the focus of the church to bear. Not something he wished to deal with right now.

"I need details, Renaud, not conjecture. Talk to your informant. Better still, bring him to me. I will hear of it firsthand."

Renaud's eyes widened. His jaw tightened. "I do not think my informant—"

Lothair sliced a hand through the air, cutting Renaud off. "This is not up for debate. I will make no decision about who I will turn until I have spoken with your informant myself."

Renaud's smile was strained. "Of course, Mon Seigneur Comte."

"That will be all."

Renaud stalked to the door.

"Oh, and Renaud," Lothair called after him. "Stop killing off my chevaliers. If one more of my men dies by your design, I will hunt you down and gut you myself. Then I will hang your entrails from your pulpit as a warning to any other *man of God* who dares to defy me."

Renaud departed, his shoulders stiff and his face a picture of controlled frustration. Lothair smiled. Did Renaud think him foolish enough to risk a werewolf's bite while knowing nothing of the consequences? That he would turn someone into a werewolf without knowing the process, not understanding if the victim was even controllable, or would survive? If Renaud believed that, then he truly was an imbecile. And he had forgotten Lothair had a potential informant of his own. Ulrik.

Perhaps a conversation with his captive werewolf was in order. For all his faults, Ulrik had a mind as sharp as Gaharet's. Alone, in the dark, weakened by silver, Ulrik had had ample time to think. About his circumstances, about Renaud and about who may have betrayed the pack. The time had come for Ulrik to cooperate.

Renaud swept from the Comte's chambers with his hands clenched into white-knuckled fists. He kept up the pretense and glared at the two guards in the corridor, and they shrank away. As soon as he was out of sight, he let the tension ease from his shoulders and unclenched his hands. It mattered not that Lothair wanted to meet his informant. The chevalier would never agree, and such a meeting was contrary to Renaud's plans.

His plans. Renaud allowed himself a small smile. Would Lothair now venture into the underground cell? Would he ask Ulrik about the turning? His smile widened. He had primed the miscreant werewolf well, poked at his anger, his grief and his desire for revenge. Lothair may well get more resistance than he expected when he set foot in that godforsaken hole. Renaud rubbed his hands together. All things considered, his plans were coming along nicely.

Chapter Twenty-Nine

Aimon trotted his horse along the trail which meandered beside a creek, following the directions Gascon had given him. Close behind him rode Kathryn, her unease battering at his senses. She clearly did not like the idea of submitting to an alpha. Having awoken within the pack, with Gaharet's commanding presence at his side, Aimon had never questioned the pack hierarchy. His wolf had recognized the authority of the alpha in an instant. A few lapses during training, until he had become at one with his wolf, had not shaken his conviction of his place.

He glanced at Kathryn, her shoulders stiff and jaw set. Being kept hidden from them, Kathryn had no such certainty. Coupled with the fire that burned so bright within her, her acceptance of Gaharet as her alpha would not come easy. He forced himself to relax. Gaharet had years of experience as the pack's alpha. Aimon had to trust him to know how to handle Kathryn.

The trees parted, and they emerged into a sheltered clearing with a small farmer's cottage nestled in the center. Despite the signs of recent repairs, an abandoned air hung over it—no signs of life and no smoke curling from the chimney hole in the roof. He had the right place. Gaharet's musky scent, and Erin's softer one, saturated the clearing.

He reined in and dismounted. As he assisted Kathryn from her saddle, the door of the cottage opened, and Gaharet ducked through the doorway, unarmed. Good. Gaharet could be intimidating enough without his armor and sword. Erin, her blonde hair loose and her feet bare, followed close on Gaharet's heels, beaming at Kathryn.

Kathryn's step faltered. Her gaze flicked to him, wary and uncertain. He gave her an encouraging nod and urged her forward. She lifted her chin, defiance burning bright in her eyes. Aimon held his breath.

"Welcome, Kathryn." Gaharet smiled, no hint of aggression or dominance in his expression. "I am sorry that we meet again in such circumstances."

Aimon's tension slid away. All would be well. Kathryn would soon be a part of their pack, protected and cherished, and the responsibility for keeping her safe would no longer rest solely on his shoulders. The thought did not please him as he thought it would. He brushed off his disquiet.

Gaharet stepped forward and reached for Kathryn's hands. Aimon's wolf roared to the surface, unstoppable. He forced his way between Kathryn and Gaharet, pulling her behind him. His hackles rose, a growl reverberated in his chest and the slide of his canines filled his mouth. Behind him, Kathryn's shocked gasp startled him to his senses. He caught Gaharet and Erin exchanging a look.

Merde.

He had challenged his alpha. Again. *What is Kathryn doing to me?*

Aimon dropped his head and bared his neck, forcefully pushing his wolf down. It did not retreat easily. His canines retracted with aching slowness and the ruff of fur on his neck receded in gradual increments, but he remained where he stood, a barrier between Kathryn and Gaharet. He would take his reprimand, but his wolf would not allow him to move, would not let Gaharet get any closer to Kathryn.

"I am sorry, Gaharet," he said, his voice little more than a growl. "I—"

Gaharet's chuckle snapped his head up. *Gaharet is not angry?*

"There is nothing to apologize for, Aimon. I understand your need to protect her." He gave a nonchalant shrug of his shoulder. "I, myself, acted similarly when Ulrik suggested Erin should be with another."

Aimon's gaze shifted between Gaharet and Erin—a mated pair. Was Gaharet suggesting…? *It cannot be. Can it?* He turned to Kathryn. His wolf pacing, a restless presence in his mind. *Could she be…my mate?*

Kathryn hovered behind him, uncertainty pouring off her in waves. Their gazes met and his wolf howled. He swallowed hard.

"Aimon? What is happening? What is wrong?"

"Don't worry," said Erin, skirting Aimon and slipping her arm through Kathryn's, steering her toward the cottage. "Gaharet didn't tell me either," she said, rolling her eyes at Aimon and Gaharet. "Men."

"Tell you what? I do not understand."

No, she would not. She had no experience with wolves. He had three years of living as a wolf and he had not grasped the significance of his feelings for Kathryn.

"I'll explain it all later," said Erin. "Gaharet needs to talk to you first, and then we'll have some girl time."

She led Kathryn into the cottage.

Gaharet clapped him on the shoulder. "Congratulations, Aimon. In such hard times as we find ourselves, this is a blessing. Come, we have much to discuss."

Aimon stared after Gaharet, his emotions unsettled. His alpha seemed so certain. If Gaharet was right, was it any wonder he had struggled to keep his distance from her? He stared after his alpha's retreating back, then followed him inside.

Aimon barely glanced about the small, cozy cottage—his attention fixed on Kathryn. In a daze, he sat next to her, his thigh brushing against hers beneath the table, unable to drag his gaze away from her. Erin stifled a giggle, and Kathryn turned to him, one eyebrow raised. He swallowed and shook himself out of his stupor. Now was not the time and place for this conversation.

"I do not know how much Aimon has told you about us, Kathryn," said Gaharet, the deep rumble of his voice demanding their attention, "but I am now your alpha."

Kathryn stiffened beside him. Aimon reached a tentative hand out to hers, and when she clutched it, emotions in his chest swelled and his wolf preened.

"Aimon has mentioned it."

Gaharet nodded. "Do you understand what that entails?"

"A little."

Her voice wavered. His wolf snarled inside his mind. He schooled his expression to remain blank and his body to remain seated. He would not interfere, but he could comfort her, encourage her. As her teacher, as her friend, her lover...and maybe her mate. He brushed his thumb across the back of her knuckles, and she rewarded him with a smile.

"It means," said Gaharet, "as a werewolf in our pack, you now answer to me."

Kathryn's nostrils flared. Her free hand clenched into a fist, and her scent deepened. Aimon thought she might shift, and he leaned closer. Gaharet's gaze bored into her, his alpha dominance rolling off him. His own wolf bristled, and he half rose. Gaharet's dark gaze shifted to him, giving no quarter. He slunk back to his seat, acknowledging Gaharet's authority, but his hand remained clenched around Kathryn's.

Gaharet returned his attention to Kathryn and waited. With her jaw clenched tight, she held Gaharet's stare for a heartbeat, then dropped her gaze to the table.

Aimon released a pent-up breath. Few could match Gaharet. Ulrik had tried and failed. But if Kathryn decided to challenge Gaharet, Aimon could not be certain on whose side he would fall. His alpha's, to whom he owed his life? Or Kathryn's, the woman who fate had chosen as his mate?

Kathryn stared at the table, conscious of the weight of Gaharet's gaze. The power rolling off him had her wanting to shrink down in her seat, or better still, flee the cottage altogether. Anne had said Gaharet ruled the pack with a fair hand, but he clearly also ruled it with a firm grip. Unlike her father, he would not view any disobedience with tolerant amusement. He was more like *his* father, whom she had always found intimidating. Stern and commanding, Jacques had dominated a room with his presence alone. She could well see Gaharet as the alpha, keeping them all in line, as his father must have done in the past. She gritted her teeth. The gentle pressure from Aimon's hand was the only thing keeping her in her seat.

"We have rules," Gaharet continued. "And traditions. Your training will involve learning what they are. It is imperative you follow them. Our safety and survival depend on it. Anything that affects the pack goes through me, and I base my decisions on the welfare of us all. If you have a problem, you come to me. Even with one of our own. Especially with one of our own."

Kathryn squirmed in her seat, but she did not raise her gaze, keeping it fixed firmly on the table. Rules? Traditions? How much more cloistered could her life get?

"But," he said, his tone softening, "it also means that I am responsible for you and *to* you. It is my duty to ensure the wellbeing and safety of the entire pack, including you. We take care of our own."

Kathryn dared a glimpse at Gaharet through her lashes. His gaze had not left her face, but his expression was not the stern countenance she remembered her Uncle Jacques for.

"It will feel strange at first, but it is my hope, in time, you will find comfort in being part of our pack."

She licked her dry lips.

"You are no longer alone, Kathryn. We will look after you. Now we know you are one of us."

Kathryn stared at her hand cradled in Aimon's. To remain separate from the pack, alone and untrained, or join them and have them shelter her, protect her, but also follow their rules and answer to yet another person. Those were her choices. Or did she not have a choice at all?

She lifted her chin and met Gaharet's gaze. "What if I do not wish to join the pack?"

Tension rolled off Aimon, and his hand tightened around hers. She waited for a denial, for Gaharet to tell her not joining was not an option.

Gaharet tilted his head to the side and tugged at his beard, his expression puzzled. "What is it you fear about becoming a member of the pack? What is it you think I would do, or ask of you?"

Kathryn squared her shoulders. "Take away my freedom, my choices."

Gaharet leaned toward her and rested his arms on the table. He smiled, though a hint of sadness crept into the lines around his eyes. "You remind me so very much of my mother, and not only because of the color of your hair. She never truly answered to anyone. Not even my father, though he was the alpha. And he loved her for it." He shook his head. "I would no more curtail your spirit than my father did my mother's, that I can promise you."

Truly? She searched his face, pushing out her senses and sampling the air. She scented no lie.

"However..."

Kathryn's hopes plummeted.

"For now, until your training is complete, and until the situation at hand is under control, there will be some restrictions. For you and Erin both. I will not risk either of you. You are too precious."

Precious? Kathryn looked to Erin, whose hand rested in Gaharet's. Erin smiled her encouragement. She did not seem at all unhappy.

"Will you join our pack, Kathryn?"

Gaharet waited for her answer, staring at her with an intensity she found disconcerting. She swallowed. Living with her secret and hiding her true nature from everyone had brought her nothing but anguish. She needed help, needed to feel as though she belonged somewhere. In the pack she would be accepted, more than accepted. Viewed as important, precious. One of only two of her kind.

She inclined her head. Yes, she would accept his authority as alpha, and would abide by his rules. She would answer to him.

He broke into a smile, nodding at her acceptance. "I am sorry we were not there for you when you needed us, Kathryn. We are here for you now."

Erin reached across the table, her smile bright, and grabbed Kathryn's hand.

"I'm so glad you're here. It'll be nice to talk to a female about stuff, girl things. It's so different from where I came from. I'm going to need a little help." She sighed and her expression turned dreamy. "What I wouldn't give for a bra and some undies. Or coffee. I don't know how anybody gets out of bed in the morning without coffee. I wonder…" She tapped her chin with her finger. "I don't suppose we could mount an expedition to Venice by any chance, or better still go to the source, to North Africa."

Kathryn looked to Aimon, confused, but Aimon looked as puzzled as she. "What is coffee?" *And what were undees and a…bra?*

Gaharet coughed and cleared his throat, raising an eyebrow at Erin.

She shrugged. "We're going to have to tell them at some point. I'm not going to be able to hide it from them forever." Erin faced them. "Kathryn. Aimon. I have my own secret. I'm not from here. That is, I'm not from the tenth century. I was born in the year 1998 in Australia, a country no one here knows exists yet."

Kathryn stared at her.

"You are from the future?" said Aimon, sputtering his words. He looked to Gaharet. "How is that possible? Wait. The amulet. She found an amulet."

Gaharet nodded. "Now you understand why I had no concern about Erin being connected with Renaud or Lothair."

"Did you know it could traverse time?"

"An amulet?" Now Kathryn was even more confused. *Traversing time?*

"Each pack member has one," said Gaharet, tugging a gold amulet from beneath his tunic. It swung on a chain. On one side a howling wolf's head, the d'Louncrais crest, on the other strange writing. "Engraved on it is an inscription. In time, both you and Erin will receive one of these. All the amulets are linked, through blood and magic, to the binding amulet, an amulet with a red stone instead of an inscription. When there is risk of our secret being exposed, reciting the inscription will activate the binding amulet, drawing you to it, keeping you and the secret of our existence safe."

"Who has the binding amulet?" she asked, looking from Aimon to Gaharet.

Gaharet glanced at Erin. She glowered back at him. It seemed Erin was no more cowered by Gaharet than her aunt had been by her Uncle Jacques.

"As alpha, I *should* have the binding amulet, but...I gave it to Ulrik to convince everyone I was dead."

"Lothair has Ulrik," murmured Aimon. "And the binding amulet."

"We *have* to rescue Ulrik and get it back."

The ferocity of Erin's tone startled Kathryn.

"I found the amulet that brought me here in an underground cell beneath Langeais Keep. It was with a headless human skeleton and a wolf's skull. A werewolf dies in that cell. A werewolf wearing one of these amulets," she said, pointing to the one around Gaharet's neck. "I didn't survive only to have Gaharet die. I won't let him die."

"All will be well, *ma petite pouliche*," murmured Gaharet, pulling Erin closer to him.

Kathryn ached at the tenderness between them, at the gentle way he brushed a strand of hair from Erin's face. How his tone softened when he called her his little filly. Aimon's hand squeezed hers. She glanced up at him. His blue eyes radiated warmth. There was that look again, the one her father had spoken of. Did Aimon truly care for her? As Gaharet did for Erin?

"We will save Ulrik and we will find this traitor," Gaharet assured Erin. He turned to Kathryn. "We need your help. Tell me everything you remember about your attack."

Chapter Thirty

Kathryn studied Gaharet as she told her story of the fateful day her aunt had died. Pain flashed in his eyes, and also anger. She did not envy this traitor the day Gaharet discovered his identity. Was what she had told him enough? Did he now know who they could no longer trust?

"I need you to close your eyes and think back to when you saw him. Can you do that for me, Kathryn?"

She nodded, and the image of the half man, half wolf, forever etched in her memory, flashed across the back of her eyelids.

"Did you notice anything other than the color of his wolf?"

She focused on the moment she had first climbed the rock, her view obscured by branches, and peered over. "He had brown hair and wore a fur-lined surcoat. I..." Kathryn frowned. "I cannot remember the color. And mail like my father's."

Her shoulders sagged. All Gaharet's men wore mail and surcoats. Four of them had brown hair. If the color of her hair and the resulting color of her wolf were any indication, four of them would shift into brown wolves. Godfrey, Aubert, Edmond and Lance, though Lance's hair now had streaks of gray.

"Do you remember how tall, how large he was?"

Kathryn shook her head. "I..."

"I know you were only a child," said Gaharet, "and he would have seemed large to you, but how much taller than my mother was he? You are similar in height to her now. Imagine it was you and I in that clearing. Was he bigger than me, or of similar size?"

Kathryn cast her mind back, doing as Gaharet suggested, imagining her in her aunt's place. She shivered. Aimon's hand tightened around hers, and she was grateful for his touch.

"Your height, your size."

"Are you certain?"

She thought for a moment. "Yes. Taller than my father, but similar in height to you."

"That rules out Edmond and Aubert. They have always been larger than the rest of us, even as boys."

She hung her head. "I am sorry I cannot remember more."

"You have nothing to be sorry for, Kathryn. What you have told us has helped us beyond measure."

"Well," said Erin, slapping her palms on the table. "I think Kathryn could use a break. While you men strategize about our next move, I'll take Kathryn for a walk to the pond. We can get some fresh air, gossip, talk about you men..."

Both Aimon and Gaharet growled.

Erin laughed and waved a dismissive hand at the men. "Oh, only the good stuff, I promise. We won't say anything bad about you, will we, Kathryn?"

Gaharet scowled. "It is not safe for you to be out alone, neither of you. I have no plans now, or in the future, to let you out of my sight."

Erin rolled her eyes. "Fine, fine. Why don't we *all* get some fresh air?"

Gaharet considered her suggestion. "Very well," he said, relenting, his frustration evident. "We will all go."

They all left the cottage. Kathryn walked beside Erin along a trail that followed the little creek, lost in thought, glad of Erin's suggestion. The fresh air, the whisper of a breeze in the trees and the gurgle of the creek flowing beside the trail soothed her frayed nerves. She now had an alpha and was part of a pack. Erin had come from the future, using a magical amulet of sorts, and talked of things Kathryn could not begin to comprehend. And thanks to her recounting of her attack, they had narrowed the traitor down to two men — Godfrey and Lance.

"Stay close, Erin," Gaharet called from behind them.

Erin rolled her eyes. "I can't wait for this training business to be over." She hitched her thumb over her shoulder, jabbing it in Gaharet's direction. "Mr. Overprotective is driving me crazy."

Kathryn grinned. "Aimon said it took him three months."

"Three months!" Erin came to an abrupt halt and spun to face Gaharet. "It's going to take me three months?"

Gaharet shrugged. "It takes whatever time it takes. You and Kathryn should be able to help each other."

"But three months?" Erin gave an exaggerated sigh. "Why couldn't I have been born a werewolf? It would've made things *so* much easier. This whole shifting, keeping form thing would come naturally, and I wouldn't have to practice so much."

Gaharet chuckled, shaking his head. "Not so. My father confined both my brother and I to the grounds of the keep for almost a year once because we struggled to maintain our form."

"Really?" asked Erin, her eyes alight with curiosity. "Do tell."

Gaharet grinned at her. "We were at an age where we had started to notice female werewolves. It only took a look, a smile or a hint of their scent, and we would transform and fight over her."

"Was the girl impressed?" asked Erin.

Gaharet grinned and shrugged. "Not really. My brother and I spent more time as wolves than we did in human form that year. It was easier. And running around naked upset the servants."

"I bet. Well, that makes me feel a little better."

Kathryn stared at Gaharet. "I do not remember seeing wolves running about the keep grounds. Nor naked boys."

"No, you would not have. We were under strict instructions, from both my father and my mother, to behave ourselves whenever you and your father visited. If I remember, the threat of punishment from my father merely goaded us. Our mother's disapproval held more weight. Her tongue lashings were legendary. Neither D'Artagnon nor I wished to risk that. And of course, there was always the threat of Anne."

Aimon chuckled. "I think we have all come up against Anne at one time or another."

"She is rather formidable," said Gaharet. "I think she may have even had my father a little intimidated." He turned to Aimon. "Have you noticed she is different with the females?"

Aimon's gaze flicked to hers, and Kathryn blushed. She turned away, and continued walking along the path, with the others railing along behind her.

"Yes, I have." Aimon's voice followed her.

She caught Erin's eye.

"I think this is a story I have to hear about," said Erin, linking her arm with hers. "When the boys can't hear us."

Kathryn smiled at her. She had made the right decision to join the pack.

The trail opened into a clearing, and Kathryn halted. "How beautiful."

A clear pool of water, bordered by moss-covered rocks and sheltered by trees, lay before them. Sunlight filtered through the canopy, sparkling off the water, and on the far side, water spilled from a rocky outcrop, creating a small waterfall that splashed into the pool.

Kathryn's skin prickled with awareness, and she turned, catching Aimon's heated gaze. Was he thinking of her in the pool? In her chemise? Him naked? Her breathing hitched, her core clenched, and her wolf hovered close. If either Erin or Gaharet noticed, they said nothing.

"Why don't you two go somewhere over there?" suggested Erin, waving her hand at the other side of the pool. Gaharet's expression darkened. "Just far enough away so you can't hear us talk. Kathryn and I have things to discuss. You two should put your heads together and come up with a way to get Ulrik out of Langeais Keep. We owe him."

Gaharet growled. Erin gave Gaharet a long-suffering look, and Gaharet sighed. "Very well, but do not leave this clearing. I want to be able to see both of you at all times."

Kathryn hid a smile behind her hand. Erin chafed at the restrictions as much as she did.

"I guess I don't have to worry about introducing you to Aimon?" said Erin, finding a comfortable spot in the sun as the men moved away. "I can see why you were interested in him. He's gorgeous. And about the right age for you, too."

Kathryn sat beside Erin, slipped her boots off, and dangled her feet in the cool water. She eyed the men sitting across the pond from them, deep in conversation. Every few moments, both Gaharet and Aimon lifted their gaze to her and Erin, but they did not appear to be listening.

"I brushed up against him when Comte Lothair summoned my father and I to Langeais Keep. I think he scented me then. Had he not, perhaps one of Gaharet's other vassals may have come to the d'Louncrais Keep in time."

"Because of Lothair's bequeathing of the d'Louncrais estate? It's a wonder one of them hasn't already." Erin smiled at her. "I'm so glad it worked out the way it did." She shrugged. "If it hadn't, I would've found a way to get you two together somehow. I would've nagged Gaharet until I got my way."

Kathryn bit back a laugh, the thought of anyone having influence over Gaharet, amusing. Yet, Erin did. And she did not appear to find Gaharet at all intimidating. Were all women from her time like this, or was it only Erin? Kathryn liked it, liked her. She had from the moment she had met her, sensing a kindred spirit. Someone who did not, would not, quite conform to the standards expected of well-bred ladies. Someone like her.

"What is it like? Where you are from? Do you miss it?"

Erin frowned, her gaze straying to Gaharet. "Some things I miss. Coffee. I *really* miss coffee. And chocolate. In time, I think the biggest thing I will miss is the freedoms women have there that they don't have here. Being able to make my own decisions, have a career, a job, other than running an estate, embroidering stupid roses and making babies."

Kathryn snorted. "I do not enjoy embroidery either."

"And the clothes. What I wouldn't kill for a pair of jeans."

"Jeans?"

"Breeches. Where I come from, women can wear breeches if they want to."

Kathryn's eyes widened.

Erin laughed. "Does that shock you?"

"Yes. But I, too, would kill to wear a pair of these jeans. My father made many allowances for me. Wearing men's breeches was not one of them."

"Gaharet has promised he'll have several pairs made for me, and I can wear them as often as I want. Just not in public."

"Truly?" She glanced at Aimon. Would Aimon grant her such concessions? She lifted a lip in a scowl. Why did she need to ask him? He lifted his gaze to meet hers, and she tilted her chin up and stared him down. His brow furrowed.

Kathryn turned to Erin. "Can you arrange for several pairs of men's breeches for me?"

Erin grinned. "Of course. I see no reason you can't wear them, too." She looked over at Aimon. "He might actually enjoy seeing you in them, but he probably wouldn't like anyone else to. His wolf would likely react badly if another man, or wolf, looked too closely. Or, God forbid, tried to touch you."

"Like earlier? When Gaharet reached for me?"

"Exactly."

Kathryn cast her gaze at the men. They seemed absorbed in their conversation. She turned back to Erin. "Why *did* he do that?"

"It's a wolf thing. Apparently. Gaharet did the same thing when I met Ulrik. It's their way of saying hands off she's mine or, as Ulrik explained it to me, I'm claiming her as mine and I will fight you to the death for her. A touch melodramatic, but nothing like a guy willing to fight for her to make a girl feel special."

"Aimon did that for me? He was *claiming* me?" Her voice rose.

"Kathryn, are you well?" Aimon's voice floated across the pond. He was on his feet, his hands clenched into fists, as he scanned the forest beyond them as though looking for a threat.

"Relax, Aimon. It's fine." Erin rolled her eyes at him. She turned to Kathryn, as a reluctant Aimon resumed his original position beside Gaharet on the mossy bank. "See what I mean?"

"But he has said nothing of this, or of a union between us," she hissed. "Though we have..." She blushed.

Erin broke into a grin. "Good for you Kathryn. It took me too long to take that step, though I wanted to, and Gaharet made it quite clear he wanted to, as well."

Kathryn looked down at her feet, splashing in the pool. "I kind of forced the issue. I disrobed in front of him and asked him to make love to me."

Erin burst out laughing. Gaharet and Aimon looked up at them. Kathryn flicked her hair over her face to conceal her embarrassment.

"Let me guess. Anne. She had to have a hand in that."

"Yes. She did. How did you know?"

"Oh, Anne. Ever the meddler." Erin patted her hand. "Don't worry. She pushed me, too."

"But…perhaps it is only a moment of pleasure for Aimon. He would not be the first man, or werewolf, to want only that. How do I know if he wants more? How did you know with Gaharet?"

Erin shrugged her shoulders. "I didn't. Not at first. I thought he just wanted sex, and once he got it, things would be over between us. When he told Lothair of our betrothal, I thought he'd only done it to protect me. And I was still determined to get home."

"Even when I met you at Langeais Keep?"

Erin nodded. "Even then."

"What changed?"

Erin shrugged. "Well, I became a werewolf for one, and Gaharet risked his life, his pack, everything, to save me. They're different to normal men, Kathryn, apart from the obvious. That's one thing I've learned. I wish Gaharet had told me right from the start. It would have saved me a lot of sleepless nights."

Bewildered, Kathryn stared at Erin. "I do not understand. Told you what?"

Erin dipped her feet into the water and swished them about. "Let me try to explain. Aimon can thank me later. It's like this. Werewolves don't come by their mates easily because what they look for in a mate, the way they view marriage, is different from your regular tenth century chevalier. Money or titles, reputation or even beauty aren't what they're looking for. It's all about finding their mate."

"Their mate?"

"Their one true love. A unique bond. You can't force it or manipulate it. It just is. It's special. Gaharet is my mate, and he knew almost from the first moment we met. He chose me."

Kathryn glanced across at Aimon. He met her gaze and smiled. "How do I know if I am Aimon's mate, or if he is mine?"

"Well, for starters, Gaharet seems to think so."

"Really?"

"And I think he's right. He *claimed* you. To Gaharet. His *alpha*."

Kathryn shook her head. "But he has not said..." Her voice trailed off.

Erin nudged her with her shoulder. "Do you love him?"

Kathryn stared at her hands and picked at her fingernails. "Maybe. I think so."

"Do you think you can trust him?"

Kathryn peeked at Aimon through the strands of her hair. He had held her through that traumatic transition in the library, her first in over a decade. Slept outside her door that first night in case she needed him. Coaxed her through her training, steadfast and sure. And he had tried his hardest to protect her modesty.

Everything he had done had been to protect her. Yes, she trusted him. "With my life."

"Then maybe you should also trust him with your heart."

Chapter Thirty-One

After a few hours spent by the pool, and a simple meal at the cottage, Aimon untethered the horses for their return journey to the keep. His gaze, as it had all day, strayed to Kathryn. *Could Gaharet be right? Is she truly my mate?* There was a rightness to it, a soul deep knowing and a smugness in his wolf's silence. A wondrous thing he had given no thought to until now. But...did she feel it too? Would she want to bond with him? Or was he merely the first wolf to have found her? How would she react when she met the other stronger, more experienced wolves of the pack?

Unease tugged at his chest. "In three days, I must meet with the others."

Gaharet nodded.

"They are going to know about Kathryn the moment they catch my scent."

He did not want to risk exposing her. Not when they were no closer to finding the traitor amongst them. Not knowing if she felt as he did about her.

"Let them meet, discuss what they have found while you remain hidden downwind. Your absence will unnerve them. They may assume Renaud has got to you, too."

Aimon pursed his lips. "Picking off the weakest of us again."

Gaharet frowned. "Whatever makes you think that?"

"I am turned, not born. I have not lived my whole life as a wolf as you and the others have."

Gaharet's dark gaze bored into him. "Aimon, your abilities are as sharp as any of us. Your wolf is strong, your senses keen, and I have taught you everything I know. Do not doubt yourself. You have survived while others have fallen. You are no less in my eyes because you were not born a wolf."

Heat suffused his neck. Gaharet believed him equal to the rest of the pack? Wolves Gaharet had grown up with, had known since childhood?

"And the others?"

"If they believe you lacking, then they are wrong and have underestimated you. Use it to your advantage." A heavy weight lifted from his chest. "But you must bear witness to that meeting. One of the others may have learned something useful. We have yet to find a way to rid ourselves of our affliction to wolfsbane and silver."

"Constance could not help us?"

Gaharet sighed, a heavy sigh with the weight of responsibility behind it. "According to her, the only cure is to not be a werewolf."

"All our plans to free Ulrik will come to naught without some way to circumvent them."

"Agreed. And we can expect Renaud to continue to make full use of our weaknesses."

Aimon grunted. "I am beginning to wish we had taken Ulrik's suggestion and killed Renaud when we had the chance."

Gaharet grimaced. "It may yet come to that."

"If the alliance between Lothair and Renaud deteriorates further, Lothair may yet save us the trouble."

Gaharet grinned. "We can only hope."

They turned as Kathryn approached, and Aimon assisted her into her saddle. He mounted his own horse and gathered his reins.

Gaharet moved to Kathryn's side. "You are one of us now, Kathryn. No longer are you alone with this. If you have questions about your training, about anything, do not hesitate to ask Aimon. For his part, Aimon will arrange so you can spend time with Erin, as much as we can manage without endangering either of you."

Gaharet tugged on his beard. "There is something else to consider. Aimon and I have a deeper connection than the others because I turned him — my saliva mixed with his blood."

"We do?"

"A part of me is in you, Aimon. And a part of Kathryn's attacker will be in her. You both have a connection to your maker."

Aimon growled. A connection with the person who attacked her? Had killed her aunt and betrayed them all? Betrayed them still?

"It will be much more subtle for you, Kathryn, because you have remained dormant and unknown to the pack for so long, but it will be there. When you meet the others, which will happen in time, if you feel anything — a sense of recognition, a familiarity, a connection with any of them — you need to tell us, tell Aimon."

Kathryn nodded. Aimon nudged his horse closer. He reached out and placed a comforting hand on her arm. Her eyes sought his. His resolve firmed. He would keep her as far away from the others as he could, for as long as he could.

"Can he sense me? Track me through this connection?"

Aimon raised his eyebrows at Gaharet. Could he? Could Gaharet track him?

Gaharet shook his head. "No. I cannot track Aimon any more easily than I track the others."

Some of the tension eased from Aimon's shoulders.

"You are safe with Aimon," said Gaharet. "He will take good care of you. Trust him. And as frustrating as it is, listen to him when he tells you something is not safe. Now we have found you, we do not want to lose you."

Aimon nodded at Gaharet and turned his horse toward the trail.

"Keep her safe, Aimon."

Aimon urged his horse from the clearing and into the forest, Kathryn following close behind. Would her connection to her maker draw her to the traitor? Despite Gaharet's assurances, Aimon was not so certain of his standing in the pack. And if Kathryn had a connection to one of the other wolves, would she choose him or Aimon?

His hackles rose, and he growled, his wolf snarling in his mind. His horse pranced about, unsettled.

"Aimon? Is everything all right?"

He forced his wolf down and regained control of his horse. "All is well, Kathryn." He would not worry her with his concerns.

When they broke from the forest, he urged his horse into a canter, knowing she would be sure to follow his lead. Kathryn pulled abreast of him, an eager smile lighting up her face and her eyes full of challenge. Loosening his reins, he gave his horse his head. Laughing, she did the same, and they raced across the meadow. He let her pass him. Her face flushed and her glorious dark copper hair streaming behind her, she was magnificent in her abandon. His heart beat in time with his mount's pounding hooves. He would not be the only one enamored with her.

Out here, away from the concerns of the world and the pack, he could well imagine Kathryn choosing him, being his. But they could not stay this way forever. With reluctance, he steered his horse along the forest trail and guided her back to the keep.

Crossing the bailey, they dismounted and handed their reins to a waiting Henri.

"Thank you for today, Aimon. For the ride and for taking me to see—"

He touched his finger to her lips, cutting off her words. Her pupils dilated, and she leaned into him, the scent of her arousal swirling around them. At her response, his mood lightened. If her reaction was anything to go by, she felt the pull as strongly as he did. Maybe that would be enough.

"It was my pleasure," he said, and he meant it. Making her happy, seeing her smile at him, drove him to give her whatever she asked for. Right now, with her head tilted back and her lips moist and parted, she was asking to be kissed. He leaned down.

K.E. Turner

"Hmm, hmm."

His nostrils flared, and his wolf snarled, but he pulled away. Anne raised her eyebrows, daring him to challenge her. Aimon scowled and stepped away from Kathryn.

"Come, come, child. I have a lovely hot bath prepared for you to ease the soreness after your ride today."

As she entered the keep, Kathryn looked over her shoulder at him and smiled. Aimon raked his gaze over her, his tongue flicking out to lick his lips. Kathryn's scent deepened, and her eyes glazed over. His wolf howled, triumphant. She would welcome him into her bedchamber again. Anne had won for now, but Aimon would have Kathryn tonight. Again and again and again. Satisfied with that knowledge, Aimon entered the keep.

* * * *

The evening meal was interminable. With Kathryn sitting opposite him, sneaking heated glances his way from beneath her lashes, Aimon struggled to pay attention to the surrounding conversation. How could he sit still and eat when what he hungered for sat across the table from him? Her eyes danced with mirth at a comment from the grizzled farmer, Brenton. Her brow furrowed at a grumble from grumpy, old Tumas. When Brenton touched her hand in conversation, it took every ounce of control he had not to launch himself across the table at the old man.

He wanted to sequester her in her bedchamber, kiss every freckle on her nose, nibble at the base of her throat and taste every inch of her, especially the sweet essence between her thighs. Its scent teased his nostrils. He could barely contain himself from dragging her from the hall — to hell with decorum. *Will this damn meal never end?*

As the food dwindled and wine jugs emptied, servants bid their farewells, and the kitchen staff cleared the table. Kathryn begged tiredness, throwing a heated glance in his direction as she left the hall. He waited several tense moments, then rose with plans to follow her.

Farren refilled his goblet, and Aimon's, with wine. "Stay a moment, Aimon."

Aimon sank back into his seat. His gaze darted to the doorway of the hall, where Kathryn had disappeared. Did Farren intuit what was happening between him and his daughter? What had happened already? Had Farren been quieter, more somber during the meal? Aimon cursed his inattention. He opened his senses and reached out to Farren. He picked up a confusing mix of anger, bitterness and vulnerability from him.

Farren tapped his fingers on the table and twirled his goblet. Aimon waited.

"I am sure Kathryn has plied you with many a question about…about werewolves, but I have a few things I must put to rest myself. If you do not mind."

Uncertainty settled in his gut, and Aimon resisted the lingering scent of Kathryn that teased at him. "Of course."

"Perhaps I should have asked you before now, maybe directed my concerns to Jacques while he still lived…" Farren's voice trailed off, and he stared at his wine goblet.

Aimon schooled his breathing and focused on keeping his body, and his mind, on the conversation.

Farren took a long sip of wine, then set the goblet down with deliberate slowness. Aimon resisted the urge to shift in his seat.

"You said they turned you. That you were not born a werewolf."

"Yes."

Farren's eyes searched his. "You do not mind being a werewolf?"

"No."

"You are not angry Gaharet turned you into something...not human?"

Aimon met Farren's gaze. "It is a better alternative than being dead, which is what I would have been had Gaharet not intervened."

"Yes, yes, I suppose it would be." Farren took another slow sip of wine.

Would Farren not get to the point? Kathryn waited... His nostrils flared, and his gaze darted to the darkened doorway. Kathryn waited, not in her bedchamber, but in the corridor, hovering beyond sight of the doorway. So close, and yet so far away. He bit back a growl.

"Do your parents know what you are? Your brother? Or did the d'Louncrais turn them, too?"

Aimon turned his attention back to Farren. *Is this what this is about? Does he want to be a werewolf, too? Like his daughter?* Gaharet would not sanction Farren's turning.

"My family does not know. Turning someone is not something we would inflict on another unless it was necessary. Jacques made the same determination regarding your sister, Elise."

Aimon's attention wavered, the scent of Kathryn's impatience tickling his nose.

Farren grunted. "Turning Elise got her killed."

Aimon's focus snapped back to Farren. *Is that what Farren believes?*

"Why did Jacques not simply marry her? If he loved her and she him, and I am convinced she did, I do not think it would have mattered to her what he was. You were dying. Gaharet saved your life. One of your kind attacked Kathryn. Elise...well...there was no *need* to turn her, and perhaps if Jacques had not, she might be alive today."

Aimon took a gulp of wine, then another, unsure what words would bring comfort, if any. Or if Farren expected him to answer or not.

"Why did Jacques do it? Why did he turn her? Why could he not have left her human?" Farren's anguish was writ clear across his face. "Is there some werewolf *code* that forbids taking a human wife?"

Aimon squirmed in his seat. "Werewolves age differently," he said. "Werewolf blood extends our lives and prevents many illnesses."

"But is that enough to risk a turning? On a woman? By far more delicate of constitution than any man."

Aimon's chest tightened, and he dropped his gaze to the table. *L'enfer.* The expectant silence and the steady beat of her heart told him Kathryn still listened, hanging on his every word. He pinched the bridge of his nose. There was no help for it. Farren would find no peace with his sister's death, and would continue to blame the d'Louncrais, until he understood. And Farren deserved to know the truth.

"There was another reason to turn Elise." His gaze slid in Kathryn's direction. His mouth went dry, and he licked his lips. "Werewolves can only... We can only procreate with other werewolves." He released a long sigh, raised his goblet to his lips, drained it, and put it down on the table with a loud thunk. "Without your sister being turned, Jacques and Elise would have remained childless."

Chapter Thirty-Two

Kathryn clasped her hand across her mouth, smothering a gasp.

"Kathryn," Aimon called out to her.

A chair scraped and footsteps moved toward the doorway. Pushing herself away from the wall, she darted up the stairs, along the corridor and into her bedchamber, slamming the door behind her. Tears smarted in her eyes.

Oh, what a fool I have been. To think, to believe, Aimon would want her because he might love her.

"There has not been a female among us for quite some time." That is what he had said. Her first day of training. The only female werewolf, and encumbered with the wealth of the d'Louncrais estate, what a prize she must seem. *A prize fool.* The chances of finding women who would consent to be turned into werewolves would be few. *Any* of Gaharet's men would want her if they knew her secret.

She clenched her fists and stamped her foot. She. Would. Not. Cry.

"Kathryn."

She stiffened. Aimon's musky scent filtered through the door. Her nipples tightened and her thighs clenched, her body immune to her anger and her sense of betrayal. His concern and regret battered her senses from beyond the door. She took a step toward him.

"Kathryn, talk to me." He thumped on the door. "Kathryn."

Not so long ago, she had resigned herself to marrying without love, had hoped only for a man she did not loathe. A good, kind, respectful man who would be willing to ignore some of her peculiarities. Did it matter if Aimon did not love her? If his attraction to her came from his biological imperative to breed? It was no different to him marrying her for the d'Louncrais estate. Yet, now, as she had begun to hope for a marriage based on love, could she accept anything less?

"Kathryn, open the door."

She stared at the barrier between them. Anne and her father all believed Aimon to have feelings for her. Gaharet and Erin thought Aimon might be her mate. But what of this new information? How much of Aimon's actions was it responsible for?

Inhaling a shaky breath, she opened the door. Aimon stood with his fist raised to pound on the door again. His arm dropping to his side, he took a step back, breathing as though he had run up every stair in the keep.

"I am sorry, Kathryn. I should have told you."

The sounds of the keep settling for the night echoed up the stairwell.

Kathryn pursed her lips. "Is that why you came? Because I am the only one you could breed with?"

He recoiled as though she had struck him. "No. That was *never* my intention. I swear to you."

The sincerity of his words hung in the air between them. "What *are* your intentions? Once my training is complete, what are your plans for me?"

Aimon sucked in a breath and closed his eyes. When he opened them, he met her gaze with a determined thrust of his chin. "You are my mate."

Kathryn grimaced. "Because I can bear you children?"

Aimon's lips thinned. "No." He tapped his chest. "I feel it here. In the very core of my being. My wolf has known it from the moment we met. I was so focused on your training and your safety, I did not recognize it as more than desire. Not until I took you to see Gaharet."

Kathryn's chest squeezed. He had not recognized her as his mate? Gaharet had told him? What did that say about his feelings for her? No words of love, only a knowing as though God, fate or perhaps the moon itself had willed it so.

"Do you not feel it, Kathryn? Are you not drawn to me with every breath you take?"

A shiver rippled through her body. She did feel it. Were her choices once again being manipulated, this time by some unseen force? Resentment and doubt weaved its way into her heart.

Aimon took a step forward, his arms reaching for her. She held up her hand, forcing him to stop. If she allowed him into her bedchamber, let him touch her, kiss her, then this conversation would be but a blur, forgotten in the heat of passion. Until the morrow.

"I need some time to think. Alone."

He dropped his hands to his side, and a muscle ticked in his jaw. He gave her an abrupt nod. The emptiness in his gaze almost had her wavering, but she firmed her resolve.

"Good night, Aimon."

She closed the door and pressed her face against the cool timber, listening to his footsteps as he walked away. She slid down the door, her eyes moistening and her vision blurring. Would she really consider marrying another of Gaharet's vassals? Take a man to her bed other than Aimon? Her body and her mind revolted at the thought. But where once she had resigned herself to marrying a man she did not love, could she now marry a man she loved deeply, with her whole heart, knowing he may never really love her in return?

Aimon stalked away and stomped down the stairs, the pressure in his chest almost too much to bear. He swept into the library, intent on imbibing enough wine to dull the ache and silence the whimpering of his wolf. Aimon pulled to an abrupt halt. Farren sat by the brazier. He had thought to be alone.

Unfolding himself from his chair, Farren refilled his goblet and filled a second for Aimon. "It looks as if you need this more than I tonight." He thrust the goblet into Aimon's hand.

Aimon raked his hand through his hair and threw himself into a chair across from Farren.

"Kathryn's temper, much like my sister's, always runs hot, but never for long. Give her time, lad."

Aimon took a gulp of his wine, and another.

"You love her, do you not?"

Aimon stared at his goblet as he twirled it in his fingers. "Yes, yes I do."

"And you plan to marry her?"

Aimon's head snapped up. "I will not take Kathryn's choices from her again by striking a bargain with you to marry your daughter." Farren flinched at his words, and Aimon grimaced. "I did not mean—"

Farren waved a dismissive hand at him. "Do not concern yourself with my feelings, Aimon. I did indeed take my daughter's choices from her, and it is a burden I must bear. Rightly so. But I am pleased to hear you will not make the same mistake I made."

Aimon stared at the floor. No, he would not, but in doing so perhaps he would be the one to lose Kathryn, as Farren had once feared would happen to him.

"Kathryn came to me this morning, wanting to know if you had made any mention of marriage to me."

Aimon's heart skipped in his chest, and his wolf paused in its sulking.

"My daughter, I believe, has developed an attachment to you. If I know Kathryn, and I do, she does nothing by halves, so her feelings are most likely strong. Have you told her how you feel?"

"I told her she was my mate." Aimon hung his head. "She did not seem overly excited by the prospect."

Farren grunted. "But did you tell her you loved her?"

Aimon stared at Farren, uncomprehending. "She is my mate. There is no greater declaration I can make."

Farren smiled and shook his head. "That may mean something to you werewolves, but not to me. And nor to Kathryn, I would imagine. Do not forget, she has lived her whole life, apart from these past few weeks, as a human. With human emotions and human understanding."

Aimon sat back in his seat. Had he not made his feelings clear? Did she doubt his true intentions because she had not fully understood what being his mate meant? To her? To him? *How is that possible?* With every touch, every kiss, he had told her how he felt about her, how much she meant to him. *L'enfer*, he had made love to her last night. Twice. And her senses were as keen as his. How could she not know of his ever present and all-consuming need for her? A desire so strong it had forced him out into the forest every night so he would not succumb to it and take advantage of her innocence?

Farren drained his wine and set his goblet down. "I will leave you to your drinking. I have done enough of it these past few weeks." He paused in the doorway. "Will you take some advice?"

Aimon sighed and inclined his head. What possible advice could Farren give to a werewolf whose mate may well choose another?

"Tell her you love her. She needs to hear it, because I suspect she does not truly know how you feel about her."

With his parting words, Farren left the room. Aimon stared after him, his wine forgotten. Could it be that simple? Was that what she had been asking for when she had confronted him at her bedchamber door? Words of love? A slow smile curled on his lips. That he could do. First thing in the morning, he would act on Farren's advice. He would tell Kathryn. Perhaps then she would accept him as her mate.

Chapter Thirty-Three

Aimon stood outside Kathryn's bedchamber and leaned against the wall, his body stiff from a night spent on the cold floor. Kathryn had slept no better, tossing about in her bed, her confusion and her hurt bruising his senses all night long. He had done this to her, with his reluctance to tell her everything. By not giving her the words she had sought. Aimon firmed his resolve. He would make it right. He *had* to make it right.

His ears pricked at the sound of horses in the bailey. Had one of the others come? No. Too many horses. He should check —

The door opened, and Anne brushed past him, leaving Kathryn standing in the doorway. He drank her in. Dark smudges rimmed her eyes and defeat screamed at him in the downward slope of her shoulders. The new arrivals could wait. Gascon would see to them and would send a servant to warn him if there was a need.

"Kathryn, can we talk?"

She stared at him through wounded eyes.

"Please?"

She pressed her lips together and gave him a sharp nod.

His tension eased a little. What he would have done if she had refused, he did not know. "When we spoke last night...I was not clear—"

"Pardon the interruption, Monsieur Aimon."

Aimon growled, swiveling to face the intrusion. "Not now, Gascon."

"My apologies, Monsieur Aimon." Gascon bowed his head. "This cannot wait. Comte Lothair is here, and he has requested your presence. Immediately."

Aimon's blood iced over in his veins. The horses. Lothair and his keep guard.

"He awaits you in the library."

Aimon sighed. His day of reckoning had arrived. He turned back to Kathryn and brushed her cheek with the back of his hand. "We will talk soon, Kathryn. I must attend Lothair. It is not wise to keep him waiting."

She pulled away, and he let his hand fall limp to his side. Her reaction stung.

"I am coming with you."

"Kathryn—"

She jutted out her chin, the steel in her eyes harder than a newly forged sword. "This is about me, is it not?"

"Perhaps, it may—"

"Then I am coming with you." She pushed past him into the corridor. "Come, Gascon. To the library, if you please."

Gascon bowed. "As you wish, Mademoiselle Kathryn."

Aimon thumped the wall with his fist, then leaned his forehead against the cool stone. There was no help for it. He followed Gascon and Kathryn.

Two of Lothair's personal guard stood outside the library, another two at the entry to the keep and a further pair guarded access to the corridor.

"Monsieur Aimon and Mademoiselle Kathryn to see Mon Seigneur Comte. As requested."

A guard moved to block them from entering. "The comte has asked only for Monsieur Aimon, not Mademoiselle Kathryn."

Kathryn stiffened and the white-hot blaze of her anger filled his senses. If Aimon wished to keep her safe from Lothair, shield her, and he did, then the guard's decree gave him the opportunity. But keeping things from Kathryn had already worked against him. He slipped his hand into hers.

"Step aside. Mademoiselle Kathryn is with me, and either she is allowed to enter or neither of us will."

Kathryn gripped his hand tighter. Had he surprised her with his support? Had he made the right decision?

Uncertainty crossed the guard's face. "Comte Lothair—"

"I will take responsibility if it displeases the comte."

After a moment's consideration, and an uncertain glance at his fellow guard who shrugged his indifference, the keep guard stepped aside and allowed them entry.

Comte Lothair lazed in a chair by the brazier, armored and armed, his hand casually resting on the pommel of his sword. His sharp gaze swept over them, coming to rest on their joined hands. Aimon pulled Kathryn behind him, shielding her from Lothair's astute gaze. He may have conceded to Kathryn being present, but he would still protect her any way he could.

Lothair's eyebrow quirked up. "Aimon, you were the last person I expected to pay the Beauchenes a visit. You have surprised me. That does not happen very often."

Aimon remained silent. He suspected he was in enough strife by being here. He did not plan to give Lothair any more reason to add to his punishment. And he was not foolish enough to try to match wits with Lothair.

"I was of the belief," said Lothair, "that you and I had something in common."

A snarl formed on Aimon's lips, but he was quick to hide it, forcing his expression to one of blank incomprehension.

Lothair smirked. "It seems you are learning, Aimon. Politics is a nasty game, and one as honest and loyal as you needs to be careful."

A chill swept over him, and he clutched Kathryn's hand tighter.

"We both know Gaharet is not dead. And we both know his betrothed is with him."

Merde. He *had* given himself away. The urge to lick his suddenly dry lips took all his willpower to suppress.

"Gaharet's other vassals do not know this." Lothair picked up the poker and thrust it into the brazier, prodding the coals to life. "And you, it seems, are in no great rush to tell them. That makes me wonder why you came here in the first place." He looked around Aimon, his gaze raking Kathryn up and down again. "I can see why you stayed." A lascivious glint lit up Lothair's eyes.

Aimon's hackles rose and his canines slid down, filling his mouth. But for Kathryn's gentle touch on his arm, he might have shifted. He forced his breathing to slow and his wolf to recede and focused on Kathryn's small hand in his in an effort to ground himself.

"I had a plan, Aimon. To flush out whoever Renaud's informant was. She"—he pointed the poker at Kathryn—"was part of that plan. You almost foiled it."

Aimon's mind raced. "Almost?" Had Lothair discovered the traitor?

Lothair grinned and leaned the poker against the wall. "The others took a more direct approach than you. Quite unexpected, really. Instead of consulting Farren, they came straight to me. Petitioned me for Kathryn's hand in marriage."

Kathryn gasped, and Aimon struggled to contain his shock. Someone had gone to the comte? More than one. Lothair had said others—plural. Aimon had never considered the possibility. Neither had Gaharet.

"Who?"

His mind weighed his options. Only one held any appeal—escape. He could flee with Kathryn, go into hiding as Gaharet had with Erin. Even as the thought crossed his mind, he discarded it. The choice was not his to make.

"Godfrey and Lance."

Aimon's nostrils flared.

"The question is," said Lothair, eyeing them both, "which one is Renaud's informant, and which one do I let have Kathryn and"—he waved his hand around, indicating the d'Louncrais keep—"all of this?"

Aimon pulled Kathryn close in behind him. He swallowed the words he wanted to shout. That Kathryn was *his* and no others. That Lothair should grant *him* Kathryn's hand in marriage.

"Kathryn *deserves* the right to choose who she weds." His words came out through gritted teeth. He met Lothair's gaze. In saying what he had, had he opened the door to losing Kathryn forever?

Lothair's eyes narrowed. "What if I insist she marry either Lance or Godfrey?"

From behind him, Kathryn growled.

His body stiffened. *No. Kathryn.* It had been an instinctive response, not a deliberate move, but Lothair's eyes lit up. He recognized what it meant.

Lothair rose from his chair and circled around them. "My, my. A female werewolf."

Aimon kept his body between Lothair and Kathryn, a buffer between this threat and his mate.

"*This* is why you came here." His gaze fixed on Kathryn, glinting with malevolent glee. "I imagine it would be a difficult thing to find a bride willing to marry a werewolf. Much easier if she is already one of your kind. It surprises me Kathryn has remained unwed for so long."

His eyes widened, and his mouth dropped open. Then he laughed. "They do not know. You have not told them."

Aimon pursed his lips together and drew back his shoulders.

"She *is* quite a prize then, is she not?" Lothair stopped circling them and stood in front of Aimon, toe to toe, eye to eye, an intimidating figure. "Does Gaharet know?"

Aimon looked away, breaking Lothair's stare.

Lothair chuckled and returned to his seat by the brazier. "You *have* been in contact with him, then?"

Aimon raised his gaze to the ceiling. Was there any point in denying it?

"Aimon?"

"Yes," he hissed.

"Mmm." Lothair drummed his fingers on his thigh. "This could still work. You almost ruined my original plan, but this…this might actually be better. If I play things right…" He stared at their hands, still clutched together.

Tension coiled in Aimon's gut. He did not like being at the mercy of their comte. Nothing good ever came from that.

"Here is what you are going to do. Send a communication out to the others. Tell them…tell them you have important information to share." A wicked smirk tugged at Lothair's lips. "Something that will change everything." Lothair stood and paced the room. "Invite them here."

"What? No!"

Lothair quirked an eyebrow.

Aimon's heart skipped a beat. "I will not risk Kathryn's safety by bringing them here."

"But Aimon, it was *your* wish she have a choice in who she marries. I am giving you what you asked for." His gaze turned hard. "You will bring them here."

Aimon raised himself to his full height, his beast close to the surface, pushing forward, ready and waiting for his command. "No."

Lothair scowled and took a step toward him, his hand reaching for his sword. Aimon stood his ground, keeping Kathryn tucked behind him.

"You would defy me on this?"

Aimon said nothing, standing firm, the room taking on a strong, musky scent. Would he shift and take on his comte? To defend Kathryn? *Yes.*

Lothair studied him, eyes narrowed. He took a step back. Aimon's wolf was close, and he suspected Lothair could sense it, feel its presence hovering just below the surface. It would be a brave, or reckless human who would take on a werewolf in close quarters.

"I see you would." He retreated another few steps, but his hand remained on the hilt of his sword. "Work with me here, Aimon. We need to flush out Renaud's informant. I imagine this is of as much importance to the pack as it is to me. I know it is not you. Or Ulrik. You are the only two vassals who know Gaharet lives, and your dedication to keeping his secret is obvious." He dropped his hand from his sword. "Gaharet must have some inkling who may have betrayed him."

Aimon resisted the urge to shift from foot to foot beneath the comte's direct stare.

"Tell me, Aimon. What alarmed you more? That two vassals approached me for Kathryn's hand in marriage, or that it was Godfrey and Lance?"

Aimon's hand tightened around Kathryn's. He thought his teeth might crack if he clenched his jaw any harder.

Lothair's eyes gleamed. "As I suspected. You believe either Godfrey or Lance is the traitor. As do I. One of those two men has colluded with that conniving excuse of an archeveque to bring me down. Whoever it is, I will stop them." He pointed at Kathryn. "And she will help me do it. She is the key."

Kathryn shrank further behind him, and Aimon longed to comfort her, tell her all would be well, but he could not be certain it would.

"Seeing the two of you—hand in hand as you are now—will test their loyalties. If they are true, they will support you and may even congratulate you. They will see the d'Louncrais estate remaining within the pack, and that will satisfy them. But for the traitor, this setback may force his hand."

Aimon had to admit, as plans went, it had a good chance of success. It also had a good chance of getting him killed and leaving Kathryn vulnerable. But what choice did he have? With the keep guard on hand, Aimon could well end up in the cell beneath Langeais Keep with Ulrik should he refuse. He would be of no use to Kathryn were that to happen.

"I will meet with them," he said. "But not here. And I will go alone."

Lothair shook his head. "No, no, no. Kathryn must be with you."

"Kathryn will stay here, safe inside this keep. I will tell them about Kathryn. As soon as I am in their presence, they will know anyway. They will catch her scent."

Lothair's eyes narrowed. "If that is true, then how is it they did not know of her before now?"

Kathryn sniffed. "I am surprised anyone could smell anything over the stench in Langeais Keep."

Aimon tensed, but Lothair ignored Kathryn, lost in thought.

"Very well, Aimon. I will grant you this one boon. You will meet Gaharet's vassals. They will smell Kathryn on you, and you will watch them and gauge their reactions. Then you will report back, not only to Gaharet, but also to me. The time will come when Gaharet is back by my side, but until then, I will know everything he does. And you, Aimon, will be the one to keep me informed." Lothair smiled at him, and Aimon found his countenance more chilling than he ever had. "And in return, I may let you keep your woman."

Chapter Thirty-Four

Kathryn stood in the hall, staring at the embroidered figures of the battle of Montsoreau, her gaze shifting from one man to the next. Aimon. Godfrey. Lance. Two of them had not done her the courtesy of speaking to her father. Nor had they called upon her to ascertain their compatibility. They had gone directly to Comte Lothair to bargain for her hand in marriage. They were willing to saddle themselves with her sight unseen, with no knowledge of her character, her disposition, and no thought of her wishes, their only thought to obtain the d'Louncrais estate. One of them had betrayed the pack she now belonged to. One of them had killed her aunt and attacked her.

Aimon had come to them. To her. But not for the d'Louncrais estate. He had come because he knew what she was. And what she was, came with inherent advantages.

Her gaze skipped to the other wall hanging of her aunt and uncle's courtship. Humans *could* be turned into werewolves if a werewolf chose a mate from beyond the pack. Her uncle had turned her aunt. And Gaharet had turned Erin. Erin's injury had necessitated her turning, but Gaharet had chosen her as his mate *before* her life was at stake. So Erin said. That could only mean Gaharet had planned on turning her, regardless.

She released a sigh as heavy as the feelings in her heart. Aimon had promised her they would talk, but after the chaos of the comte's arrival and departure, he had set about sending communications to Edmond, Aubert, Lance and Godfrey, calling them together. Then he had saddled his horse and ridden out of the bailey without a word or a fare-thee-well. She scowled at his embroidered image on the wall hanging. He was making a habit of that.

The familiar scent of her father warned her of his approach.

"An interesting piece, this one." He stood beside her, taking in the battle scene before them. "Did you and Aimon talk?"

Kathryn shook her head. "He tried first thing this morning, but…"

"Comte Lothair interrupted."

She gave him a defeated nod.

"I hear he defended your right to be present. Few men would do that."

Yes, he had, and it had thrilled her no end after his initial rejection of her request to be a part of the conversation. But her triumph had been short-lived.

"Lance and Godfrey have petitioned the comte for my hand in marriage."

Her father grunted. "What did Aimon have to say about that?"

She met her father's gaze. "That I had a right to choose who I should wed."

Her father smiled and patted her on the arm. "He is a good man. He will make you a fine match."

"But…"

Kathryn turned her attention back to the wall hanging. She reached out and ran her fingers over the fallen embroidered figure, his blue surcoat stained with blood, and his long white-blond hair spread around his head like a halo.

"But he did not petition the comte for my hand in marriage."

Her father took her shoulders in his hands and turned her to face him. "You wanted the choice to be yours, Kathryn. He is trying to give you what you want." He raised his hands to her face and tilted her head to look at him. "You have a decision to make. You are an intelligent, strong woman. Lord knows, you have always had your own mind. But if there is one piece of advice I can give you, it is to think with your heart, Kathryn, not your head." He dropped a kiss on her forehead and stepped back. "Aimon will return soon. Talk to him. Do not leave things unsaid between the two of you."

Her father retreated from the hall, leaving her to stare at the wall hanging, lost in thought. She had a choice to make. What no one seemed to consider—not Comte Lothair, her father, nor Aimon—was the fourth option available to her. Now a member of the pack, she was no longer alone. The threat of being destitute if her father died was gone. If that were to happen, the pack would care for her. Gaharet would see to it. Now Kathryn could choose to not marry at all.

* * * *

Dusk slowly crept across the sky as Aimon rode into the bailey of the d'Louncrais keep. A good portion of his day he had spent with Gaharet, making plans and trying to cover all contingencies. Damn Lothair and his interference. Aimon had wanted to keep Kathryn's identity hidden until they had found her attacker. But it was not to be. He could not defy Lothair.

Aimon slid from his saddle and handed his reins to Henri. He needed to talk to Kathryn, and he had little time before he must leave to meet the others — to do Lothair's bidding. He found her in the hall, seated near the fire, her dark copper hair spilling down her back like a river of flame. The very sight of her had his pulse speeding up.

She stiffened as he approached, but she did not turn to greet him. "Where did you go? You have been gone all day."

Aimon grimaced. He had not told her of his intention to consult with Gaharet. A deliberate move, but necessary. She would have insisted she join him, and he had not wanted her privy to their discussion. Things had needed to be said, strategies put in place should he not return from the meeting. Of course, it had angered her.

He skirted her chair and crouched before her. "I went to see Gaharet. To warn him, to seek his advice and to plan."

"I could have come with you. To see Erin." She searched his gaze, seeking answers. "Oh. I see. You did not want me there."

He looked away, avoiding the accusation in her eyes. She got to her feet and brushed past him, moving around the fire, putting it between them.

"What have you and Gaharet decided?"

Aimon stood and stared at her across the fire. "Gaharet is bringing Erin to the keep. He will guard the two of you until I return."

If he returned. There were no guarantees. It all depended on how the traitor reacted, whether the others would support him... He had defied a direct order from Lance by coming to the d'Louncrais keep. That would not be received well, despite his having a valid reason. He may not get the chance to tell them why.

"I do not suppose you would consider letting me come with you? I have control over my wolf now. I could help you."

Aimon raked his hands through his hair. "I understand why you want to be there, Kathryn. I do, but it is not safe. Our betrayer will be there. He has already had a hand in murdering our kind. He may see this meeting as an opportunity to ambush the rest of us. I will not put you in harm's way."

She shook her head, her copper locks falling about her face. "Of course."

He winced at the bitter note to her words. "I will need to have my wits about me. I cannot afford to miss something because I am worried about protecting you. With you here, with Gaharet watching over you, I will know you are safe. As safe as you can be."

He skirted the fire and took her hands in his. His heart rejoiced when she did not pull away. "If things go awry, if someone breaches Gaharet's defenses, unlikely as that is, you and Erin can lock yourselves in the training room and wait for help to arrive. I hope it will not come to that, but knowing you have that option will put my mind at ease. Promise me you will stay in here in the keep."

Her father had once told him she would never break a promise. He was counting on Farren knowing his daughter.

He released her hand to tilt her chin up, forcing her to meet his gaze. "Promise me, Kathryn. Please."

Her eyes softened, and she licked her lips, drawing his gaze.

"I promise."

Her voice was soft and breathy, the scent of her arousal teasing his nostrils. He inhaled deeply, stepping closer, and cupped her face. He sighed, touching his forehead to hers as another familiar presence filled his awareness. Gaharet had arrived.

"I know we have not had a chance to talk, and there is so much I want to tell you. Right now, we do not have the time, but know this. Like Elise was for Jacques, and Erin is for Gaharet, you are the only woman for me. I love you, Kathryn. The inner fire that burns so bright within you, your courage, your determination. The way you revel in the forest, letting your hair down and removing your boots to run barefoot. How you ride horses with reckless abandon." He smiled. "Lord knows, I even love your temper. And were you not a werewolf, were you not attacked and turned and had remained human till this day, I would love you still."

Her eyes widened, and her lips parted on a gasp. He took full advantage, taking her mouth in his, putting everything he felt, every emotion she provoked, into his kiss. He released her, leaving her dazed and her mouth moist from his kiss.

"Gaharet and Erin are here. It is time for me to confront the others. Stay safe, Kathryn. For me."

With one last squeeze of her hand, he left her standing by the fire. Aimon did not look back. He would see this through. He must. For her. And perhaps, when he returned, she might choose him as her mate.

Chapter Thirty-Five

Aimon stepped out of the keep to find Gaharet waiting for him. Night had fallen, and the moon hung low in the sky, yet to reach its zenith. Its color gave him pause.

"A blood moon rising. What does it portend for this meeting?"

Gaharet turned to face the moon. "Perhaps something. Perhaps nothing."

"Nothing good."

"Do not be so sure, Aimon. A fourth full moon of the season rose on the night Erin arrived. She called it a blue moon. The reason for that escapes me, for the moon did not turn blue, but that night changed both of our lives. In a good way."

"My mother would say blood will be spilled this night. Perhaps I go to meet my doom."

Gaharet grunted. "Your mother has ever listened to idle gossip and superstition. Do not let her words trouble you. While you will meet our betrayer tonight, you will not be alone. Both Edmond and Aubert are loyal. And formidable. They will not let you fall."

Aimon grasped the pommel of his sword, its familiarity comforting. "Take care of her for me."

"Of course. Be safe, Aimon. We will be here when you return."

Wishing he could have Gaharet's confidence, Aimon made his way across the bailey, passing through the gate and stepping beyond the walls. Steeling himself for what was to come, he entered the forest.

He approached the clearing, trepidation coursing through his veins. Had he made the right choice in calling the men here? So close to the d'Louncrais Keep? So close to Kathryn? Here, in this small meadow, he had trained her. Taught her how to control her wolf outside the safety of the training room. Taken her on her first run as a wolf from here. And he had made love to her for the first time in this clearing. Her first time.

The scent of their coupling still permeated the clearing, heady and strong. With their keen sense of smell, the men could not fail to notice. Nor would they miss how close it lay to the d'Louncrais Keep. A place Lance had forbidden them to approach. But Aimon needed every advantage he could get, and the evidence of what had taken place in this clearing would go far in staking his claim over Kathryn. At least to the men.

He pushed out his senses, searching for a hint of anything out of place. Gaharet had warned him to be on the lookout for wolfsbane, and the strange absence of any scent and the deadening of sound that signaled its use. Night animals scurried about, birds settled in their nests for the night and the smell of damp earth and pine surrounded him. All was as it should be.

He entered the clearing, his wolf hovering close and primed for the arrival of the others. He did not have to wait long. Edmond and Aubert were the first to arrive, for which he was profoundly grateful. Dismounting, they tied their horses off and stepped from the cover of the trees, their noses twitching. They shared a look, then as one, turned to stare at him.

"Aimon?"

He met Edmond's stare, sensing no hostility, only curiosity. Through the filtered moonlight that flickered beneath the forest canopy, Lance and Godfrey appeared. They, too, dismounted, leaving their horses in the trees to graze before entering the clearing.

Lance raised an eyebrow. "You have something you wish to tell us, Aimon?"

Godfrey snorted. "I think the smell of sex in this clearing says it all. You found Erin, and you have mated with her."

"Use your nose, Godfrey," said Edmond. "It is not Erin. We know her scent. This is someone else."

"What other female werewolf could there possibly be?" demanded Godfrey, but he sniffed the air again.

Lance's gray gaze bored into him. "Would you care to explain, Aimon?"

Aimon took in the men, gauging their mood, as they looked to him for explanations, the physical distance between them matched only by the remoteness of their emotions. His body tensed in readiness, as his gaze darted from one man to another.

"You are right, Edmond. It is not Erin." With but a few words, they would know of Kathryn's existence, and she would no longer be safe. "It is Kathryn Beauchene."

They stared at him, their eyes wide and their mouths agape. Night insects chirped, an owl hooted, and an expectant stillness settled over the clearing.

Lance broke the silence. "Kathryn is one of us?"

Aimon gave them a slow nod, not daring to take his gaze any off them. "Yes. Kathryn *is* one of us."

"Is she your mate?" asked Aubert.

Aimon hesitated. Kathryn was his mate, but he had never been more aware Kathryn had yet to acknowledge he was hers, had yet to tell him she loved him too. "I think she may be."

"Yes!" Edmond punched the air with his fist. "It is about time our luck changed."

Aubert moved to him and clapped him on the shoulders, a broad smile splitting his normally gruff visage. "Congratulations, Aimon."

He released a pent-up breath. The twins' delight was genuine. He looked over at Lance and Godfrey.

Lance looked worried. "You turned her? And had her out here, beyond the keep walls so soon?"

Godfrey blew out an incredulous breath. "You have been a wolf a mere three years yourself. What were you thinking?"

Aimon clenched his hands at his side. Did Godfrey and Lance think so little of him? Did they truly believe he would attempt something as risky as a turning without the sanction of the pack?

He squared his shoulders and faced down their rebuke. "I did not turn her."

Aubert grunted. "Somebody did."

The men eyed each other before turning back to him.

"Aimon?" queried Lance. "Do you know how Kathryn came to be one of us?"

Aimon stared at each of them, paying particular attention to Lance and Godfrey, watching for any sign—a twitch of an eyebrow, a lip curling in a snarl. Nothing.

"Kathryn was attacked."

Lance's eyes narrowed. "Attacked? When?"

"The same day, the same place and by the same wolf who killed Elise d'Louncrais."

The men drew back, as though struck.

"A wolf killed Elise? One of us? Impossible," said Godfrey.

Lance spun away before turning back to face them. "Who of us would do that? And Kathryn would not have been much more than a child. That one of us would have attacked a child..." He rubbed his hand over his face and stared at the ground.

Edmond tapped his finger against his chin and looked at his twin. "What are the chances of having two rogue wolves in the same century?"

"Not good," said Aubert.

"Then...if my calculations are correct, Godfrey was right. Ulrik is not the one who has betrayed us. Neither is Aimon. But whoever did is standing right here in this clearing."

Godfrey snarled. "I resent your accusation, Edmond. Pray tell us how you came to this conclusion."

Edmond crossed his big arms across his chest. "When Elise died, Ulrik was in Bretaigne, sent there by his parents. He could not have been responsible for her death. Or for the attack on Kathryn. Aimon was not yet one of us, and we all know Gaharet would never have killed his own mother."

"Another pack?" suggested Lance.

"Have you ever, in all these years, caught the scent of a werewolf not belonging to our pack?" asked Edmond. "I have not."

Aubert shook his head.

"No. It is not another pack. One of us would have encountered some sign of their presence years ago," agreed Lance as he paced the clearing. "What about D'Artagnon, Gaharet's brother?"

Aubert frowned. "He died in battle years ago."

"Did he though? We never found his body."

Edmond shook his head. "Several of us saw him crawling from the battleground with heinous injuries. And I cannot accept D'Artagnon killing his mother any more than I believe Gaharet did. Her death devastated them both."

"We are forgetting we have a witness." Godfrey turned to Aimon. "Kathryn."

All eyes turned to him again, and Aimon met their gazes. He had to choose his words with care, or they would scent a lie.

"Kathryn remembers very little about the attack. She was able to tell us the color of the wolf, though."

"And?"

"Brown. The wolf who attacked her had brown fur."

"Well." Edmond looked around the clearing. "That does not narrow it down at all."

Aubert turned to his twin. "Rules out D'Artagnon."

Edmond inclined his head. "Truly. I would not call his wolf brown. His fur is as black as Gaharet's."

Silence descended amongst them. Aimon waited and watched, his gaze flicking between Lance and Godfrey.

"So, Aimon," said Godfrey, breaking the uncomfortable lull in their conversation. "How is it you came by all this information? The knowledge that Kathryn is one of us? Were you not supposed to be tracking Gaharet and his mate? Were we not *all* ordered to stay away from the Beauchenes?"

"Why did you petition Comte Lothair for Kathryn's hand in marriage?" countered Aimon.

Edmond shared a look with his twin. "Godfrey? You petitioned Lothair?"

"I have spent all week pouring over scrolls and texts, trying to find a way to circumvent wolfsbane, while Aimon has spent his time bedding the last female werewolf, and you question *me*?"

"Godfrey is right," said Lance. "I made it clear none of us were to approach the Beauchenes."

Resentment flared in Aimon's chest. "None of us were supposed to approach the comte either. You also petitioned Lothair for Kathryn's hand in marriage, Lance. Would you care to explain *yourself*?"

Lance met his stare, unperturbed by Aimon's accusation. "I made no secret of my intentions to ask for the d'Louncrais estate. You, however, have flouted a direct order from the pack. Perhaps you would care to enlighten us on why? And how you know of any petition to Lothair?"

Aimon calmed himself. Anger would not serve him now. He could not make a mistake and compromise Gaharet. Nor could they ever know he now answered directly to Lothair. "Very well. I caught her scent at Langeais Keep. I thought my nose confused by the stench of it, or a lingering effect of the wolfsbane. As Godfrey pointed out, I have not been a werewolf for long. I assumed I had it wrong. I planned to ride to the d'Louncrais estate, wait until the Beauchenes arrived, catch Kathryn's scent again and confirm my error. Then

I would be on my way, carrying out the tasks Lance assigned me."

"I gather that is not what happened," ventured Edmond.

"No. I was not mistaken. I approached Farren Beauchene with the truth of it, and he disclosed the circumstances of Kathryn's turning. He knew of us but had kept his daughter unaware. She did not know we existed and thought herself to be cursed. Frightened, with no training, she had resisted her wolf for over a decade."

Godfrey gaped at him. "Resisted her... That is not possible."

"I assure you it is, and she has," said Aimon, unable to keep his pride in her from entering his voice.

Shadows flitted in Lance's gray eyes, and his lips lifted in a smile. "If that is the case, then she is quite a remarkable woman indeed."

Chapter Thirty-Six

Kathryn slumped onto a stool and stared at the fire, her lips still tingling from Aimon's kiss. He had said he loved her. That he would have loved her still had she not been a werewolf. She touched her fingers to her lips.

"It's only been a few weeks since I was here, but I'd forgotten how immense this room is." Erin's voice broke through her reverie.

Kathryn rose to meet her and hugged her. "I am so glad to see you, Erin." She released her. "Is it not dangerous for you and Gaharet to be here? The servants, the farmers…someone will see you."

"No need to fret now, child," said Anne as she bustled into the room carrying two mugs. "There is a celebration in the village. All the servants have the night off so they can attend. Only myself and Gascon are in the keep tonight." She handed a mug to Kathryn and one to Erin. "Chamomile brew for the nerves."

"There's a celebration in the village tonight? That's rather convenient," murmured Erin.

Anne chuckled. "We leave nothing to chance, dear girl. Now, sit by the fire, relax and let the men do what they do best — take care of things."

Kathryn grimaced. "I have had more than enough of *men* taking care of things for me."

"Now, now, Kathryn." Anne wagged her finger at her. "Do not go getting any ideas about leaving the keep. Or you, Erin. This meeting is dangerous, and neither of you have the experience as wolves to risk yourselves out there tonight. Gaharet and Aimon would never forgive themselves if something were to happen to either of you. Sit, drink your brew and stay put."

Erin planted herself on a stool. "Yes, Anne."

"Kathryn?"

Kathryn wilted under Anne's stare. "Yes, Anne."

"Good. I will be in the kitchen should you need anything. But have no doubt, if I suspect either of you are planning something, I will not hesitate to lock both of you in the training room for the night. Do you understand?"

Kathryn looked at Erin, and they both nodded.

"Good."

With a satisfied smile, Anne left them to their brew.

"Formidable, isn't she?" whispered Erin, as Anne's bulk disappeared through the door.

"Oh my, yes. She does not care one bit we are werewolves. You know, she threatened to rap Aimon over the knuckles my first night here."

Erin chuckled. "She scolded Gaharet like he was a naughty little boy the first time I met her."

Kathryn gasped. "And Gaharet allowed it?"

"Yep. It was one of the most astounding and amusing things I'd ever seen. I think if he'd challenged her, she might've grabbed him by the ear and dragged him from the room. Now *that* would've been a sight to see."

Kathryn giggled. She could not envision Gaharet letting a servant treat him so, but Anne was a force to be reckoned with.

"So," said Erin, before taking a sip from her brew. "How are things going with you and Aimon?"

Kathryn's smile slipped, and she stared down into her mug.

"That good, huh?"

Her fingers clenched around her mug, and her gaze slid to the embroidered wall hangings, settling on the one of her aunt and uncle.

"I learned something—" She bit off her words.

"Something about Aimon?"

Kathryn turned her attention back to her mug. "No. Something about werewolves."

"Oh. Does it change how you feel about Aimon?"

"I…"

Kathryn shifted her gaze to Erin. Did Erin know? "I overheard Aimon talking to my father. It appears werewolves can only have children if they mate another werewolf."

Erin's eyebrows rose. "Say what now? Gaharet never mentioned that."

"Before you came, there were only seven werewolves left in the pack, and no females. There are five unmated males out there." Kathryn waved her hand toward the forest. Somewhere amongst the trees, five men met to discuss her. "Gaharet said I was precious. Now I understand why."

She turned her gaze back to the wall hanging of her aunt and uncle's courtship. "All of Gaharet's vassals are fantastic matches — a rise in status and fortune for many women. But would any woman feel the same if they knew what they had to become? Would they not falter in their pursuit of such a match if they were told they would have to go through a turning?" Kathryn drew in a deep breath, releasing it with a heavy sigh. "I understand now why Gaharet's vassals have not married. The risk of exposing our secret, should they reveal all and face rejection, is too high."

Erin gave her shoulder a comforting squeeze, drawing her attention back to her friend. Was she not angry Gaharet had kept this information from her?

"It might surprise you what a woman will do for the man she loves." Erin gestured at the wall hanging of her aunt's courtship. "Your aunt braved the turning for your uncle. And though I never had the chance to make that decision, I chose to stay here in this century. A place so far removed from my home, from everything I knew, so Gaharet and I could be together. Think about it, Kathryn. If you weren't a werewolf already, would you choose to become one so you could be with Aimon?"

Kathryn sat up straighter. She had never considered it from that perspective. Would she?

"I..." She got to her feet and paced in front of the fire. "Oh, I do not know what to think. Then there is Lance and Godfrey. What if either of them challenge Aimon for me? What if Anne is right and the men take care of things? And what if I do not like the outcome?"

Erin shrugged. "Then go to the meeting."

"But I gave Aimon my word I would stay here."

And there was Anne. She had once wondered if Anne would drag her back to the keep by her hair if she disobeyed orders. She did not doubt it now. And she would have to get past Gaharet.

"Aimon will forgive you, Kathryn." Erin's forthright green gaze met hers. "But will you forgive yourself if you let them make your choice for you?"

Kathryn stopped pacing. "You are right." She handed her mug to Erin. "I must go. I have to be at that meeting."

Erin grinned. "Go. Don't let those men make your decision for you. And Kathryn," Erin called after her as she raced from the hall. "Be careful."

Kathryn nodded and slipped into the corridor. She did not know where the men were convening, but with her wolf senses she could follow Aimon's trail. The faint mutter of voices from below told her Anne and Gascon were in the kitchen. The flicker of light beneath the library door suggested her father had retired there. That left only Gaharet to sneak past. She was not naïve enough to believe that would be easy.

She did not find him in the corridor or lingering beyond the keep entrance. Cautiously, she followed Aimon's scent, grateful he had not stopped at the stables to get his horse. She crossed the bailey, passed the darkened store houses and the smithy and approached the keep walls. With all the servants at the celebration in the village, did Gaharet man the gate? For certain someone would guard it.

A guard stepped out of his hut to greet her. Not Gaharet.

"Good evening, Mademoiselle Kathryn. Shall I open the gate for you?"

"Please." She danced about on her toes, impatient to be gone.

The guard stepped forward, shifted the heavy beam that barred the entrance, and swung the gate open. Kathryn's gaze darted about.

It cannot be this simple.

She stepped beyond the keep walls and raised her nose, taking in the confusion of scents of the servants, the guards, the farmers and the many people who had entered the keep over the last week. She caught Aimon's fresh trail, heading toward the forest. She peered into the darkness. Where was Gaharet? He must be around somewhere.

The gate closed behind her with a thud, and she jumped. She stared up at the moon, its usual glow tinged with red. A flutter of unease brushed against her mind, but she would not let anything deter her. Not a red moon. Not Gaharet.

Still no sign of her alpha. Could it be she had chosen an opportune moment? Had he been one of the voices floating up from the kitchen, believing her safe in the hall with Erin?

She should not waste time. Any moment now, he would discover her missing. With a determined stride, she headed for the forest, following Aimon's scent.

"Going somewhere, Kathryn?"

She froze. Out of the darkness, a tall shape coalesced. Had he been standing there all along, watching her? *How did I not catch his scent?*

"Gaharet."

He came to stand before her, towering over her, strength and power rolling off him in waves. It made her want to shrink away and dart back inside the walls, back to the hall to sit by the fire like a dutiful woman should. She straightened her spine and jutted out her chin. Dutiful woman be damned. That description had never fit Kathryn before. She was not going to conform to it now.

"I am going to the meeting. If I do not go, they might…"

She closed her eyes and blocked out Gaharet. Would the likes of Lance, or Godfrey, listen to Aimon? Listen to her? Would they care what she wanted when there was so much at stake?

"Might what, Kathryn?"

Kathryn opened her eyes but did not meet Gaharet's gaze. Instead, she focused on his family crest, the howling black wolf emblazoned on his surcoat above his heart.

"I know now why I am so precious to the pack. I am the only unmated female, and they are going to squabble over me like a group of street urchins thrown some coin. They do not care what I want. Except for Aimon. And he is so much younger than the others, and…"

She dropped her head and stared at the ground. Gaharet would never let her go.

Gaharet placed his finger under her chin, forcing her to look at him. "Then perhaps it is time you told them what you want."

"I… Wait. You are not sending me back to the keep?"

Gaharet dropped his hand and stepped out of her path. "No."

She eyed him warily. "Are you sure? Are you not afraid for my safety?"

"No. Aimon will not let anything happen to you. Nor Aubert and Edmond. Perhaps Godfrey and Lance would protect you, too. As you say, you are our only unmated female." He gestured to the forest. "They are in the clearing Aimon took you to for training."

Kathryn hesitated. "What if I do not wish to wed at all? Would the pack still protect me?"

Gaharet cocked his head at her, amusement dancing in his dark eyes. "Is that what you truly wish, Kathryn?"

"Maybe." She dropped her gaze. *Was it?* "No."

"Then go. Claim your mate."

Kathryn took a few steps forward, expecting Gaharet to change his mind at any moment and call her back. When he did not, she increased her pace until she was running toward the forest. Why he did not stop her, she could not begin to fathom. Nor did she care.

"Stay down wind, Kathryn, and tread lightly," he called after her. "They will not know you are coming."

So that was how he had caught her by surprise. Heeding his words, she slipped into the forest. Too many people had made decisions on her behalf. She would not let them make this one without her.

"I hope you know what you are doing."

Gaharet eyed the man who stepped from the shadows of the wall. "I know my men, Farren. I know the best way, the right way, to handle them. She is the only one they will listen to."

"This is my daughter's safety we are talking about here. How can you be so sure?"

"You know nothing of our kind, Farren." He softened his lips into a hint of a smile, taking the sting out of his words. "Werewolves mate for life. And the female's agreement to mate is paramount. The male can chase her, woo her and try to impress her, but it is the female who does the choosing." Gaharet shrugged. "That is our law, here, now, as it has been for centuries. Neither Lance nor Godfrey can take that away from her. And the others will defend her right to choose. I guarantee it."

Farren grunted. "I pray you are right."

"Come. Let us adjourn to the hall and avail ourselves of Anne's chamomile brew. It will calm your nerves."

As Gaharet turned away, a hint of a scent, so familiar and yet lost to him so long ago, tickled his nose. He halted and scanned the darkness. He lifted his nose to the breeze, searching for it again. Nothing but pine, oak, damp earth and the whiff of wood smoke from the keep.

"Gaharet? Is something wrong?"

He shook his head and followed Farren through the gate. "A memory, nothing more." Wishing it were otherwise was foolish. D'Artagnon was long gone from this life.

Chapter Thirty-Seven

Heeding Gaharet's words, Kathryn shifted her path to stay downwind and picked her way through the forest with care. She avoided the four horses tethered nearby and stopped short of the clearing. Five large men stared at each other, arguing, the clearing awash with tension and the faint reddish glow of moonlight giving their faces an eerie cast. Hiding behind the trunk of a large tree, she opened up her senses.

The first thing to hit her was the unmistakable scent of sex. Kathryn pressed her hands to her heated cheeks. *L'enfer. How can I face them now?* Every one of them could not fail to be aware of the intimacy she had shared with Aimon. That she had lain with a man outside the sanctity of marriage.

She turned, took two steps back toward the keep, then halted. People had talked about her before, whispered snide comments when she had walked into a room. Was she prepared to let a little embarrassment stop her from having a say in her future?

Kathryn spun around. No, she would not. She returned to the large oak and crouched behind it. Again, she opened up her senses and pushed past the lingering evidence of her and Aimon's tryst. A mixture of anger, confusion and curiosity, all underscored with the musky scent of wolf, wafted from Gaharet's vassals.

Her gaze shifted from one man to the next. Which one had attacked her? Would she be able to tell? Would she feel a pull toward the man who had made her, turned her, as Gaharet had suggested? Could it be Lance? With his back to her, he gave nothing away. Or Godfrey? Anger radiated from the chevalier. It was not the hulking twins. Gaharet had already established that. They looked on, more curious than riled, exchanging an occasional look between them. They intimidated her still, but she sensed no threat from them. And Aimon, shoulders stiff, legs parted in a wide stance, he withstood the assault of their words as one would a gale force wind.

"And what of the tasks set for you?" Godfrey glared at Aimon. "Or were you so enamored of Kathryn they did not once cross your mind? Our pack verges on the brink of extinction, Lothair has Ulrik chained beneath Langeais Keep, we have a rogue wolf in our midst, and you..." Godfrey huffed out a breath. "What have you been doing? Bedding the *only* female werewolf."

Heat returned to Kathryn's face. Aimon snarled. How uncouth of Godfrey to mention it. And in such base terms.

"I completed my tasks." Aimon's voice was little more than a growl.

"Did you give them the same attention you gave Kathryn? Did you doggedly pursue them as Edmond and Aubert did Renaud? Have you spent every waking moment chasing down leads, burying yourself in useless information as I did?"

"I went to the clearing. I visited the witch's cottage."

"What did you find, Aimon?" asked Lance, cutting off further accusations from Godfrey.

Kathryn held her breath. Would the others sense a lie?

Aimon paused, breathing deeply, as though containing the anger that swirled around him proved difficult. "It was as we thought. Gaharet was in the clearing. As was Erin. And Ulrik. Lothair and Renaud, too, with the keep guard and some mercenaries."

Kathryn let out her breath, long and slow. Aimon's words, chosen with care, rang of truth.

"The wolfsbane had wilted, and had minimal effect, but I could discern the circle they created with it. A perfect trap."

Edmond frowned. "We all scented the wolfsbane and felt its effects. We have to presume Gaharet and Ulrik did, too. What would entice Ulrik into the trap?"

"All the mercenaries were dead, killed outside of the circle," continued Aimon. "Except for one. But...I found blood inside the ring of wolfsbane, not belonging to him, Ulrik or Gaharet."

"Erin." Lance threw back his head and stared at the night sky. "Ulrik fought Gaharet for Erin. That is the only thing that makes sense. Erin must have been injured in the fray." He rubbed his face with his hands. "We should have seen this coming after Ulrik challenged Gaharet over her at his keep."

"If that is what happened, where are their bodies?" asked Godfrey. "Did you find them?"

"With such a confusion of scents I..." Aimon raised his hands, and an expression of defeat crossed his face.

Godfrey's lip curled. "And in your wisdom, you did what? Nothing. You did not think to consult with one of us, to call on someone with more experience. No doubt one of us could have teased the truth from that clearing."

Aimon flinched and Kathryn repressed a growl, her fingers digging into the bark of the tree. How dare Godfrey imply Aimon lacked the skills, lacked honor?

"But you had other things on your mind. You wanted to return to the d'Louncrais Keep. You had found a female werewolf, and you did not want to risk losing her to one of us."

Aimon growled at Godfrey. "What was I supposed to do? Who was I supposed to trust? Kathryn said a brown wolf attacked her. That absolves Ulrik, but—"

"—not any of us," finished Lance.

"For what it is worth, I did not expect to find my mate. I never expected to fall in love with her. I thought only of protecting her and keeping her safe."

Kathryn stifled a gasp. He had told them, declared his feelings to the pack. Warmth infused her body, and she stared at Aimon, unable to shift her eyes from him. His gaze flicked toward her, scanning the forest. Could he sense her presence? She pressed closer to the trunk of the tree.

"Has Kathryn agreed to be your mate?" asked Lance.

Aimon shifted his gaze back to the men in the clearing, his Adam's apple bobbing in his throat. "No. Not yet."

Kathryn pressed a hand to her chest at his wounded expression.

Godfrey smirked. "Well then, she may not settle for you, the newest member of our merry little band. Perhaps she will choose one of us."

Aimon snarled, and his wolf roared to the surface.

Surprise flitted across Godfrey's face. "You think to challenge me, young pup?"

Aimon roared, and his face contorted as his bones shifted. He ripped his sword belt off and reached for his hauberk.

Godfrey bared his teeth, his canines sliding clear and his face contorting as he unbuckled his sword and cast it aside. "So be it."

No. They will not fight over me. Kathryn abandoned the safety and anonymity of the forest and raced into the clearing. She placed herself between the two partly shifted werewolves, arms held aloft.

"Stop!"

"Elise?" Godfrey recoiled from her outstretched hand. "How is this possible?"

Aimon's hands dropped to his sides, and he took a step back. His bones shifted, and he settled back into his human form. "No, not Elise. Kathryn."

The men stared at her, the anguish in Aimon's eyes making her heart skip. He had been trying to protect her. As he had all along.

"There is a striking resemblance," muttered Aubert.

"Do I not have a say in this?" Kathryn spun around, pinning each man with a glare.

Edmond chuckled. "And spirited like her, too."

It unnerved Kathryn to have her back to any of them, so she gave it to the man she trusted most. Aimon.

"You have more than a say, Kathryn." Lance stepped forward. "By our law, you have the right to choose."

Kathryn backed away from Lance. *I do?* She narrowed her eyes at him. "Like you gave me the choice by petitioning Comte Lothair for my hand in marriage?" She turned her glare on Godfrey. "Or you, too? Treating me like I am no more than a prized cow, or a piece of expensive horseflesh to be bargained for and sold to the highest bidder. And now you fight over me. As though the last one standing will get to claim me by default."

Godfrey flinched, and a slow flush crept up his neck. He held up his hands and stepped away from her. "The choice is yours, Kathryn. You are the only female of our kind. In these times, that is a rare and precious thing. And you hold the fate of the d'Louncrais estate in your hands. But know this. A claim once stated cannot be unmade, so choose well."

"Your choice, Kathryn." Lance swept his hand out, taking in all the men. "But Godfrey speaks the truth. Any claim you make is final. Make sure you are certain of your choice."

The moment of truth. Who would Kathryn choose? Him? One of the others, more experienced than he? Did she feel a pull toward her attacker? Who knew how quickly that connection could resurface. Aimon's stomach clenched, tying itself in more knots than a fisherman's net.

Kathryn gazed around the circle at the men, settling on each of them, studying them. Each time her focus shifted, Aimon's heart skipped a beat. Edmond and Aubert, after a quick glance at him, stepped back and would not meet her gaze. Lance smiled at her, and Aimon's hands clenched into fists. Her attention moved away from Lance, and Aimon released his held breath. She turned to Godfrey, lingering over him longer than the others. Aimon's mouth went dry.

Finally, her eyes met his. A gentle smile tilted the corners of her mouth, and she came to him. Keeping his hands fisted at his side lest he reach for her, he waited. She placed her hand against his cheek, and he leaned into the gentle touch, the others fading into the background.

"I am sorry," she said, her eyes full of regret.

Aimon's heart cracked, but he did not look away from her. He could not.

"I am sorry, Aimon, that I did not tell you back at the keep that I love you. That, like Jacques was for Elise, you are the only man for me. You are my mate. I choose you."

"I…"

Wait. She loves *me? She chose* me?

He stared down at his mate, his heart near bursting with emotion. With a groan, he pulled into his arms and took her mouth in his, sealing their fate.

"Kathryn has chosen," said Lance. "So be it."

Aimon released her lips, nuzzling his face into her neck, loathe to let her out of his arms.

"I thought I had lost you," he whispered against her skin.

"Never. It has always been you, Aimon. From before we met, through all my training, to this moment right here, right now."

He pulled back, staring into her eyes. "From the moment I caught your scent at Langeais Keep, you had my attention. When I saw you in the forest, your hair down and bare toes peeking out beneath your dress, you stole my heart."

He kissed her again, deep and lingering.

"Hmm-hmm." Lance cleared his throat beside them. "We still have much to discuss, but I think it wise we leave things for now. Unless any of us have found anything important." Lance turned to Godfrey. "Nothing of interest in your father's tomes?"

Shadows flitted across Godfrey's eyes, and he hesitated. The fine hairs on the back of Aimon's neck rose.

"I have found nothing that can help us with our affliction to wolfsbane or silver."

Though Aimon sensed no lie in his words, Godfrey was hiding something. Of that, he was certain.

"Edmond, Aubert, anything on Renaud?"

"Plenty," grumbled Aubert.

Edmond rolled his eyes. "None of it is of any use to us. But he did give us the slip one day. We suspect he has a secret way in and out of the chapel. If we have to sleep on his damn doorstep, we will find it."

"Good. Aimon, did the witch tell you anything useful about wolfsbane?"

Aimon shook his head.

Lance grunted. "We will keep looking. We have to find a way to negate Renaud's advantage."

"What about our rogue wolf?" All eyes turned to Godfrey. "What happened to Elise and Kathryn cannot go unpunished."

"Nor his betrayal," said Edmond. "It has cost us too many and too much."

"Unless one of us has something to confess, it leaves us at an impasse," said Lance. "I am not convinced it is one of us."

"But what of Renaud's knowledge of us?" Edmond pinned Lance with a hard stare. "It had to come from someone."

"We all have retainers on our estates. Anyone could have overheard something. It has happened before. We were lucky, and Jacques was able to contain it. Maybe our luck ran out."

Godfrey eyed Lance dubiously. Aubert and Edmond shared a glance. Knowledge of them, yes, Aimon could believe that getting out. But knowledge of the amulets... And there was still the wolf responsible for Elise's death and Kathryn's turning.

"We will meet again in a sennight. Perhaps one of us will know more by then."

"Not here." Now the pack knew of Kathryn, Aimon did not want them anywhere near her.

"The crossroads at Langeais," suggested Godfrey. "It is out in the open. No chance for an ambush to be laid there."

"Very well. In a sennight. Stay safe." Lance turned to them. "Congratulations to the pair of you." He smiled. "Perhaps this is a sign of better things to come for us."

Edmond and Aubert stepped forward and clapped him on the shoulder, offering him their best wishes.

"You have your hands full with that one." Edmond chuckled, giving Kathryn a wink.

Pink stained her cheeks, but she did not look away. Instead, she raised an eyebrow at Edmond and lifted her chin. Edmond threw back his head and laughed. Aimon grinned. He did, indeed, have his hands full with her. And he could not be more pleased.

Godfrey studied them from across the clearing, his brow wrinkled in a frown. Aimon's smile slipped. Godfrey opened his mouth to say something, then closed it again, bending to retrieve his sword. He buckled it about his waist, then the older chevalier met Aimon's gaze. With a brief nod, and a last glance at the others in the clearing, he turned on his heel and strode into the forest toward his horse. Aimon watched him leave. Never before had Aimon seen the softly spoken chevalier quite so agitated as he had tonight.

"Stay safe, Aimon." Edmond and his twin moved toward their horses and mounted up. "And protect her. She is the future of our pack."

"I will."

"Welcome to the Langeais Wolves, Kathryn. You can count on us to look out for you."

Aubert nodded his agreement with a hint of a smile on his lips. The twins turned their horses and rode off into the gloom of the forest.

Lance untied his horse's reins. This may be the only chance Aimon had to confront him about his lies, but... Aimon tightened his arm around Kathryn.

"Something bothering you, Aimon?" Lance glanced around the clearing. "Something you found you did not wish to share in front of the others?"

Aimon opened his mouth to speak, then closed it again. If Lance had betrayed them... Could he take Lance on? Could he win against the older, more experienced wolf if it came to that? With a subtle step forward, he placed his body between Kathryn and Lance.

Lance raised his chin at the move. "I will never replace Gaharet, Aimon, but I am here for you. Trust me as Gaharet did."

Kathryn gazed up at him, her eyes full of confidence in him. He had to get to the truth. "Why did you lie about being at the clearing where Lothair captured Ulrik?"

Lance gave him a rueful smile. "You really did go to the clearing like you said?"

"Of course I did. I found it as everyone had said. Everyone except you."

Lance moved away from his horse and away from Aimon. He rubbed his chin as he paced about. "The truth?" He glanced at Aimon.

How fast could Lance shift? Faster than he could, but his armor would slow Lance down. As it would him. "The truth."

Lance stopped pacing and looked down at the ground. "I am a little embarrassed by the truth."

Aimon waited, his muscles tense and his wolf hovering close.

Lance's gaze flicked to Kathryn. "I am ashamed to say I was with a woman. No one special. I lost track of time and I missed the rendezvous." He looked off into the darkened forest. "When I saw the score of mounted men returning to Langeais with Ulrik, I knew something serious had happened. Then Gaharet did not return." His defeat hung thick in the air. "Gaharet was my friend. I have known him since he was a child. I let him down that night, Aimon. What if I had been there? Could I have prevented what happened? Or at least stood by his side?" Lance turned to face him, anguish written in the tight lines around his eyes and the pinching of his lips. "I *should* have been there. Instead, I was wasting time with some woman whose name I cannot even remember."

The truth of Gaharet's survival lodged in Aimon's throat. He wanted to trust Lance. Believe his grief was real. He opened his mouth to ease the man's guilt. The breeze shifted and a familiar scent tickled his nostrils.

Godfrey.

Aimon shut his mouth. He would not be telling anyone Gaharet was alive. Not tonight.

Chapter Thirty-Eight

Aimon waited in the clearing until he could no longer sense Lance and Godfrey and he was alone with Kathryn.

He wrapped her in his embrace and nuzzled at her neck. "Mate," he whispered against her skin.

She pressed herself against him and murmured her agreement. His cock stirred. He would like nothing more than to take her here in the clearing. Again. Bury himself in her welcoming heat. Imprint himself on her in a way no other man ever would. He pulled away from her.

She growled her discontent, her arousal spiking the air.

"We should get back to the keep. Gaharet will be anxious for news." He dropped a kiss on her nose. "You promised me, Kathryn, you would stay in the keep."

"I know, but—"

"Seeing you entering the clearing almost made my heart stop."

She poked a finger at his chest. "And I was supposed to sit at the keep while you fought the others for me? Wondering if you would return injured? Or at all? Knowing you faced them alone, and I had not told you I loved you?"

He wrapped her in his embrace and dropped a kiss on top of her head. "Say it again."

She frowned. "I do not—"

"Tell me you love me."

A slow smile spread across her face. "I love you, Aimon Proulx."

He planted a kiss on her lips. "I love you, Kathryn Beauchene. And I plan to tell you often for the rest of our lives." He released her and took her hand in his. "Come. Your father will be frantic if he has discovered you missing." He led her through the moonlit forest toward the keep. "Tell me, how *did* you sneak past Gaharet? That is quite the feat."

"I tried, but he caught me at the gate."

Aimon halted. "And he let you come?"

"I thought he would turn me back, maybe lock me in the training room. Instead, he told me where to find you."

Aimon scowled. Gaharet had sent his mate into danger? After vowing to protect her? He started walking again. He would have words with Gaharet about this, alpha or no.

"Do you think he knew how the others would react? That they would let me choose?"

Aimon considered her words. "Perhaps. There is a reason Gaharet is the alpha. He is strong and fair, but he is also shrewd." They cleared the forest and made their way up the hill to the keep. "It may be, as you say, he had some sense your presence would be needed."

He squeezed her hand. "I thought for a moment you would not choose me. That the pull from your maker might have influenced your choice."

She tugged on his hand and pulled him up short, not two steps from the keep gate. She cradled his cheek in her palm, and he leaned into her gentle touch. "Nothing I felt for any of them would ever change what I feel for you."

"*Ma belle renarde.*"

He dragged her to him and kissed her, a tangle of tongues and teeth and passion. Lifting her against him, her legs wrapped around his waist, he pressed her against the keep wall, grinding his ready and willing cock against the vee of her thighs.

A clearing of a throat brought him to his senses. Kathryn growled as he attempted to slide her from his body. Her hands gripped his hair and tried to pull his mouth back to hers.

"We have company," he whispered against her lips.

She stiffened. With an embarrassed huff, she unclenched her thighs from around his waist, dropped to her feet, and straightened her dress.

"Pardon me, Monsieur Aimon. There is a messenger here to see you," said the gate guard. "An urgent dispatch from Comte Lothair."

Lothair wanted a report already? *Merde.*

A man stepped forward, grinning, giving Kathryn a lascivious stare. Aimon growled and snatched a folded parchment from the man's hand. It had the comte's wax seal stamped on it.

"Off with you now," said the gate guard. "You have fulfilled your duty. Delivered your message. There is a celebration down in the village tonight. All the men are there. And the women. You may find a welcome there."

With a shrug, and one last lecherous glance at Kathryn that had Aimon's wolf pushing to the surface, the messenger departed.

"Mademoiselle Kathryn, Monsieur Aimon, Mon Seigneur Gaharet awaits you in the hall."

Aimon nodded his thanks, and he made his way to the keep, Kathryn in tow. Upon entering the hall, Erin raced to Kathryn and enfolded her in a hug.

"I'm so glad it all went well." She pulled away. "It did all go well, right?"

Kathryn smiled up at him and clasped his hand in hers. "Yes. It went very well."

"That's a relief."

Gaharet smiled at him across the table and raised his goblet in salute. "Congratulations Aimon, Kathryn."

Aimon took in Farren's relief at his daughter's return. "Thank you. But…"

Was he going to challenge Gaharet on his decision to let Kathryn go to the clearing? Now it was over, and Kathryn was safe? Aimon let the matter drop.

"You have a dispatch from Lothair, I see." Gaharet's astute eyes missed nothing.

"Yes, I—"

"Come, come, now everyone. Sit down at the table," said Anne, shuffling into the room with trays of bread and meat. She placed the platters on the table as everybody gathered around. "Time to eat. Time to celebrate." She beamed. "Two of my young men mated. I was wondering if I would live to see the day."

"All thanks to you, Anne." Erin grinned and took a seat at the table. "Mmm." She leaned forward, sniffing the tray of barely cooked meat.

"Now, now, I cannot take all the— My dear, why are you so pale?"

Erin shot up from the table and raced from the hall, one hand clutched over her mouth and another on her stomach.

"Erin?" Gaharet pushed his chair back.

Aimon shared a look with Kathryn. Was something wrong with Erin? Werewolves did not get sick. Was it something to do with her turning? Or the herbs the witch had used?

The sounds of Erin retching in the corridor reached their ears, and Gaharet shoved past a startled Gascon.

Anne's enormous girth blocked his way. "Now you just sit down, Gaharet, and eat your meal. I will take care of Erin."

Aimon tensed. Standing between an alpha and his mate was not advisable for anyone, not even Anne.

Gaharet's lip lifted, revealing large canines, and a growl rumbled deep in his chest. A shiver ran up Aimon's spine and his wolf slunk into the depths of his mind. Kathryn shifted closer.

Gaharet towered over Anne, his musky scent strong and pungent. "My mate is ill, Anne. I would be with her."

Anne stood her ground, and Aimon's respect for the old cook grew.

"She will be fine. Nothing a bit of ginger brew will not fix, I suspect. Sit down. I will fetch it now."

She bustled off toward the kitchen.

"Ginger brew?" Gaharet called after her.

Anne stopped at the door and smiled. "I believe, if her reaction to the smell of the meat is anything to go by, your mate is with child, Gaharet. You are going to be a father."

Gaharet slumped into his seat, a slow smile spreading across his face. "I am going to be a father."

Aimon met Gaharet's gaze and grinned. Their pack would survive. Once again, there would be offspring.

As congratulations flowed around the room, Kathryn's hand slipped into his beneath the table. Perhaps they, too, would soon follow in Gaharet and Erin's footsteps. The thought of Kathryn's belly swelling with his child... His grin widened. Kathryn smiled at him, her eyes dancing with all sorts of heated promises. He rubbed his thumb against her soft skin and her eyes glazed over, dark swirls lingering in their depths. He would have her alone again soon, and they would begin their own journey to parenthood.

"Farren," said Gaharet, bringing Aimon's focus from his mate and back to the table. "Would you organize the chaplain please? Tell him he will need to perform a discrete marriage ceremony for two couples. Best to make things legal, at least in the eyes of Lothair."

"Of course. Will you be returning to the keep? Should Kathryn and I perhaps join Aimon on his estate?"

Aimon choked on his wine. Kathryn and his mother in the same house? *He* spent little time at his family home. The risk of exposing his secret was too great.

Gaharet shook his head. "I am afraid this is not over yet, Farren. Erin and I must remain hidden at the cottage for a time. You will remain here. As should Aimon and Kathryn. Even should I return, this will remain your home."

"But—"

"You are family, Farren. More so now that Kathryn is one of us and mated to Aimon. This keep is big enough for all of us, and I have been alone with these empty rooms for too long."

Aimon's chest squeezed. Family. And a place where he would truly belong. Kathryn, too. He fingered the unopened communication from Lothair in his hand. Would Lothair's words shatter this moment of happiness, of hope?

He broke the seal.

Aimon stared at the elegant writing across the page, seeing it, but not truly believing its import.

"What does it say?" asked Gaharet.

Aimon read it again, making certain he had not misread or misinterpreted the meaning.

"It says — Aimon. I trust you have had no hand in this latest incident. Ulrik Voclain has escaped Langeais Keep."

* * * *

He slunk into the clearing, his nose to the ground, his black fur ruffling in the breeze. Scents familiar to him tickled at his memory. Others, from the mated pair, from their coupling in the clearing, were new to him. He padded about, teasing out the individuals, until he found what he was looking for. The one scent embedded in his psyche, never to be forgotten. His lip curled back, revealing large canines. His attacker. The one who had betrayed him. The one who had cut him down on the battlefield and given him the scars that crisscrossed his back. The one he had trusted.

He turned his one good eye toward the direction of the large walled building where wolves lived as men. He had vague memories of living in such a place. Living as a man, not as a wolf. He had watched such a wolf, black-haired, bearded and dominant, standing guard outside the wall. A yearning so strong had clenched at his entrails. He knew this man-wolf. Had once called him family.

He turned back to the scent he had traveled long and hard to find. The black wolf was not what he was here for. He was here for justice. Picking up his quarry's scent, he followed it and disappeared into the forest and away from the building he had once called home.

Epilogue

Aimon startled awake. Pressed against his side, his naked and beautiful mate thoroughly satiated and exhausted by their lovemaking. Unsure what had interrupted his slumber, he brought his wolf close to the surface. Even tucked away in Kathryn's bedchamber in the d'Louncrais keep, with Gaharet, Farren and all the keep guards, it behooved him to remain alert. The traitor was still out there.

Kathryn whimpered and tossed in her sleep. "No!" She writhed about on the bed, pushing away from him, her hair a tousled mess of copper and her face twisted in anguish. "No! I am not yours. You cannot take me!"

"Kathryn." Aimon slipped his arms around her and pulled her in close. She struggled against him, but she was no match for his strength. "Wake up, *ma belle renarde.*"

Kathryn exploded from her nightmare, almost wrenching herself from his arms. Her chest heaved, and her body shook as her eyes darted about the darkened room. "I saw him." She gulped in a deep breath. "The one who attacked me... He was trying...to make me...his." She rolled toward him and buried her face against his chest and sobbed. "He tried to take me away from you."

"Ssh." He rubbed his hand up and down her back. "All is well, Kathryn. I am here. You are safe. I have you, and I will let no man or wolf harm you. I promise you. No one is taking you away from me." He lifted his hand to her head, cradling it against his chest, and stroked her hair. "Calm now. It was just a dream. There is no one here but you and I."

Her hands petted his chest, as though she needed confirmation that he was real, that she was awake and not still held in the clutches of her nightmare.

"You said you saw his face." He continued to stroke her hair. "Did you recognize him?"

She pulled away—her face pale and streaked with tears. "I..." She scrunched up her face in a frown. "I...I did see his face, but..." She stared at him, shadows of uncertainty flickering across her eyes. "Now I cannot... It is like the memory is there, and yet I cannot see it."

He pulled her back into his embrace, hiding his disappointment. "Do not fret, Kathryn. The memory is there. It will return in its own good time."

"Wait." She pushed him away again and stared up at the ceiling. "His sword. I remember. It had a jewel on the pommel."

A jewel? An affectation for wealthy chevaliers, it was not common, for it could change the balance of a sword. Neither his nor Gaharet's swords were adorned with such. Nor were Aubert's and Edmond's. But both Godfrey's and Lance's were. Was the traitor mere moments away from being revealed?

He tempered his excitement. "What color jewel, Kathryn?"

"I... I... Oh." She covered her face with her hands. "I do not remember."

Aimon smothered his frustration and pulled her into his embrace. The answer was there. So close and yet so far. Without knowing who had betrayed them, Kathryn was still very much in danger. As were they all. He could only hope she remembered soon, and they could take this traitor down before any more damage was done.

Want to see more from this author?
Here's a taster for you to enjoy!

The Wolves of Langeais:
Wolf's Redemption
K.E. Turner

Coming November 2024

Excerpt

Langeais, Frankia
999

The clang of the grate above had Ulrik Voclain on his feet. His chains rattled and the silver shackles around his wrists and neck shifted, brushing over red and blistered skin. He hissed, steeling himself against the pain. Footsteps descended the steep steps cut into stone—confident and purposeful. He faced the stairs, tilted his nose and sampled the air, his visitor closer than he would have liked when he finally caught his scent.

Lothair, Comte de Anjou.

Ulrik's lips curled in a snarl and anger burned a fiery trail from his gut to his throat. He drew himself up to his full height but repressed the growl threatening to form. The man who had taken everything from him, who had thrown him in this dank, godforsaken hole, would not see him cowering. But to unleash his rage would serve neither him nor his pack.

"Ulrik Voclain."

Lothair stepped into the tight space, a candle held aloft, its meagre flame doing little to stave off the darkness. Ulrik smirked. The lack of light did not make *him* uneasy.

Anger flashed in his comte's eyes, the air tainted with its sharpness, but it was gone as quick as it had appeared. "Laugh all you like, Ulrik. I may not have your ability to see in the dark, but *I* am not the one chained to the wall."

This time, Ulrik could not suppress his growl.

Lothair set the candle on the bottom step and surveyed the small, airless space, his hand shifting to rest on the pommel of his sword. Ulrik rolled his lips, quashing his grin. Even now, chained and bound in silver, Lothair saw him as a threat.

"How do you like my little cell, Ulrik? My *oubliette*? It is impressive, is it not?" Lothair brushed a hand over the rough stone wall. "Secure, unpleasant and hidden beneath the bowels of my keep. I never imagined I would use it to contain a werewolf." Lothair's gaze settled on him, malevolent glee flashing in the depths of his eyes. "Ironic, you should be the one to end up secured in here after what your family sacrificed to save you from this very thing."

Ulrik roared and lunged for Lothair. His chains snapped tight, keeping him well beyond the reach of his comte. He howled, filling the cell with his anguish and his loss. Nervous shuffles and anxious whispers from the guards above filtered down the stairs, along with the heavy stench of fear so strong he could scent it even in his weakened state.

Amusement danced in Lothair's eyes, but he took a cautious step back. "Tsk, tsk, tsk. Always the hothead." He shook his head. "Calm yourself, Ulrik. We do not want rumors of a beast beneath my keep spreading now, do we?"

A growl rumbled in Ulrik's chest, but there was no force behind it. The silver of his shackles kept his wolf repressed. He had never felt such loneliness within his own thoughts. Where once the comforting and familiar presence of his wolf had filled his mind, a constant since birth, now only a deep silence remained.

Damn the silver. Damn Archeveque Renaud and his wolfsbane trap.

If there had been any other choice... If he could have saved Gaharet, his alpha, without stepping foot within that ring of wolfsbane... Had his alpha's mate's life not hung in the balance... He breathed through his rage until it settled into a calm acceptance. There had been no other choice. If not him, Gaharet would have stepped into the trap. Ulrik could never have allowed the unholy alliance between Lothair and the scheming archeveque to imprison their alpha. Not while he still breathed. The pack needed Gaharet more than it needed him.

Lothair paced in front of him, close but not close enough. "Archeveque Renaud came to see you." Lothair's lips twisted in a sardonic grin. "Did you think I would not know? That my men would not inform me of his visit? Ha! Renaud is a fool if he thinks I would not suspect his game." Lothair tilted his head to the side, regarding him. "What did he offer you? Freedom? Vengeance?"

Ulrik glanced away.

"Ahh. Both. Very free with his promises, is our archeveque. And what, pray tell, was the archeveque's price? No." Lothair held up his hand, halting words Ulrik had no intention of speaking. "Let me guess. He wanted you to bite me. Turn *me* into a werewolf, rather than I choose a sacrificial keep guard or some lowly chevalier to turn. The perfect excuse for him to use all his newfound skills at binding werewolves. The church to the rescue of the people of Langeais, saving them from the wicked and now cursed Comte de Anjou. What a coup for Archeveque Renaud."

Lothair took a step towards him. Ulrik met his stare. "Renaud may see you as an easy target, an open festering wound he could poke a few times and stir into action. I know you are too smart to fall for his promises."

Ulrik's nostrils flared, and his hands clenched into fists. Renaud's offer had tempted him. He could not deny it, not to himself, but he had not given his life freely for his alpha, only to turn on him now. Not again. He stepped back and let the tension ease from his chains, if not his body.

The knowing smugness that settled across Lothair's face rankled, but Ulrik held it in. For all the rumors of his loose grip on sanity, the comte had an uncanny ability to be one step ahead of any scheme or plot against him.

"I always win, Ulrik. You know that."

Ulrik gritted his teeth, but he kept his expression neutral.

"And I always get what I want."

Ulrik repressed a snarl. "Do what you will, but I will not bite you or anyone else. I will not help *Renaud*" — he spat the name out — "and I will not help you create an army of werewolves."

Lothair shrugged. "We shall see."

Ulrik steeled himself. From the moment he had thrown himself into Renaud's wolfsbane trap, putting himself at the mercy of his comte, it was always going to come down to this. Lothair would use whatever methods necessary to achieve his goal, and that promised Ulrik pain and suffering. "I will *die* before I give you what you want. You may be the Comte de Anjou, but I will never kneel before you again. I *renounce* you. I rescind my oath to serve you."

"You think to taunt me into killing you swiftly?" Lothair hummed his amusement. "In the end, you may wish for death, but I assure you, it will not come anytime soon. You are too valuable a commodity, and you possess knowledge I require."

Ulrik sneered. "I will tell you nothing."

Dark eyes turned flinty, a steely determination dancing in their depths. "Oh, you will. Renaud has an informant. One of your own. I" — Lothair pointed his finger at Ulrik's chest — "have you. The days of drowning your sorrows in wine and women are over. It is time to get your head in the game. Work with me and you may be one of the few members of your pack to survive."

Ulrik's nostrils flared. Confirmation they had a traitor amongst them. Who? Lance, their oldest and most experienced surviving wolf? He had stood by his alpha and supported Gaharet's leadership of the pack. The twins, Aubert and Edmond, big and brutish? He had always thought them steadfastly loyal. Aimon? The newest member of their pack turned after the battle of Montsoreau had left him mortally wounded. Could he have designed to infiltrate their pack at the behest of Renaud? It seemed a risky move. If not for Gaharet turning him, Aimon would have died. Or Godfrey? Quiet, scholarly and ever the strategist? He had his own secret. Did he know Ulrik had uncovered his predilections? Did he suspect the others had knowledge of them, too?

"Is Renaud not forthcoming with all you need to know?" Ulrik sneered. "He is not much of an ally for you, is he, if he keeps things from you?" Or was it the traitor to their pack that had been less than forthcoming? Either way, Ulrik would sow whatever seeds of discontent and distrust he could. Lothair was enemy enough. It would only aid them if he could break up his alliance with Renaud. "Why should *I* tell you anything?"

Lothair grinned. From beneath his tunic, he removed a small gold disc on a gold chain. He dangled it in front of Ulrik, the disc spinning. A howling wolf's head on one side and a blood-red stone on the other. The binding amulet. The one Gaharet had given to him in exchange for his own. Their hastily planned deception rested on his possession of it.

"Remember this? Renaud tells me it is the alpha's amulet. That you killing Gaharet, *as you claim*, makes you the new alpha. Only problem is…" Lothair stepped closer, lowering his voice to a conspiratorial whisper. "I know Gaharet is not dead."

Ulrik kept his breathing even. Lothair was baiting him.

"You may have duped Renaud with your little ruse. It appears to have also fooled your pack. But not me. Gaharet is not dead, and *you* are no alpha." Lothair stepped back and resumed his pacing. "Since only the alpha can turn men into werewolves, your usefulness extends as far as the information you can provide. For everything else, I must hunt Gaharet down."

Ulrik rasped out a laugh. "You question my claim, yet you believe every word out of that treacherous archeveque's mouth."

Lothair paused in his pacing, an eyebrow raised. "And which piece of information of Renaud's should I discard?"

Ulrik met Lothair's stare, letting his comte see the truth of his words. A truth he had never thought to reveal but was now the one thing that could keep his alpha safe. "Any of us could have helped you turn men into werewolves, helped you create your werewolf army. Even the one who betrayed us. All it takes is a bite—our saliva mixed with another's blood. It need not come from Gaharet."

Lothair's lack of surprise at his revelation fanned the sparks of unease in Ulrik's gut. *L'enfer*. How had he once thought he could best Lothair? Risked his pack, challenged his alpha—the man he had, in times past, called his friend—determined to have his vengeance against the comte. He would not make that mistake again.

"And the turning itself?" asked Lothair. "What does it entail? How does it affect the one being turned?"

Ulrik glanced about the small room not taking anything in, his mind racing. He had said enough, and only then, to keep Gaharet safe. He shifted on his feet, wincing as the silver of his manacles touched unblemished skin and raised fresh welts. He would say no more.

"I see." Lothair grunted and turned to leave. "Then I must hunt and trap Gaharet."

Ulrik filled his lungs with the stale air of his cell, exhaling slowly. That he was even considering revealing the secrets of his pack turned his blood cold, but... Though he may not survive this, Ulrik would see

Gaharet lived. He owed him that. He swallowed, his throat dry from his days of confinement as much as from what he was about to reveal. "Wait."

Lothair turned. Silence hung heavy between them. Lothair gave him a hard stare. "I am waiting."

Ulrik gritted his teeth, the words clogging his throat. "Pain. The turning is agony," he said, forcing the words out.

"How much? For how long?"

"Three days. Or more."

Lothair grunted. "Three days, you say? Bearable."

Ulrik barked out a laugh. "Bearable?" He fixed his gaze on Lothair. "Let me save you your delusions. Many do not survive. Some go mad." If he could guarantee Lothair would die during a turning, he would bite the comte himself. "You should ask Aimon about his turning. He was not born like the rest of us."

Lothair blinked, the only hint of his surprise a flicker of a frown as he made the connection. "The battle of Montsoreau?"

Ulrik inclined his head. "Ask Aimon how he *screamed* for days on end, strapped to a cot to protect him. To protect us. I can still remember his torment. How he begged us to end it. To end him. Ask him how many months it took to learn how to control his wolf." Ulrik paused, letting his words sink in. "Aimon was lucky. He had us to shield him, to train him. When he was at his most vulnerable, we were there." Ulrik allowed himself a vicious grin. "I imagine Renaud is eagerly awaiting an opportunity to catch you at your weakest."

Lothair stilled. What little air there was in the cell seemed to be sucked into the silence.

"You think you have it figured out?" Ulrik sneered. "That you have outsmarted us all. But you know nothing. About us, or what you are asking for."

Lothair fixed him with an impenetrable stare, the corner of his lip curled in a sardonic half-smile. He tossed the amulet and caught it in his hand. Palm out, he revealed the reverse side, the blood-red stone glinting in the candlelight. "I know this amulet, with its red stone that reeks of blood magic, denotes more than the alpha."

Ulrik's heart stalled in his chest.

With a flick of his wrist, Lothair tossed the amulet and Ulrik followed its arc across the cell until it landed in the dirt at his feet. "I also know if I try to kill or capture another werewolf, if they recite the inscriptions on *their* amulets, if they disappear…" He jerked his chin at the gold disc on the floor. "I need only be near that one, with its red jewel instead of an inscription, to find them. That it will draw them in like a beacon for lost souls."

Ulrik tried to keep his emotions under control and his breathing even. How had Lothair known of the true purpose of the amulet? The inscription? The bloodstone? Had the traitor told Renaud? He did not think so, for Renaud would have used that information to good effect. And he had not.

Lothair chuckled. "I always win, Ulrik." His smile vanished. "Never forget that." He turned on his heel, grabbed the candle and climbed the stairs.

The grate above screeched open, then clanged shut and the comte's footsteps receded. Ulrik eyed his surroundings. He must escape this hole in the ground. Staying, holding out as long as he could, was no longer an option. With only seven of them left, not a single female among them, and one of them confirmed as a traitor, things had never been more dire for the pack. Or his alpha. Gaharet had to be warned. But how in God's name would he get free of this silver?

About the Author

K.E. Turner can't remember a time when she wasn't writing stories or reading books — as a teenager in class instead of doing math, in her lunch break at work, or at home when there's housework to be done. With a love of history, mystery, suspense, paranormal, and romance, she likes combining more than one element in her stories.

She writes spicy paranormal romances and romantic suspense, with strong but good hearted heroes, smart, sassy heroines and an often unexpected villain or two, to shake things up.

A Western Australian based author, she lives with her husband, two dogs, two cats and a menagerie of farm animals on their property in the southern region of the state. A hopeless romantic, she enjoys beach sunsets, sitting by the wood fire with a good book, and a nice shiraz.

K.E. Turner loves to hear from readers. You can find her contact information, website details and author profile page at https://www.totallybound.com

Home of Erotic Romance

Sign up for our newsletter and find out about all our romance book releases, eBook sales and promotions, sneak peeks and FREE romance books!